In a London Fog

by

Elizabeth R. Lawrence ©2008

ISBN

978-1-4357-6068-4

All rights reserved

No part of this publication may be reproduced or transmitted in any form or by any means, electronic or mechanical, including photocopy, recording or any information storage and retrieval system, without permission from the copyright owner.

Contact information

E.R. Lawrence

erlaw1@yahoo.com

Use of a name of anyone living or dead is purely coincidental.

In a London Fog

In a London Fog

Acknowledgement……………………………………I

Dedication…………………………………………II

When You Are Old……………………..………...IV

Chapter One …………………………………...1
    English Visitors
    A Farewell Party
    The Nature of Desire

Chapter Two …………………………………..22
    Love by Post
    The Letters
    The Photographs

Table of Contents Cont'd

Chapter Three …………………………………..68
    Journal Entries
    My Irene Dunne Flat
    Guy Fawkes Day
    Penny

Chapter Four …………………………………..114
    Half a World Away
    London & USA
    Bombshells

Part Two

Chapter Five …………………………………...230
    England 1992
    Their First meeting
    Their Second Meeting
    Their Third Meeting
    A Late Visit

Chapter Six …………………………………….333
    Going Home
    Home USA

Epilogue ………………………………………...355

In a London Fog

Acknowledgement
With love to Margaret Singleton for her kindness and understanding over the years. To Tony, Matthew and Kingsley Singleton for everything nice.

Elizabeth R. Lawrence

Dedicated to
The Real David

In a London Fog

WHEN YOU ARE OLD

When you are old and gray and full of sleep,
And nodding by the fire, take down this book,
And slowly read, and dream of the soft look
Your eyes had once, and of their shadows deep;

How many loved your moments of glad grace,
And loved your beauty with love false or true,
But one man loved the pilgrim soul in you,
And loved the sorrows of your changing face;

And bending down beside the glowing bars,
Murmur, a little sadly, how Love fled
And paced upon the mountains overhead
And hid his face amid a crowd of stars.

--William Butler Yeats

In a London Fog
by

Elizabeth R. Lawrence

Chapter One   English Visitors

It was hot, blistering hot on a July day that summer of 1966.. Julie was ready for the pool in the rear of the apartment complex. Jason, her twenty one year old son, had come home to report that a British group was already there Tina, nineteen, her dark hair pulled into a ponytail, was helping her mother braid her own dark hair. A full braid fell over one shoulder when the phone rang.

"We're getting company," Julie said, when she hung up. "Cora has family visiting her from England and wants to know if they can be my guests at the pool. I said it would be fine."

"Are they part of the brain drain group already in residence?" Jason asked.

"With Cora we're not talking about brains," Julie answered, trying to fix her hair again, then giving up when she had trouble. "Her sister is visiting her with her family. They don't have a pool. This is a port in the heat."

She was wearing a dark blue, one piece Esther Williams type bathing suit cut high in the legs with a sheer open white blouse over it. . It would do. It would have been too late to change anyway for they arrived rather quickly.

Tina opened the door when they knocked. In minutes the apartment was full with Cora calling for something cold to drink. With her was a smiling matronly looking woman, a child of about eight or nine, a man who faced away from her view, her cousin, Kitty, and her husband, Russ,.

Julie headed toward the kitchen. "I'll get some iced tea ready," she said, turning away.

She had the tea ready quickly enough but the ice cube tray was giving her trouble. She couldn't get it out of the freezer. Jason had already gone back to the pool and Tina was in the living room making friends with the little girl called Janet.

Looking from the kitchen toward the living room, and smiling, she called out, "I need someone strong enough to help me with this ice cube tray."

By the time she turned back the unknown man had come to help her. They were facing away from each other as he reached into the freezer. He had the tray released quickly.

"That was easy," he said, smiling at her

"For you," she answered. She looked at him and smiled and at that very moment she had to grip the table in front of her to keep her balance. My God, she thought. I actually want to put my arms around him.. I don't know him, but it's as if I do. His British accent added to his fair haired mustached mystique. She caught her breath as she straightened up.

He was looking right at her. "Are you all right?" he asked, gently.

"I don't know, but I think so, yes," she answered, smiling. "Thank you for your help.." She hesitated. "We weren't introduced."

"David," he replied. "And you must be Cora's friend, Julie." He smiled, taking the tray of glasses and iced tea from her. His hand brushed hers and in an electric instant the tray rattled in his hand.

"Are *you* all right?" she asked, softly.

"No. Yes, I, I think so." The tray tilted as he looked at her and one of the filled glasses crashed to the floor.

"My God," he whispered before Russ rushed in. "What just happened here?"

The soft question was mirthful but the words hung in the air between them as Russ helped them deal with the broken glass.

Russ, a tall, thin fop of a man with a pencil thin mustache was an American. He had lived and worked in England for a time so, once they were in the pool area, he functioned well among those in the British group. He seemed to think that what he perceived as British culture rubbed off on him.

Russ and Cora were fairly new in the area. Julie thought them a perfect match as first class idiots of both countries. Cora , the simpering has-been beauty and Russ the dandy at her beck and call.. Cora was not one of her favorite people nor was Kitty, but she could bear them in a crowd, especially once she got them all outside and introduced to the British group already there.

Julie mingled with everyone including those among the other British people who were there with their families. After introductions and a refreshing swim in the pool she relaxed in a shaded area in a pool side chair. David, who didn't swim, was pleased when Tina helped Janet. A winsome child, she was soon surrounded by other children, British and American.. David and his wife, Addie went separate ways after meeting Richard and Emma, the new resident Brits. He sat near them while Addie sat closer to Cora and Kitty, apparently catching up on local tales and family gossip.

Conversations filtered through laughter and whispers to where Julie sat doodling pencil sketches on a drawing pad. She sketched what she saw and heard. Interesting how Cora and Kitty dismissed her attention for she saw them as cunning women who spoke of their escapades with the wealthy men they knew. They would not have appreciated the caricatures she was doodling of them.

Cora's tale of how she'd met Julie was less than factual, but she knew Cora's vanity would not permit her to say she had applied for a job where Julie had interviewed her. She didn't present herself well. She was overly made up and had no working history. Almost fifty, but claiming herself younger, with cosmetics lumping into the creases in her face, she couldn't even consider her for a receptionist in the sales office. With misgiving she'd put her in the sales group where she might earn a commission. She quit after the first day. Julie kept her image intact by diplomatically telling her she was overqualified for anything else. From that interview Cora had learned Julie lived in a newly built house nearby and she had latched on. That was a few years ago, before Julie's move to the townhouse at the apartment complex.

Cousin Kitty, a striking white haired woman in her late fifties, was living in a lavish New York apartment building owned by a wealthy married American man she called Stan. . She had met Stan at the gaming club she and Cora had frequented. They spoke of the men they'd met there and what they had to do to maintain their life style as they got older. Kitty agreed to live with Stan on a trial basis, but only if he would give her enough money to give her some independence. He gave it to her.

"I took it," she said, "then I left him because he gave it to me right in front of the cabbie." Whispers and laughter as she added, "I didn't let him near me until he put money in my bank account."

Cora told about a woman she knew who had followed her American friend to the States when he was transferred from England even after he returned to his wife and family there. Peals of laughter swallowed the rest of her words.

Addie was obviously older than David. She was a simple, matronly looking woman with few of the pretensions of her sister or her cousin. Whatever her natural hair color she kept it in a soft pale brown color. She had grown children, even a couple of grandchildren. Someone among the Brits asked Cora if she was David's mother.

With a seventeen year age difference it was a logical question. The age difference didn't bother them; that was not uncommon in England. Young men married older women. Older men married younger women. It was an economic fact. But Cora and Kitty had yet to reconcile her marrying a man who worked for the London Metropolitan Police when she could have had her pick of rich men.

"At least he's a detective," Cora sniffed..

"It's a steady job," said Richard, "And it has real estate perks for buying a house.."

"An older woman usually brings something to the marriage, too," said Emma. "Property or a bank account, whether they've been married before or not."

"And with his career just starting," Richard added, "he probably wanted stability. "

For his sake Julie was glad David had gone to check on Janet and couldn't hear them.

As conversations rambled pictures were taken. Julie took a couple of David and Addie and David took a couple of her with a hair braid still falling on a bare shoulder. As it got late parents gathered their children and began moving along paths to their apartments. David and Julie found themselves walking together on the path behind everyone else.

"Hello, sweet Julie," David said, softly

Hello, you beautiful man." Julie said, barely breathing her thoughts aloud.

She heard his intake of breath.

Russ joined them. He had been to a liquor store so the pool party was now a cocktail party with Russ acting as bartender. Tina made Janet a small root beer float; Julie sipped soda, and Jason rummaged around to put snacks on a couple of tables. Cora used the phone to make arrangements for a dinner party at the Hideaway. She identified the party as guests of a wealthy prominent American man in the area. Then Russ rushed around to get everyone back to their house where they would dress for dinner and meet at the restaurant. Julie and her children were told they were welcome. Jason had other plans but Tina would go along for Janet's sake.

"Or she'll be stuck with all grown ups."

Julie had just waved to those already in the car as David came up behind her. He had had too much to drink, too little to eat and was still on Greenwich MeanTime.

"I had to use the loo," he said, "and I think I found your bedroom."

Someone in the car hit the horn as Russ rushed back for David. The door opened just as David put his arms around her. With a disapproving look Russ hustled him through the door to the waiting car outside.

"But I only wanted to kiss her goodnight and thank her for her hospitality," she heard David say before the car door closed.

She hesitated about showing up at the dinner. Common sense said beware. It's just a summertime flirtation, said the devil in her. But Tina had promised Janet she'd be there and, oh, for heaven's sake, it's just a dinner.

Still, she dressed carefully choosing a soft, silk, summer dress from Mexico. She'd bought it at an upscale second act store and this was the first time she'd be wearing it. It was bright orange with a multicolored splash of flowers placed everywhere. The silk material draped over curves. It needed no bra for the upper folds of the dress enclosed her breasts leaving them firmly, but loosely covered. Wide straps fell over bare shoulders to a bared back. High heels, not sandals, went with it. Whatever happened David would still be almost a head taller. She took the time for her hair. Fixing the braid into a bun atop her head she wove a piece of the silk orange fabric underneath. It was like the accent of a tiara. Gold earrings were her only jewelry. She carried a small green purse pinned with a bright orange flower.

"Wow!" exclaimed Tina when her mother was downstairs. "Wait till they see you! You look fantastic. I just wish.." she stopped.

"Wish?"

"You weren't so lonely, and you didn't work so hard, that's all."

"Work isn't the problem," Julie said. "Lonely is. And. at forty-one, it's an unpleasant fact of life that is sometimes hard to handle."

"Yeah, I guess," Tina responded, tying a white ribbon around her ponytail and putting a light jacket over her own pretty flowered dress.

The valet parked the car as Julie and her daughter entered the restaurant. Janet ran to Tina leading her back to her seat while Russ and David stood up at the table to greet them. Russ helped Janet and Tina as David pulled a chair out for Julie. She was seated next to him.

"I'm a little embarrassed," he said, smiling. "I'm sorry about that goodbye."

She acknowledged everyone before turning to look at him. Smiling, she said. "I'm sorry about your bad timing."

He looked at the menu. "So am I." he said,

Conversations around the table focused on plans already made for excursions to New York, to Washington, DC, to Atlantic City and to other towns around the New Jersey, Pennsylvania area.

"It's a lot to cram in in only three weeks," said Russ. "But if Addie can handle it.."

"Will you be coming with us?" Janet piped up, looking from Tina to Julie.

"No," Julie answered. "We will be at work. But we'll share the trip with you if you'll send us a card on your travels."

Tina wrote their address and phone number on a paper napkin, before handing it to Janet who gave it to her father.

"I'm sorry you're not coming with us."

"I'm not," Julie answered, softly. "I would hate it." At David's surprise she added, "This may be a once in a lifetime trip for you. My being with you could only spoil it."

"I'll call you," he said."

She waved him away when he lingered after walking them to the car. "Now go, she said, smiling, as Russ's horn sounded. "Have fun." She drove off even before he walked away.

"Did you enjoy yourself?" Tina asked.

"Not really," Julie answered. "Lonely is still lonely. This was a delusional moment."

There were no calls and cards that came were obviously written by Addie or David in Janet's name. They had toured the New York area, visiting all the tourist places they could manage. Kitty, with Stan, had wined and dined them at Stan's country club. In Washington they toured whatever was open to tourists. David visited the FBI building. During his visit apparently he was told that since he was not a US citizen he wouldn't qualify for anything with the FBI.. Julie wasn't sure that was correct but she didn't bother checking it out.

She was in the moment. There seemed no point in seeing beyond that. That's not what she wanted either. She just wanted to feel alive.

Cora phoned the evening of their return to say they were back. She also invited her to a farewell party for Addie the following evening.

"David thinks you should be here."

Julie managed to plan her schedule so that she was leaving the office by three. That gave her plenty of time to have dinner with her children. She didn't dress up; she merely exchanged a simple blouse that she'd worn to the office for a flowered halter top to wear with the skirt.

In a London Fog

The Farewell Party

It was close to nine when she got to Addie's farewell party. Russ opened the door after she rang the bell. Music came from a stereo. Addie was on the phone talking to Kitty who was calling from home in New York. Janet was playing with Cora's dog with Cora curled up in a club chair nearby. David moved from his seat on a sofa as Julie entered. She seemed to be the only guest there.

"I'm either too late or too early," she said, handing David a gift wrapped package. "It's an empty photo album for pictures of your trip." She hesitated. He had been in her thoughts for the whole of those three weeks. "And it's to wish you a safe journey home." As she spoke she was struck by the finality of her words. She blinked back sudden tears. "Consider it a memento," she said, turning away.

"Touching her chin David turned her face to look at him. "Do you think I'll forget?"

"If we have any sense we both should," she said, quietly..

"Dance with me," he said, softly, brushing a tear from her cheek. His voice and his clear blue eyes were shadowed with repressed emotion.

"When you didn't call I thought…"

"I tried to call but I didn't know how to use your public phone system." he whispered, "and there was no one with me I could ask."

Their eyes locked as they danced, a slow dance that held them in place. Addie was still on the phone. Russ and Cora were whispering. Janet spoke up.

"Dad," she said, "why are you looking at her like that?"

Dad had not heard her. Addie got off the phone to take her to bed. Cora and Russ feigned indifference to play with the dog.

"I hadn't planned to come on this trip at all," he said, "By the time I had a change of heart I couldn't get a ticket on the same flight so my return trip will be delayed by a day."

They didn't hear the music stop but when Russ said it was getting late and began to turn off lights it was time to go.

"We have got to talk," David said, as he walked her to her car. "We only have one night left. When they took the dog out of the kennel today I said I'd walk him tonight. Pull away now as if you're going home but double back. I'll find you. Will you do that?"

"Yes," she said.

"Don't put it past Russ to follow you," he cautioned, stepping away from her car as Russ appeared in the doorway.

Her stomach in knots and her thoughts racing, she waved at David now standing with Russ. If Russ will follow me Cora is sure to phone to make sure I'm home so I'll go home to get her call before I turn back, she thought. She wished she'd had the thought when David was near her. She talked to the night sky as she drove hoping sky borne telepathy would carry the message to him. Delay your walk, she whispered, or walk in circles until I get back.

She was home in time for Cora's call.

"Yes, I am sorry to say goodbye," she said, anxious to get off the phone when Cora seemed to want to prolong the conversation. "I have to be at work early in the morning so right now I just want to shower and get to bed."

She counted to ten after she hung up, then counted to ten again lest Cora call back before she got to her car. Russ's car was in the drive when she drove past. There was no sign of David or a medium sized dog until David emerged from a corner news shop near a convenience store.

"I walked every dark street in the area. When I didn't see you I looked for a phone. This is where I found one." He tried to control the dog as he got in the car. "It was another public phone. I was trying to figure out how to use it and look over my shoulder at the same time, and I had to keep this dog quiet. And I was looking for you. I finally got someone there to help me but your phone was busy when I managed to…"

She explained. "That was Cora."

The dog, his leash still in David's hand, settled down between them as David leaned toward her, trying to reach across the animal.

"This will never do," he said "We can't seem to get a minute alone. Now we've got a watchdog. I can't stay out much longer or Russ will be out looking for me now."

"If we can get the dog in the back seat," Julie said, reaching into a side pocket on her car door, "we might have a couple of minutes to ourselves." From the pocket she retrieved a half open package of stale cookies and a red rubber ball. She held the package of cookies to the dog's nose and threw the ball and the cookies in the back seat. The dog leaped over the head rest to get to the items .

"Do you have a dog, Julie?"

"Had," she said, as David slid closer. "He was a German Shepherd called King."

David was close enough to put his arms around her. He kissed her. It was a tender kiss.

"Oh, my darling," he whispered. "Do you know what you've done to me since I saw you?"

She kissed him, holding him closer to do it. It was not a tender kiss. It was a passionate, hungry, kiss from a woman who had waited too long. "Do you know what you've done to me?"

He groaned, his hands grappling with the ties of her halter top until he found her breasts. She let him devour them as they burst forth.

A minute, two minutes, maybe five or six timeless minutes alone until headlights from a car came toward them and they drew apart. They adjusted their clothes as they separated.

"I don't know how this happened but this is insanity." He gasped, exhaling. . "I can't let you go like this but I must. We have got to calm down but we must talk. I'll be 3000 miles away shortly. If you'll be patient with me we'll work things out from there." He paused, looking at her. "Once Addie and

Janet are safely airborne I'll be coming back here. If Russ was a real man he would get out of the way to let us have at least one night together." He spoke softly, touching her face. "And maybe our brains would start functioning again. As things stand, unless you come to see me off when I leave, this will be our last time together for God knows how long."

"I know," she said, gently. "And they know you'd rather be somewhere else."

"With someone else is the problem."

"I doubt I'll be invited anywhere now."

"I'm inviting you, my darling. If they make a fuss about it you can drive me to Kennedy in your car. I'll cover the expenses."

There was time for only a small kiss before she dropped him off where she'd found him. He and the dog were walking toward the house as Russ stepped from his car.

"What are you doing out?" David asked.

"I wanted to look for you," Russ began, "but the air conditioning in the car isn't working too well. I don't think it needs Freon but I'll check in the morning. What happened to you?" he added. "We thought you got lost."

"In a way," David said, handing Russ the torn and empty package, "I stopped in a store down the road and got some cookies for the dog."

"He seems to have enjoyed them."

"Couldn't get enough," David said, with a short laugh as they went in the house.

Julie knew the flight number and the time Addie's flight would take off. Later, at the office, when she knew all had gone well, she pictured his return from Kennedy with Cora and Russ. What she didn't know was how morose David had become when they were back.

Before leaving for Kennedy a florist had delivered flowers he had ordered the previous day. For Addie and Cora yellow rose corsages For Janet red roses as a wrist corsage. They had worn the flowers to the airport. Searching through the empty boxes scattered about to find the phone number of the florist, he phoned an order for a corsage of red roses to be delivered by the next day. He would pay with another Traveler's check.

As it got late David paced, going to the door again and again. She should have been there. Had Cora or Russ said anything to keep her away? They wouldn't dare. Oh, yes, they would came the thought. He picked up the phone to call her just as the doorbell rang.

"This is for me." David said, moving in front of Russ "I'll get the door, if you please."

"You're late," he said, kissing her cheek. "But I'll forgive you now that you're here."

She was dressed casually in a two piece yellow knit suit that skimmed her curves, and with it a sleeveless pale pink top. Her hair was up, fixed as before in a bun that was covered by a pink and yellow scarf. Tan heels and gold earrings completed the outfit.

"You look edible," David whispered, "like an ice cream parfait. And you smell delicious."

"I didn't expect you," Cora said through clenched teeth.

David smiled. "She's my guest."

"Well, at least you're smiling again," she said. She turned to Russ "I'll have a drink."

Russ busied himself with the liquor cabinet as David turned on the stereo.

"What about you?" Russ asked Julie.

"Soda or ice tea would be fine."

"Don't you drink?" David asked.

"Not very often and not much when I do."

"I think my last night in the United States calls for something special. We'll have a farewell toast later." He held out his arms. "We should have had tonight," he said, "but we can still dance."

As they came together he gave her a Shakespearean quote he had penned while he was waiting for her.

The Nature of Desire

"No sooner met but they looked. No sooner looked but they sighed, No sooner sighed but they loved, No sooner loved but they asked each other the reason, No sooner knew the reason, But they sought the remedy.

She looked at him with tears in her eyes after she read it. "Exactly," she said. "But you're leaving much too soon for any remedy."

Daggers flashed from Cora's eyes as they moved together. For a while they were oblivious of their surroundings as they held each other. Then, catching a glimpse of Cora, Julie whispered, "We've stirred up a hornet's nest. I don't think I should stay much longer."

Cora didn't think so either. Speaking directly to David she said, pointedly, "You have to be at Kennedy early tomorrow."

David nodded as Russ turned off the stereo. He raised his glass to Cora and Russ before turning to Julie. "We'll see each other in the morning," he said, clearly, "but I want to thank you now for a most memorable time."

Julie gulped the liquid in her glass to get it past the lump in her throat...Clearly emotional David finished his drink. Cora turned away. Russ just stood there. Then Julie was in her car

The idea of being stuck in a car with them for hours, even with David there, was suffocating. But the thought of not seeing David again was enough to motivate her to get up and get going when the alarm buzzed in the morning..

She put on the same yellow knit outfit she'd worn the night before. This image, as well as Shakespeare's words, were what she wanted him to remember of their last night together.

She saw only pain in his eyes when he glanced at her as she entered the house. He didn't look at all happy. Not even her arrival seemed to affect him.

"He's been like that since we reached Addie on the phone this morning," Cora said, not seeming the least concerned about her presence or his mood. If anything she seemed to be enjoying it. "If you're going to come along maybe you can cheer him up so we can get going."

"We're not going anywhere," Russ said as he came in from the outside drive where his car was parked. "Not unless you want to sweat out the trip in a very hot car."

"What's wrong now?" Cora asked, petulantly, almost stamping a foot.

"The air conditioner isn't working," he answered. "Its already hot out there, and the temperature will be up in the 90s today.

"You can't fix it?" she asked.

"No," Russ answered. "And we haven't got time to get help. It will be a long uncomfortable trip on those highways."

David came to life. "Julie has a car."

"With air?" Russ asked.

"Yes," David answered, remembering their moments with the dog in the car.. "Think it will work?" he asked, turning to her.

"It's a fairly new car," she answered. "I haven't had any problems yet. But," she laughed at the thought. "The back seat may need to be swept out first."

David understood immediately. "I'll take care of that," he said. He had a broom in his hand rather quickly as he and Russ went out to check out her car. As he swept out the crumbs he tossed a small rubber ball to Russ.

"For the dog," he said.

By the time they finished the florist had delivered a red rose corsage that David pinned to

Julie's yellow shoulder top in full view of Russ and Cora. By that time he had his suitcase in the trunk of Julie's car, and Cora had worked out the seating arrangements.

Russ would be the driver. David would sit in the front seat beside him, and she would sit with Julie in the back seat. The ride would have been cool even without the air conditioner. Neither a glance nor conversation was possible between them.

A moment of freedom came once they were at Kennedy. David had to check in. Russ went with him. Cora made a trip to a ladies' restroom leaving Julie alone at a small, round table in a lounge area. She was still alone when David sat next to her.

"I need to hear your voice," he said, in utter frustration. "Say something to me before they get back."

"I love you," she said, softly.

"Oh, my darling," he whispered.

"You have my address. If you want to stay in touch you will have to write to me first."

They'd had their moment, one sad love-lit moment, before the appearance of Cora and Russ ended any further conversation. Both were in shock at finding them alone. Russ had stopped at a rest room while Cora lingered with her makeup in the ladies' room.

She glared at Russ.

Julie used the silence to take out the Polaroid camera she had brought with her. She took a couple of test pictures. She even got Russ to take a picture of the table where she and David were sitting with Cora. She would crop Cora from the photo later. If nothing else she had a color picture of David sitting with her before he boarded his flight home to England.

Elizabeth R. Lawrence

Chapter Two   Love by Post

My dear Julie,
     Here I am, back in the filth and depravity that is my lot in London. I am so depressed.
     I miss you so much I have written a poem, not something I usually do.
          "Gaolers I had four, you know,
          Or maybe it was five. (the dog)
          "No where could I move or go,
          "Most guarded Englishman alive.
          Just one moment in your arms,
          Your lips I gently kissed,
          Just one moment of your charms,
          "Oh, how much love I've missed.
          I miss your voice, your eyes, your hair,
          I love you so, you know.
          And for your love and my despair,
          3000 miles I'll go."
     Please forgive my poetry. It is not something I usually do. I am so lost I can't even think of how to put the words I want to say on paper. But I want to post this right away. Even by air it will take four or five days for our mail to reach each other. I will have to be patient to wait for your reply. I wish I had taken one of the Polaroid pictures you took. I feel so cut off now.
     I don't know how this happened, Julie, but I love you.   David

In a London Fog

Letters meant to fill in the space between them as they got to know each other continued their longing and frustration while Cora and Kitty continued to hover in the background.

In one letter, responding to David's obvious frustration, Julie wrote: "If they had left us alone to do what we wanted to do on sight, we might have sizzled for a while and maybe burned out naturally. Now I don't know..."

"I know," he answered. "Your sweet face haunts me every hour of the day. I, too, picture us together. I have an ache where I ought not, just for you and because of you. Only when I have enjoyed the promise of your lovely body will I be able to think straight."

She was delighted by the unexpected delivery of a dozen red roses a few days later. A handwritten card came with them.

"Thoughts too long to be expressed,
 And too deep to be suppressed.
                    Love David.

She had pressed his red rose corsage safely in an album. Before doing anything with these she cabled a thank you to David's office.

He responded by cable at once.

"Roses? Not guilty. Will do better."

At that very moment she knew who had sent them. At first she was simply going to write to tell David. No, she thought. I know what she wants. She dialed Cora's phone.

"Hello, Cora," she said, speaking happily. "I thought you'd like to know I've just received a dozen roses from…" She heard Cora gasp.

"From?"

"David."

"What color roses?" she asked.

"Red." Julie said.

"Red roses mean love, you know."

"A card came with them."

"Sometimes florists write the cards," Cora volunteered. "What did it say?"

"Why don't I bring it over," Julie replied. "You might know the writing."

Cora, looking like a has been from an old talkie movie opened the door when she got to the house. There was no way Julie could reconcile David's relationship to this woman. The thought itself was a turn off.

Cora showed no surprise as she read the card. "But why would he send roses now?"

"He's probably thanking me for the use of my car," Julie answered, with enthusiasm. "I wish I could thank him and …"

Cora was suddenly energized. "With the time difference," she said, "he might be home now. I can call from here and talk to Addie. If he's home she'll put him on the phone."

Cora had done exactly what Julie wanted her to do, As a result she had managed to hear David's voice even though a confused David couldn't hear a word she said with Cora chattering behind her. .She wasn't making much sense anyway. Her voice was too choked with her effort to keep her feelings out of it.

Because their letters had a four to eight day gap David didn't learn of Cora's involvement with the first dozen roses until much later. By that time he had sent her two dozen roses with a card signed *"The Real David."*. When he finally got the letter he wrote: "What a bitch of a thing for Cora to do. Why would she do such a thing?"

Sweet innocent, she thought. "Once you said you hadn't sent them I knew she had and the reason was clear. She wanted to know if we were communicating. By my seeming so open she believes we're no longer in touch."

All guilt aside she didn't mention Addie. She saw Addie more as a mother than a wife who was treating David more like a dutiful son than a husband. Julie had responded to the man in him. The man had responded to her as a woman.

Until they could work that out there was no going back.

"In one of your letters I received today," he wrote, " you asked if I knew you, particularly from your letters.

Darling, whatever happened in the past, does it matter? (A lot was put to me to frighten me off before I left.) My attraction to you was so obvious. You can't imagine the pains they went through to tell me about you. Your past is past and so is mine. Today we are so far apart we may as well not know each other. But tomorrow..? I can tell you now, I knew you within ten minutes of meeting you. All that I wanted to know anyway. Let me explain.

Elizabeth R. Lawrence

    My job, I think, has a lot to do with it; it is second nature to me to weigh everyone as soon as I meet them. You? You have warm eyes, dark and sweet. They tell me that you are overly generous, that you have been hurt, and that you worry inwardly. Your eyes told me other things later, including come to bed. How I wish I could right now, in the middle of this hot summer day.

    I did so love your last letter. If I could have touched you I think we would have crushed each other. I feel so much for you; words can't tell you how much. . When I join you in the ultimate of love's acts, then I shall be able to tell you and show you exactly how much.

    I must stop teasing myself so I'll change the subject! Among a drawer full of letters I can't find the one with your birthday. Will you remind me, please?

    I now must leave on business, darling. I hope I can get back and post this today.."

    (Three days later. It is now Tuesday the 23rd of August.) I am so sorry . My only excuse is that I work eleven hours a day. Saturday is generally the best day for me to find time to write to you as, during the afternoon , although I am still busy I normally find time to clear all the paperwork that built up during the week and can scratch around on my own business.

    As you can gather, from the news you have had there, it is pretty hectic at the moment. We don't like this running about armed to the teeth playing cowboys and injuns! It's not healthy!

There's a book I must get you on the history of the British Police. It might interest you and will, at least, show you why we are seldom armed. (It was a bit of a shock to see even your traffic police armed to the teeth!)

I am longing to hear your voice on Wednesday. I only hope the office is reasonably empty so that I won't have too much of an audience."

The letters, which arrived in pale blue air mail envelopes, had become the highlight and heart of Julie's still busy but changing life. Her job at the sales company, from where she had interviewed Cora, kept her busy during the day. Her work meant interviewing the sales people, dealing with real estate problems, interacting with management and helping with the paperwork, but it was a job, not a career. It didn't make for a full life when she went home to the quiet rooms of her townhouse apartment.

Tina was spending the end of summer working and living at a friend's Wildwood shore motel. Jason, still at his job at the Mall, was busy with his friends, but he was interviewing for a job that would take him to New York. With her children moving on with their lives the phone didn't ring as often. Noise stopped. Silence lingered. Echoes began.

She slept alone with thoughts of David. She wanted to talk to him, to walk with him, to share her love with him. She wanted his love. She wanted what he wanted even if it was just a kiss. She lived in a park like setting that would have suited them both. She had his picture; she had his letters and she had all the space they would have needed to hold each other if he wasn't a married man half a world away.

David's letters echoed her longing.

She didn't dwell on thoughts of the young man she had married years ago. She had spent too long dealing with his credit card debts, and working to help pay creditors, as he drifted from job to job after finishing college. Foreclosure had taken their newly built house. Bankruptcy took what little assets they'd accumulated. She salvaged what she could, filed for divorce and moved with her children into the apartment complex near her parents and life went on.

On weekends she took her aging parents grocery shopping with her. She got them to their doctors' appointments and picked up their medicines. Sometimes she just sat with them and let them talk as they ate together. Lonely was lonely for them, too.

The pool was still open and, when she had time, she enjoyed the company of Richard and Emma, the resident Brits who had settled in a nearby apartment with their young children. Cora and Russ had visited them a couple of times but Richard had discouraged their visits.

"We have very little in common," he said, without going into detail.

They showed her cards David had sent that said how much he enjoyed meeting them at the pool.

He'd sent a funny sketch he'd done to the children with a little note from Janet enclosed. They were, she knew from his letters, things he could write from home and she was delighted but, at the same time, she wanted to cry. They had already been apart too long.

The next pale blue air mail envelope held typewritten pages on regular typing paper.

'My darling, darling girl, I am still trying to recover from that wonderful phone call. I went cold inside when I heard your voice. It was such a thrill. Unfortunately, I can't reciprocate. I don't think the Commissioner would want to pay for such a call and there is no way I can have it charged to me. It was sweet of you to phone but don't do it again. Save the money towards airfare and get to me.

The buildup to this was fantastic. In the early afternoon I drove to Duncan Police Station and was engaged for some time. While I was there one of the lads telephoned me from Lancer to say that someone had phoned from the States and would call again at 5 PM.

At 5 PM I was at the Romany Police Station (I wonder why that makes me think of you? Your hair, maybe?) so I couldn't take your call. I managed to get back for 7 PM and WOW!

By that time the office was packed, each man half cocking an ear to hear what was going on. As you can guess the word has got around among the fellows. You would have laughed at some of the ribald comments I had to put up with. As I think I have said before, they are a good crowd of villains and, apart from the usual leg pulls you come to expect the lot, unlike Russ, can be relied on 100%.

I so regret not getting more letters off to you. I so regret late posts when I am called away

I received two letters from you today, including photos, none at all yesterday and I pined all day so I know how you feel. Darling Julie, I wish for so many things now. Life is so short. Why can't we just seize our chances and run away? Why can't our dreams all come true?

I've been called away twice while writing this. My darling, darling, lovely girl.. I am so sorry that I have not sent this letter, particularly today. I have been so busy I have not been able to write more than a few words at a time. I have, during the course of my duties, to visit Pubs (bars to you) to meet informants and the like. Of course, this means that, sometimes, I consume more drink than I should. Anyway, what I am trying to say at the moment is that I am half cut. (stoned or bombed) so I must be real careful what I say. I do try to exercise a great deal of restraint in my letters, you know.

I wanted to say so much about that bitch of a trick of Cora's but it's not worth my time right now. Darling, even if I'm late I do hope there is something in the post for me tomorrow. I won't delay this one any longer if I can help it. I love the photographs you sent me together with the framed one of us at the airport. I am gazing at it in rapture. You look so attractive I could eat you.! What a stupid fool I am! Oh, what the hell! I can't make sense. Don't want to. I have tears in my eyes just for want of you

In a London Fog

Darling Julie, why did you have to complicate my life? I have never even looked at another woman. With just a glance between us you have ruined me, destroyed me absolutely. Suffice it to say I will love you always.

Don't worry about American vs English expressions. I will tell you about them one day. Just write and tell me you love me. That's the same in any language. I can say it in French, too, but I can't spell it.

Dear sweet face, as I look at you you almost come alive for me. I can almost hear your voice. Such a gentle voice, I can remember every intonation and inflection. But nothing except "I love you." Please love me and think of me. I miss you so very much."

Julie read and reread the letter hearing his British voice in every word. Whatever had started in a glance had gone from a spark to a tiny, burning, flame. 3000 miles separated them but an ocean had not put out the desire. But how many times, and how many ways can you put it in words on paper?

When she hadn't heard from him in days she wrote a couple of letters as one act plays "to be staged in London." The first was titled:

The Unexpected Arrival

<u>Me:</u> (getting off plane) Oh my goodness. They ALL look like David.

<u>You:</u> (Peeking at photo in your pocket) That must be her. The one in yellow.

<u>Me:</u> (Scanning the look-alikes and wearing brown) I wonder if he'll show a badge or something.

You: (Passing me to get to the girl in yellow): Pardon me?
Me: (Hearing your voice and losing mine): David?
You: (Nervously) Speaking to me?
Me: (Taking your arm) For many weeks on reams of paper..
You: (Wondering if you can handle me) I have a shack down by the river Thames.
Me: (In the shack) Kiss me.
You: (Gurgling).Are you sure Cora isn't hiding somewhere around here?
Me: (Melting in your arms) Who is Cora?
You: (Gasping for air) The shack is slipping. The tide is coming in. I can't swim. I'm going to drown..
Me: (Sighing) Me, too.

      FADE OUT to second play.
      "The Surprising Arrival"
      Same Cast – Dorchester Hotel

Me: (Pinching nose to sound British) May I speak to Detective David Gregory, please?
You: (Official voice) Speaking
Me: (Outraged citizen) I want to report a crime.
You: (Bored) Name and address. please.
Me: (Holding nose) Dorchester. Room Seven.
You: (Annoyed) That is out of my district.
Me: (Suffocating) There is a note attached to a body to be delivered to David Gregory in person.

In a London Fog

<u>You:</u> (Alert) A body? For me?
<u>Me:</u> (Trying to breathe) It says come alone or..
<u>You:</u> (Anxioux) Be right there.
<u>Me:</u> (After perfuming room) Titter titter..
<u>You:</u> (Knocking) Open in the name of the Queen!
<u>Me:</u> (Prostrate on bed) Come in
<u>You:</u> (Looking past me) Where is the body?
<u>Me:</u> (Moaning) Come closer.
<u>You:</u> (Leaning over) Miss??
<u>Me:</u> (Turning face to meet your lips) Kiss me.
<u>You:</u> (Losing official composure) I'm on duty.
<u>Me:</u> (Holding you) I hope so.
<u>You:</u> (Not resisting) This is wrong.
<u>Me:</u> (Arms around you) Charge me with the crime later.
<u>You:</u> (Groaning) I'm only human.
<u>Me:</u> (Sighing with pleasure) Me, too.
            FADE OUT

He got mixed messages from her two plays.

"When will you arrive?" he asked. "Please forgive me for taking so long to write to you. The days are just not long enough to cope with the rubbish, let alone the additional trouble we are having with these shootings. Today I started at 9AM and don't expect to complete the work before 11 PM.

I have received your beautiful letters. You must be so annoyed with me after all this time. But, before I go on, I must tell you I love you.

I've missed not being able to talk my heart out at least every other day. I adore you and long for you constantly. You have been very discerning in your advice to me as far as Addie is concerned.

She has noticed how quiet I've been since our return and last night this came to a head when she taxed me with it. Her words to end the argument were, "You have left something behind in America. You had better go back and clear it up if that's what you want to do." I felt like jumping on the first plane but, darling, I have strings like six inch ropes tied to me!"

"If I had any sense," she said, talking to Richard and Emma after confiding in them, "I would run away as if he had the plague."

They agreed. "You should get out more."

"Out where? I haven't met anyone who interested me in years. I don't think we spoke more than a few words to each other and look what's happened. Most people I meet at work are married, too. Maybe I need a hobby."

"We're signing up for a course in handwriting analysis at the high school two nights a week." Emma said.

She gave Julie a mimeo copy listing other classes. A few days later Julie signed up for an art class she might enjoy. It filled her time and she interacted with everyone there, but she didn't meet anyone that interested her in or outside the classroom.

Maybe, by now, she thought, trying to understand her feelings for David, they would have fallen in bed and lost themselves in each other's arms. Or maybe they would have found they had nothing in common beyond that urgent desire. Or maybe he was right. It was insanity.

Take off the blinkers, she told herself.

"Tell me about you," she wrote.

"About me," he wrote, in answer to her question. "I've led a quite simple life as an ordinary bloke who grew up in a Catholic family with four brothers and two sisters. I left school early but soon signed on for training in the building trade. Because of the war I spent as much time in air raid shelters as I did with my tools. However, by the time I finished I was a carpenter. The royal army took me for the next two years. Of course, since I was now a man who worked with wood, they decided I belonged in the metals department in the technical area where I proceeded to ruin a Spitfire (one of ours, of course). They then put me in charge of twenty-two men and sent me around England where I might do some good and less damage.

(May I do some damage control here? It has been too long since I've told you I love you.) I love you, sweet Julie. I love you.

To continue: I went back to being a carpenter, but I didn't fancy it as something I wanted to do for the rest of my life. By then I
was more adventurous so I applied for a job with the Metropolitan Police. (Now I fix or build

things in my home or make things I enjoy making.)

When I saw the specimens among the over seventy applicants taking the tests I didn't think I had a chance but surprise! I was one of twenty chosen to return. There was a great deal more testing but eventually I became a policeman. (bobby to you.) That work entails traffic duty as well as everything else. Once you're out there you're pretty much on your own. The work was interesting and I enjoyed it but I wanted to go further so, after the two required years, I tested for work with the C.I.D. (That's the Criminal Intelligence Department) where we deal with vice. (investigating not indulging). There were more tests, many involving the law. I have had many successes and some disappointment, most due to my lack of education, but I am now C.I.D. Detective Constable David Gregory.

Get over here, my darling. I adore you and long for you. Somewhere to stay? Worry about that when you arrive! I hope to be able to get you a small flat not too far away. These are the least of our problems. Excuses are mine."

That last paragraph reminded Julie of an old movie she had seen as a child. It had starred Irene Dunne and John Boles. The title was *"Back Street."* It was a love story that seemed sad. She didn't understand why it was sad but she remembered crying at the heartbreaking end.

The memory disturbed her.

"Don't get too angry with me. You are always in my thoughts, night and day. Love me always and forgive me for being your long distance lover."

"Darling, I love you," he wrote in another letter. "This has been a rough week as far as work goes. Apart from the usual run of the mill stuff we had a call from a building site. Workmen were pulling out some old drains when they found a body about five feet down. Straight away this becomes a murder enquiry. Then we find that the body has been there since 1530! Interesting story. Will tell you someday.

Hurry up and come to me. I wish you could come in the spring so that you could see England at its most beautiful. But that's too long to wait, isn't it? In fact, forget I said that. I want you very much. Now.

I shall have to drop this now and do a bit more later. My enemy, time, is to blame again! I bet I make you mad. One of these days you will receive a deluge of letters. Promises. Promises."

"So sorry, my sweet darling," he said in another late letter. " So very, very busy. Will write later. Don't worry. (See enclosed news clipping.) All my love. In haste."

"I know how you feel," he wrote in the next letter. "We are all very busy at the moment and find it difficult to find time to eat! The last two days have gone by and I have had only two cards from you. I miss your letters each day I can tell you so don't punish me by not writing, will you? You ask 'What do you do each day?' The simplest thing to do is to describe today.

7 AM: Hammered the alarm through the top of the bedside table to stop it ringing and promptly went back to sleep. 7:45 AM: Woke to cries of "Dad! Dad You're late!" Leapt out of bed and staggered back with the shock. 7:50AM Got in bath and got out. Water too hot. Shaved, dressed and wandered into kitchen fresh as a daisy.. Had breakfast and leapt into battered old car to do a half hour journey in twenty minutes . 9:20 AM: Only 20 minutes late. Wandered into office trying to look as if I'd been about since half past eight. Looked in tray. Blast! No letters. Picked up several files and bits of paper. Put them down and had a cup of tea in the canteen. 9:40 AM: Had first peep of you in drawer then got down to type some reports to spin the time out until 11 AM. Hoorah! A card! "Write!" Blushed and rushed out to do the morning calls. Housebreaking and the like.

To continue (one hour later...) Returned to station at 1 PM. Made necessary entries in various books. Drove Detective Superintendent (head mosh of the CID, our Division) to local Public House (bar) to meet an informant. Had a sandwich and a couple of gins for lunch and listened to a load of rubbish about nothing. Returned to the station at 2:30 PM. Just about to do more paperwork when somebody shouts , "Suspects loitering outside Lancer Gaol!" Run down two fights of stairs, jump into the CID nondescript, drove out of the garage, three hairy monsters jump in, and with two other cars, lights, bells and klaxons going, we roar up Lancer Road through all the traffic, sliding all over the place in the wet and arrive at the Gaol sweating and about ten years older. False alarm. Relax. Light cigarette. Amble back.

Broke off here. 10PM: I am going home. Will complete AM tomorrow. I LOVE you.

...Another day. No sense in continuing. I got called out and was engaged until 8 PM. When I returned had to take a number of statements which kept me until 10 PM. Couldn't complete this. You can see what its like however.

Now. Today I received your sweetest letter together with your telegram which was phoned over to me. Darling, I am so sorry. I love you so much it hurts me, too. I will send you a cable first thing in the morning.

It is now 9:10 PM, Sept 1st. Over a month of loving you. I have to pick something up in the morning which I want to enclose if it is okay so will hold this.

I love you so much. I can't wait for the photos you are going to send. Please, don't get upset when you don't hear from me. (Once again I had to leave!) Now Friday Sept 2nd. 10:30AM: Getting this in the post now. I hope you like the enclosures . I don't think they're very good but still. The picture I have left in the folder you can keep in your bedroom. You had better turn his face to the wall when you undress though. He is not above a peek now and then. Please forgive this lack of mail. Same reason for this as the bags under the eyes, long and late hours. Look after that sweet mouth. I love you very much. Forever."

Sept 3rd. By the time you get this you will have my photos. What did you think of them? I thought they were terrible. Do I really look as haggard as that? Mind you, I am very tired just now. I think I could sleep for a week and it shows. How much do you love me? I often wonder in spite of a drawer choked to the brim with your letters now. I must go through them to answer any questions I missed earlier. It will give me another excuse to look at your face anyway.

In one of your letters you asked how much 300 pounds was or was it 300 dollars? Anyway, 300 pounds equals approx. 900 dollars. Simple way to break a pound up is to say it equals three dollars, although the correct rate is $2.82 per hundred pound sterling.

Notes in common use are: 10, 5 and 1 pound with British pound symbol. (not dollar sign) and 10/ (ten shillings) There are twenty shillings to the pound; there are twelve pennies to the shilling. Coins are English Crown (or dollar) which is 5/- shillings and Half Crown 2/6d. Florin (two bob) equals 2/- and shilling equals 1/-. Sixpence equals 6 d. Copper equals three pence or three penny bit

(3d) One penny is 1d, and half penny (or ha penny) is ½ d.

Three shillings and five pence would be written thus: 3/5d. Any note can be broken down. 1 pound equals 2 at 10 or 8 half crowns, etc, etc. Must leave on business. I love you.

Monday. 2 PM. After all the above rubbish let me tell you I have been thinking about you more than ever over the weekend. I worked on Saturday as usual and had Sunday off. I spent the time making a unit up for the kitchen. It is most peculiar how a phrase from one of your letters will suddenly come to mind just out of the blue and you are in my thoughts for hours. I will enclose a couple of your letters with answers to questions right on them. Letter 1 A. I loved you when I saw you. B. We both knew, didn't we? C I want you very much. 2 A. You must keep up your strength for me. B. You know I'd come to you if I could. C. Because I love you D. Yes. I can hear your voice on paper. You have a soft, sweet voice. . Get over here.

This is the sweetest letter you have sent. I shall want to see this again. Both the enclosed are sweet letters. Why should I part with them? Make sure you keep them for me to see, if possible, just before I make love to you.

Dear, darling, unattainable one, I want you so much. Think of me now and again, Will one day write a sensible letter. I love you. "

Elizabeth R. Lawrence

Their Photographs

The black and white studio pictures he had sent crossed with the color Polaroids she had sent to him. She got his first. The one he had left in the folder had been enlarged. In two she saw an unsmiling serious man, in one a tired man, in another the obvious policeman with a strong jaw, but none were haggard. The one in the folder was a strong, gentle, kind, man. That was the one she knew. She did what he asked, putting it on the bookshelf headboard of her bed, next to the color Polaroid taken at the airport that brought him to life. A copy of that one was also in her wallet. She lived with the others for a while before putting them in the album that held another airport copy, the rose corsage and Shakespeare's words.

"I love your pictures," she wrote in her letter. "But they made me cry. Adding a line from the poet, Edna St. Vincent Millay, she wrote, "*And who are you that loving you, I should be kept awake, as many nights as there are days, with weeping for your sake...?*" I've only kissed you once, David. Why should I feel this way? I love your pictures but I want the flesh and blood you to come to life."

With the help of one of the women from the art class she had posed for the Polaroids to send to him. The class had been drawing faces, not figures, from various magazines. Taking home a Playboy Magazine Julie chose from poses she could use. When they were finished she had photos modeled after the lacy, peekaboo pictures, not the nudes. In one, with her hair falling on her shoulder, she is wearing a wide brimmed red hat with a short see-through black lace nightie. In another, in dark slacks and a low cut top that barely hides her breasts she points a gun near a sign that reads: Have gun, will travel. In another, barely clothed, with spectacles at the end of her nose, she is reading one of his letters. There were a total of six, all in similar provocative poses. Her letter went with them.

His reaction to the Polaroid pictures was typically masculine. On Sept 12th he wrote: *"Good Gawd! *?//***::@""&ooo!!* I have just picked myself up after looking at those photographs! Whew! I feel all hot under the collar now. Why did you have to do that to me after such a hectic day?

Dear, dear Julie, I think they are beautiful and only wish I could put them up all around the office. Couldn't possibly do that though. The other monkeys would nick (sorry, steal) them. Ye Gods! I shall be done for the rest of the week now! What a gorgeous woman you are, Julie!

Change the subject immediately, David. Before I do may I say I have waited for three days without a letter but it was worth it! You ARE beautiful, you know. Wow!

Darling, this, I'm afraid, must be a short note as I must get cracking on some more work. (It is only 8 PM.) While I am on the subject I must point out that we work the hours we do, not for more money, promotion, or anything else, but only because we have to owing to shortage of staff, and the love of the job. It is very rewarding, you know.

Elizabeth R. Lawrence

Enough of that. When can you get over to me? It is important that Addie should not have any idea that you are coming for what I intend to do is leave home as usual in the mornings (I can always arrange to be called out at night, too) and spend days and days and nights and NIGHTS with you. The lads here will cover for me. As I explained , they are a good crowd of MEN. Besides a bedroom, I also want to show you a little of London, too. After those last photographs I am not so sure of the last bit though.

Please forgive the gap between letters but we have had a couple of nasty shootings during the week, one a ten year old child (I think I told you about that), the other, a meth drinker (bum). Not very pleasant, either of them.

Thank you for your sweet letters and those wonderful photos. I love you very much, you know. In fact, I am told I talk in my sleep. Although my wife won't tell me what name I used I can make a pretty fair guess.

Darling, I will end this with the last of that Shakespeare quote: "<u>No sooner knew the reason but they sought the remedy</u>."

I am looking forward to the remedy. Love me. I love you very much, my darling.

15th Sept 1966. Hello, my love, I am just snatching a few moments in another hectic day to tell you I love you and think of you constantly. I have tried to find time during the day to put my thoughts on paper, but I'm afraid this whole Division is like a mad house at the moment.

The day seems empty so far for I haven't had a word from you yet. I so look forward to getting your mail every day. Yesterday produced three, together with your card. The letters were very sweet.

Your remarks on Cora have been noted. I think she is a professional liar. She was known as Lita in England so I often have to think twice before I make the connection with the name Cora. Any letter she writes should not be too difficult for her. We haven't heard from her in some time and are wondering what the delay is. By the way, when she reads our letters to you, take them with a pinch of salt for, as yet, I haven't sent my love to you direct via Cora for obvious reasons, so she is obviously putting it on a bit anyway.

So that you can have a bit of a giggle I will explain a few facts and you can compare them with Cora's version.

The life story of David Gregory, Esq continued.

The basic pay for this job amounts to 73 pounds per month before income tax, although with Detective duty allowances, etc., I get a good deal more. (73 pounds equals $219.00 approx.) I think your New York city cop gets about 200 pounds per month. Some comparison!

I married Addie ten years ago. Janet was born a year later. Addie has two grown children and two grandchildren that call me Granddad.

We live in a suburb of London, very heavily populated and not very pretty. I own a terraced house (with a fair mortgage) also not very pretty but very middle class. My car would make an American laugh but, to the English, it is a little above the middle price range and very fast. I work at least eleven hours a day, six days per week, sometimes more. My daughter attends an ordinary London County Council Junior School until she is eleven, when she will have to take an exam for a better school. What else? Oh, yes. My garden is a mess. My garage is falling to pieces and so is the fence. That should give you something to get on with.

Now, before I go mad I must tell you that I love you and that I can't wait to touch you. And, blast it, I shall have to pack this up for a while and dash out. To be continued:

Fri. 16th Sept. 1:20 PM. Impossible to do anything at the moment. I can't seem to settle in one spot long enough .Please excuse me. This is so rushed I can't make sense of it so don't know if you will.

I received two letters from you this morning. They cheered me up no end. I do notice a day when I don't get a letter for, when I read them, I can hear your voice. There is no doubt your letters are you.

Let's turn for a moment, to your questions on love. I shall never forget the feeling I had when, at the airport, you said, so simply, those wonderful three words. I can remember your face and the absolute feeling of tenderness I had at that moment.

I find I can't express exactly what I felt. I just haven't the time to sit and think. All I can say is I have never heard those three words spoken with such feeling, tenderness and love. It was a little more than a whisper, yet it meant so much for it was something that I had no right to say.

We were stumbling around it from the moment we met but once I knew how you felt I had the right to express my feelings. How can I tell you how much I love you? I can only say my feelings are akin to yours, that I treasure every thought of you and remember every trivial little contact with you. I literally long for you and pine for you like a sick dog. I have a normal desire to possess you (in fact, I want you like hell) but, at the same time, I have such a tender feeling for you. I can't explain. Wait until I hold you. You won't have to say much either but, boy, let me get my hands on you!

Love by post!! I could laugh sometimes if it wasn't so tragic. It's not fair, you know, all this time going by and, if we were nearer all our thoughts could have been put into practice. Darling, it is so simple. I love you with everything in me that is tender. I want you with everything that is savage. I need you with everything impatient. Oh, that I had a thousand pounds! I would hammer your door down.

I love you, darling. I can't make sense. I'm in love! Your David.

8PM. Darling, before going home thought I would knock out a few words while I have a minute on my own. I love you.

Elizabeth R. Lawrence

I have had a scan through my treasured photographs to get in the right atmosphere and now feel in the mood to ravish you. (With respect, of course,) I couldn't tell you which photo I like best. I like them all. No. I love them all even though they're a substitute for the real thing. I must say you look younger than I thought. Darling, you are very beautiful. You are lovely. You are gorgeous. How I wish I could kiss that sweet face right now. One day I shall hold you and say all the things I can't say on paper. Right now I would settle for just one look in your eyes!

Like you, I have put us both in crazy situations (in thought) and would love to have the time to put them on paper. In my situation we reach a peak of love only to find our friend?? Cora peering at us from some weird vantage point and I collapse on the floor giggling.

Darling, I love you so much. I shall kiss you from the top of your pretty head to the tips of your pretty toes as soon as I can lock you away in a room somewhere. (Before, if possible.) The picture I have of you in my mind is so real I can almost feel and smell you. Please, let me know in plenty of time before you come so I can lay something on. I can't stand the thought of spending fleeting minutes with you and dashing away. I must have time, time, time. What I have in mind for you cannot be completed in three months, let alone three weeks!

I must get away from here before I get caught for another job. My darling, I love you and want you very much.

I came across the the enclosed newspaper in my drawer, while I was trying to make room for your letters, and thought you might be interested. The job itself was very interesting. Do you think the picture looks like me? Notice that, apart from the fact that they used the wrong name. they promoted me. Shows you can't believe everything you read in the newspapers!! The other chap is my Detective Superintendent, the fellow I spend most of my time with. A nice old boy; due to retire soon.

Must go, my sweet darling. I love you and think of you always. I conjure up your face almost every hour in the day. Goodnight and sweet dreams, my love.

Mon. Sept 18th.. Darling, I am so sorry that the letter I posted today was delayed. I haven't been near the station for days having been engaged on the rest of the Division so I couldn't post it. It didn't contain much news anyway. I hate this practice of sitting down to scramble a few words on a bit of paper. I would like to give a little thought to what I am about to say. Perhaps it is better this way but I feel I am not at my best when rushed. (at anything.) I am sorry but I do my best.

I intended to be a little serious when I first started this letter and wanted to be neat, tidy, and cool about it. But how can I when I have to rush around to get a few minutes alone to write? It is almost like having Cora on my tail! Heaven forbid!

Elizabeth R. Lawrence

The following day. Tues. Not a bad day today. Has been very quiet but you can bet that now I have settled down for a few minutes things will begin to happen. Never mind.

I loved the letters I received today. Yes, I do think of you as much as I say. Today I was driving through the Mall at Buckingham Palace, through Westminster, over the Thames, and saw London in a new light. I thought how nice it would have been had you been with me. The buildings looked so beautiful in the sunshine. This is the time I should be showing you around. You will love London; such a mixture of old and new. You should be here RIGHT NOW. Why aren't you?

You asked me in one of your letters what England was like, was it always raining, etc., and what clothes should you bring .

Well now.. No, it isn't always raining. In fact, we haven't had any rain for weeks. It is so pleasant now that I am sitting about in shirt sleeves, something an Englishman is reluctant to do. It isn't considered polite. When you come in October (I hope and pray) it will be getting cold and we should have some rain then. Towards November we can get fog which is particularly nasty. It won't be too bad though and, with you around , we must have an Indian summer. The sun is sure to shine. Clothes? Warm ones. (You will not need much in bed anyway.) Come in rags, You will still look the most beautiful girl in town!

Have I ever told you what a beautiful woman you are? If I haven't I must be mad. If I have once more won't hurt. I want you like mad, my beauty, Spring, summer, autumn or winter. So come when you will. If you are cold I will cuddle you. If you are hot I will fan you. Just let me see you, that's all!

Ah, if only one of us had money!

Do you know I suddenly felt like a ponce? I had better watch out or I will lose you to some rich guy. I wonder what would happen if all of a sudden you weren't there? I'm getting morbid at the thought so better pack this in.

I love you, darling, and promise I will write later in the week. Think of me. All I have are some photos. I long for you. There are women and there are women, Julie. To me you are one of the most beautiful creatures in the whole world. I love you. U and only U.

Wed. 21st Sept. Dear sweet Julie, Is it telepathy or pure coincidence? I went to the Post Office to post a letter this morning in which I tried to explain what the weather would be like and what you should bring to wear, only to find, on my return, a card in which you berated me for not doing just that. I am amazed.

At the risk of repeating myself come as you are at the moment. (I hope you are not in the bath.) Seriously, bring warm clothes . (You look a darling in anything.) It will certainly be cold, I can assure you of that, so you will need something warm to wrap up in.

Isn't it exciting? The thought of you being here makes me tingle. All I hope is that I will be able to spend plenty of time with you. Please give me plenty of warning. I need to make arrangements, as you can guess. I wonder if, when we meet again, you will be able to say the things that have passed between us by mail? Will we be stuck for words?

Broke off once again! Can I ever have time to complete a letter in one go?

It is now 2 PM the next day (Thurs.) and I find myself with not too much to do. It is wonderful to be able to relax and think sweet thoughts of you.

As I came past the Houses of Parliament this morning I noticed tourists taking photographs. I pictured myself taking a photograph with you in the foreground. What a shame you are not here. Everything is so beautiful. When you come you will miss all the green trees; the Guards will have their pretty uniforms covered with drab grey, and everything will be dull. Why aren't you here now?

I mustn't complain. When I think about it, if all goes well, you should be here before long. I wonder what you will like most about London? It will be nice if we can see some of the countryside, too. Surrey and Kent are much like New Jersey and Maryland. I wish I could take you all over England but you would need months for that. (Can yu manage it?)

I so look forward to seeing you. I love you very much and want you here. I must not get impatient after waiting all this time. But, oh, how I want to touch you.

4:35 PM.. I can't believe it! How on earth did I find time to sit down twice in one day to write to

In a London Fog

you? As usual, I received a card and a letter just after I had posted one to you. Such a sweet letter. I love you so much. I wish I could put my thoughts on paper in such a lucid way. I was amused at your card and reference to clothing once again. For your information it is still very warm here although a little chilly in the mornings together with a slight fog.

I so miss you, darling, and I want you;

The rush hour in London is well under way and, from my office, I can see thousands of cars pouring out of London all rushing to get home. Lucky devils. How do you think I feel? I know I shall be on duty until 10 PM.

I'd love to know what impressions you've formed of London, Let me know and I'll tell you how near you are.

I have to charge off into the wilds of Kent very soon so I suppose I must put an end to this. I had a few moments peace and couldn't resist the temptation to tell you that I love you. I shan't say a word to you when I first meet you. I shall just feast my eyes on the beauty of you. (<u>You</u> try working that one out. Perhaps you won't do it to me.)

I am just about to have a quick look at my picture gallery and then off. Remember I love you and have you on my mind <u>all the time.</u> You come with me to the strangest places! I love you. It won't be long before I retire (At least, eight years doesn't sound long if you say it fast.) How would a house in Cherry Hill, New Jersey look called Gipsy Cottage? Just dreaming. Never mind Love me NOW!

5PM. Sept 23. Darling Julie, I bet you're wondering what has happened? Three notes in three days? I only wish I could do more. I have been confined to an office all day today. Have plenty to do but I am bored.

At the moment I am trying to conjure up a picture of you swaggering about with those few flowers I gave you just before we parted. You did look attractive. No wonder I am all a Ga Ga. I love you.

Thank you. I had two letters today. I feel like a lovesick kid looking for them each day. The fellow that brings them up from the front office for me today said, "Christ, Almighty, is somebody over there writing a b----ing book?"

I'm sitting here half watching the P.C. on point duty outside, and wishing that my life, at the moment, was as uncluttered and uncomplicated as his. I wish I had his free time. Eight hours on the beat and he is done. No worries or cares. But still, he hasn't got a beautiful American girl to think about.

Tell me why it is that, after such a brief meeting I should be swamped with memories of you? Trivial little snatches of conversation a touch, a glance, all suddenly leap into my mind to remind me of you. When I think about it I must have set my sights on you the moment I saw you across that kitchen table. It's a wonder I didn't ravish you there and then. I wish I had. No, I don't. You ARE beautiful! That's for sure!

I am wondering what we have done to upset Lita (sorry, Cora) as we haven't heard from her for ages. Perhaps it is this concocted story that is taking so long. Should be interesting.

Panic, panic, panic.. I just went to my drawer to have a look at your letters and couldn't find the two I received today. After a frantic search I found one but can't find the other. There is such a gigantic bunch there now it must be there somewhere.

I wish you you had been with me over the past two years. It has taken me that long to do my kitchen the way I wanted it. Apart from the obvious reasons, I would have been glad to have you to help me as number two carpenter! Pass the 'ammer, mate! Make a right pair, wouldn't we?

Don't think the cost of living is lower here. If anything, in some respects, it is a lot higher. What's money anyway? (If only...)

Right. Its off again; The mad scramble to get out on a job that's just come up is on so I had better get going.

Remember, I love you and want you very much. It won't be long before I can show you.
Love me? How's that fellow in your bedroom behaving?

Tues. Sept 27. Dear, sweet Julie, I intended to let that suffice but you have asked for a reply to your last letter. I received it today after a long patient wait. With two others, of course. (Slow post office your end or mine?) All right, read the first sentence above. Enough said? Do you understand that I am so interested in you that nothing would matter to me as far as you are concerned? Now, I had better watch out or you will try to read between the lines. There are no spaces. What I can't find the words to tell you is that I love you and nothing else matters. I love you for what you are to me, not for what you have been or what you will be, but for who YOU are You could have a million or nothing, all I want is to hear you speak, see you move, and adore you. (Tomorrow if possible.) You could <u>tell</u> me anything. That doesn't matter. What is important is what I have <u>seen.</u> I told you I am an expert on character.

My darling, lovely, female, beautiful and attractive woman until I can whisper in your ear don't worry about what I think. I <u>KNOW.</u> Just wait until I can whisper in your ear. Wait until I can touch, feel and smell the beauty of you .

No. Why wait?

If I could be near you my silence would tell you more than I could ever write here for this love by post does not suit me one bit! One caress, one word and one look is more important than reams of paper. Do you understand what my limited command of English is trying to explain, my sweet faced darling? I love you.

Gaze at the stars, my imaginative darling, my gifted gipsy. I just feel tender, that's all. I wish you could have everything in the world you desire. I love you so much I would take one step back to let you have it, too. That would be some sacrifice!!

Look behind the cold eyes of old hard face in the photograph you have. He is as soft as hell underneath and he loves you so much. I wish I was there with him. I could ogle you night and day.

Think of me, my darling. May your dreams come true. Be faithful or else! Love ME. Goodness me. Now who's making demands!!? I love you, darling. Remind me to kiss your lovely eyes. I will write to you soon when I can be a little more sensible about you. I want to kiss you so much. I DO! So much! Love me.

Wed. Sept 28. Darling, Have a few moments alone and I can think of you.

I received a sweet letter from you today after mooning about waiting for it to be delivered. The fact that you may be here in three or four weeks hasn't yet sunk in. When the truth eventually dawns on me I shall have to galvanize myself into action and make some sort of arrangements for your visit. I shan't convince myself its true until I see you at London Airport.

I love you. To continue: How I wish you could have been here now, if only for the weather. We have had a wonderful late summer. Not a speck of rain for weeks and almost continuous sunshine.

As far as work is concerned the pace has now slowed down a little (I am touching wood) and I had a little more time to relax during working hours. I feel I need a good rest as I am now as white as a sheet with bags under my eyes you could do your shopping with! Some fresh air and rest would do me the world of good. (Here, as usual, I must leave you on business. I love you.

Elizabeth R. Lawrence

To continue: Now Thursday, 29th. In the middle of my lunch someone told me there was a letter for me and I have just read it. If only you could see what you do to me. I am so choked up inside. I suppose we English are cold, but only on the exterior, inside the same as anyone else. When I think about it I suppose its just English reserve. Show nothing but think a lot.

Anyway, put it on record that I'm in love.

Four weeks! How can I wait? By the way, check with the British Embassy as to what sort of visa you will need. Don't forget you will be a lovely alien but an alien nevertheless. If you think of staying to work you have to have a particular visa. Yes!

Hell, it sounds as though I'm trying to extend your three weeks already. Darling, I love you and am waiting like a lovesick kid to show you things in London that you couldn't see anywhere else in the world. I do so hope that you will enjoy your visit. What a pity it must be so secret. I love you very much, my darling. Wish I could kiss you and show you how much,"

Today I heard that a friend was going to Scotland for nine days in November. I have been trying to talk him into letting me have his flat while he is away.

I didn't get very far with that. It is now Friday, 30th, 5PM. after a rather hectic day. I will leave the subject mentioned above as he is not too keen.

I received a wonderful letter from you today, so candid and sweet. It has cheered my day because, for the first time in weeks, it has poured with rain. Some of the bad weather you have had, I should think.

Here we go again! Will have to complete this later. I love you, darling, so much.

I am so sorry for the delay. It is now Monday, 3rd October. I know I should be shot for this but since the last few words I wrote I haven't been near the office. Now, a bit more quiet. Darling, this is such a mess. I can't be tidy. I just haven't the time. Talking about time. It seems to be spinning by and still we are no nearer.

Frustrating, isn't it? I happen to love you very much. D'you know that? Thank you for the letter received today. Most unusual. I don't get any mail on Mondays as a rule. A pleasant welcome for me when I got in.

Now, about this CORA! There is no doubt she is going crackers. . There was NO letter from Addie simply because we haven't had a word from them. So how the hell she can attribute remarks to Addie and me from a nonexistent letter, I don't know. The poor girl is nuts, or "barmey," as we say. You can see what I mean when I say you should not trust her with anything personal. God knows what this story about a stand-in for me will sound like when we do get it. I shudder to think. I telephoned home during the day, (mine, not yours, worse luck) and Addie told me she had received a parcel containing one or two things Janet had left behind and a comic strip! No letter. No nothing. How crazy can you get?

Enough of that. She isn't my gaoler anymore and, unless she is peering over your shoulder as you read this, what the hell. . If she is let her have a good look at the next line. Glasses on? I am in love with Julie Martine and when I can get my hands on her I am going to kiss, cuddle, and have sex, sex, sex, and still more sex. I love her! So there!! It's no joke though, is it? She spoiled my chances before and if I have anything to do with it, it won't happen again.

Darling, I love you. I have been so busy of late but I can assure you that you have never ben out of my thoughts for one single day. The very thought of you fascinates me. While watching television late Saturday night, I almost fell out of my chair, for a girl sang a song that brought you straight to my mind. I heard it the first time I looked at you and realized what a gorgeous creature you are. At the time you had looked at me and passed on to rivet your attention on someone else. Just how daft am I? A man enraptured by a love song! I won't tell you what it is. In fact, I can't think of the title and I can't hum the tune here, so you will have to wait until we can hear it somewhere together.

Darling, I had better post this. I'm sure you have waited long enough. Please, remember I adore you, then you may excuse me for being so long even if you can't forgive me. I want to TALK to you! I love you, Julie Martine. Come and kiss me!"

Sat. Oct 8. Sweetheart, Before I apologize or say anything else, let me say how delighted I am that

In a London Fog

the date is fixed! Now get here on that date or else! **<u>Don't put it off for any reason.</u>** I have arranged for a furnished flat for you for two weeks commencing 25th Oct, 1966. I couldn't get it for any longer for the following reasons:

The fellow who rents the flat is a young colleague of mine whose wife is a nurse. She has taken a job which will take her away for two weeks. At my insistence he blackmailed his wife into letting me use his flat. Not me exactly, but you. As far as she is concerned I am a single man living in a Police Section House. (That can be explained later.) Now, I haven't seen the flat, have no idea what it is like, how it is furnished, or anything. I am just taking a chance that it will do. It will be somewhere to rest your head anyway and save the cost of a hotel. You are left with no other alternative. Get here on the 25th Oct.! Right?

I am thrilled to bits. I can't wait for your arrival. Have made the necessary arrangements for a cover story to meet you. etc. I am now chewing my fingernails and waiting.

Please excuse the delay. As usual it has hen one long struggle to find time to eat let alone anything else. So sorry you have such a bad cold. Cheer up. If you can't get rid of it bring it over and give it to me. Now, get steaming! Don't think about it. DO IT. Now! Get here by the 25th October or you are in trouble! Have you got the message? I love you so much I feel that my hands are reaching out across the Atlantic to drag you over to me, my darling.

I love you, Julie. Bring your cold and red nose. I will kiss it. Just remember, I can't wait much longer. I will go MAD!"

Tues., Oct 11-Dear, darling Julie, Since Saturday I have received no less than three letters, each written in a different mood, each having a different effect on me, as you can imagine. In one you're frightened about what we're're doing; in another your cold is getting better. From that one I can feel you getting better, for with a few words you made me go hot under the collar and feel I could take on the American Army to get at you. Why do you feed my imagination like that? It's bad enough already.

I am sitting here during a pause in the mad, mad rush and trying to cram all I can into a short note to you, and all I can see or think of is you. (Reading your card now.) My goodness, if only I could have been there when you were in that state of dress, or undress, and in that state of mind! I would have gone crazy! You had better not tantalize me to much. I don't want to be an animal, (the first time anyway!)

Have you stopped to give a thought to how it will be the first time we are locked up, alone, and together? I have! My God! What thoughts! I must drop the subject and tell you that, above all else, I love you tenderly. Whatever else I might want my basic desire is to just hold you, feel you close to me, and love you. I'll go mad and rape you many times afterwards! (Sure am teasing myself!)

In a London Fog

Now, I have got my mind of the subject of sex. I can get my one track mind on other things.

Your friend? And my relation, Cora! She mus0t be mad!! That's all I can say. Her conversations with you prove that. The letters which she alleges have come from us are nonexistent. We haven't had a word from her for ages let alone this fabricated story she is supposed to have sent. Nothing. Think this illness she has had ? has set her crazy. I knew, from what I have heard of her in the past, she was a professional liar, but this, ? I can't credit it. She must roll them off just for the sake of it. I shall persuade Addie to write her a note tonight and see what sort of story you get from the real thing. Poor darling, what she is doing to you.

I am so sorry this is such a hurried thing but I must make use of the time I have free. You once said, "Write what you feel and how you feel and don't worry about spelling or the English." I do just that, don't i? My God! What a mess!

I long for the 25th of October. If you must ignore the heart cry in my last letter and wait a little longer I wil understand but thrash you for it. Please, get here if you can by then for you know the set up I have here for you. No complications. If you feel you can't make it, let me know by return and I can cancel. Avoid telegrams if you can. There is always a risk attached to them and nothing must spoil my wicked plans for you. Oh, darling, if only you knew what even one hour alone with you would mean! After all this time, how will I manage to be gentle? Have just sat and thought of you for about five minutes... What pictures! What thoughts!

Julie, do you know what a gorgeous woman you are?

I had better close this and grab a meal for I don't know when I will get the next one. Just remember that I love you very much and want you here in London with me. Then, and only then, wil I whisper my thoughts of you. Come, and let me love and caress you, my darling. I will have you on my mind all day now!

Gipsy, I want you very much. I love you."

London. Oct 13th. Dear, sweet Julie, for whom I can hardly wait. I read with interest your account of the bust-up with "Cora (Lita) I can well imagine how you felt. I know she can 'rabbit.' Once she starts she just can't stop, most of it verbal rubbish. A pity. Still, on her own head be it. You know, I really think she is mental. I know that Russ has a hard time now and again with her. I guessed, too, that the upset with her daughter wasn't one sided. Such a shame but what can you do?

Oct 13th. Not long now. I am waiting for that letter to say that you will be here come hell or high water. As I said before , I can stand the disappointment if you don't get here as expected but, I had better hear soon or I shall be in the same state as Cora. Over here, by the way, we still call her Lita and I still have to stop and think each time I write her name.

Packed in suddenly there. Big panic on..Now back.

In a London Fog

Do you know I find it difficult to think how I am going to fill your time while you are here? GAWD! Will I never get any peace!? Back to normal once again. As I was saying I have ideas (lovely ones), but we can't do that all the time. (Or can we?) Other than that I have got to organize places to go and things to see to fill three weeks. You had better make a mental note of all the things you want to see and do and let me know so that I can make some plans. I can't think straight. You had better get here before I really go mad!

It is now Monday, Oct. 17th. I didn't get very far, did I? I should think this will be the last letter I will send before your arrival. I haven't had a letter from you over the weekend so hope there wil be no delays. Anyway, unless I hear from you to the contrary, I shall be at the airport to meet you so keep your eyes about. If I should be delayed SIT STILL AND WAIT for I will be there. That's a promise. I only hope there will be no note in the post tomorrow to say you are not coming. It would kill me.

Someone just dumped a load of paperwork in my tray which means I will be working late tonight. Will say goodnight now. Don't disappoint me tomorrow, please, for I love you and want you very much.

Roll on 25th for you will be here. Get a window seat so you can get a good view of England as you come in. There is no where in the world like it! I love you so much. Hurry up! Now, sit back, relax and enjoy your flight. Will be waiting.! All my love until then.."

London. Western Union Cable. Oct 21,
To hear you wonderful. News terrible. If you cannot come suggest wait until June. Letter follows. Love. David

Oct 20th. London. Dear, sweet Julie., I feel so disconsolate for I know you won't be telephoning me on the 25th. What a terrible thought! It was so lovely to hear your voice again though how I can lose all my senses and be unable to come up with anything constructive? I don't know.

We're a couple of amateurs at what we're doing, Julie, and we're not world travelers, are we? But I have thought many things I could have put your mind to rest about. For instance, as far as money here is concerned you would have a roof over your head, and food and entertainment and me, me, me. Oh, hell, I might see you on the 25th anyway! Julie, you have sent me crazy again and it only took one phone call!

When you telephoned I was in another office secure in the knowledge that I wouldn't hear from you until 11 AM, (our time). This meant I had to gallop up two flights of stairs and fight my way through an office full of cackling idiots to speak to you. No wonder I hadn't much to say. Oh, Julie..

Please, ignore my telegram. The reason I said wait until June was because I shall be really flush by then and you won't have to worry about a penny for yourself or the family. And I had in mind the thought that you'd have good weather. But to hell with it. I can't stand the suspense anymore. Just get here. You won't have to work. Why the hell couldn't I talk to you when you phoned? I feel like a daft schoolhoy!

The thought just struck me that if you do leave as arranged this will be waiting for you when you get back. You can sit back and scream
your head off with laughter at this rubbish. I do hope you wil read this when you return from holiday and not next week when you should be here with me.

In view of the time I had better get cracking and get this in the post. I love you, Julie, and want you here so much. I am longing for you, my darling. I will be so disappointed if I don't get that phone call.

On Tuesday next.. Darling, what shall I do if you don't come? I love you. Why do you tantalize me?"

Chapter Three   London 1966

Julie was frightened about what she was doing even as she boarded the plane. She was frightened for herself and for the David she had come to know in his letters. He was right. They were a couple of amateurs who didn't know what they were doing; and they weren't world travelers either and, for all his bravado, he was frightened, too. Whatever her fears, however, she was compelled by her longing and his desire to cross the ocean to be near him again.

She'd had to arrange things at home first. Lee, one of the company managers, approved her request for a leave of absence, calling it a business trip. Jason and Tina thought she needed a vacation. They would watch over their grandparents and take care of things at home. Although she told them where she was going, and that she would visit David, she asked them not to discuss it outside the family.

Because of her fears she hadn't followed up with another cable to David to say she was on her way after all lest she change her mind again at the last minute. He'd had only her last cable saying she was having second thoughts. As a result she had to wait for hours once the plane landed at London Airport.

She waited from 6:20AM, GMT, to phone him at his office at nine. By 8:30 she couldn't wait and, of course, he wasn't in. It seemed an eternity until he called back and her knees buckled when he

In a London Fog

spoke. She actually had to lean on the wall for support.

"Welcome to England, Julie!" said his disembodied voice.

She was in England and David was on the phone only a few miles away. She could barely speak. "I've been waiting so long, David."

"I know, darling, but you'll have to wait a little longer." he said, "so sit tight and rest while I make sure that flat is still available."

She waited more hours. She sat down, stood up, walked around, sat down to write a note home, paced and searched each passing mustache looking for his face. She wondered if there would be instant recognition when he came in sight. There was.

She saw the top of his head as he came through the door and she knew him even before he looked up toward the balcony and saw her. She almost fell to the floor below when he smiled. She didn't expect her stomach to lurch as it did as he walked toward her and, though she may have appeared steady, she almost fell against him when he touched her at last.

She would have put her arms around him and kissed him in that bustling airport lobby but, although his smile was warm it was a reserved Englishman who took her arm and led her to his car. He kissed her cheek when she was seated next to him.

"How was your flight?" he asked while he drove from the airport onto a major highway.

Elizabeth R. Lawrence

Suddenly adjusting to being driven on the wrong side of the road while still coping with that waiting time exhaustion she could barely speak. "I think I was in shock that I was actually on the plane," she said, "because I really don't remember a thing. I think it was uneventful."

"Did you see England as you came in?"

"Yes," she said, "but not too well. I didn't get a window seat."

He smiled, glad that she'd remembered what he'd written. "You look lovely in that silver coat," he said, softly, reaching over to touch her cheek.

""This was perfect for the plane because the fabric doesn't wrinkle," she said, nestling his hand with her cheek as she spoke, "and I didn't have to pack anything bulky. I'll buy something here for the weather."

At that moment they became aware that they were touching each other. David needed both hands on the wheel and Julie needed to breathe again so they concentrated on the drive.

When he finally stopped the car they were in a London area near his police station. It was not the picture post card London she'd expected. This was a somewhat rundown area with all sorts of old buildings crowded on city streets that teemed with traffic all going the wrong way.

David walked her up a dark flight of stairs to a second floor flat in one of the old buildings. It had a small hall sized kitchen, a bathroom with a separation from a toilet, a lounge and a bedroom. It was scantily furnished but it was clean and pleasant enough. The bedroom had a bed, a chair, a bureau with a mirror and windows to the street view outside. When she smiled to let him know it would do he rested her carryall bag against a wall and took a deep breath, obviously relieved.

He had written something about England being a mix of the old and the new but she didn't think he was referring to modern appliances or indoor plumbing.

There was no hot running water in the tiny kitchen or the bathroom, no central heating, and the toilet was flushed with a pull chain.

"And I was looking for help with an ice cube tray," she said, with a smile. "I'll need a lot more help here."

"At your service," David said, helping her remove her silver coat as he removed his suede, tan, shearling jacket.

"Maybe it's just a poor neighborhood," she said, "but I feel as though I'm in a time warp. It's as if I've just stepped out of the 20th Century."

"Remember, my darling," he said, as he put her coat on the chair with his jacket. "London had to dig itself out of bomb damage after the war so progress has been slower here."

"We take a lot for granted, don't we?" she said, speaking as much to herself as to David."

Without pen and paper to speak for them, even to hide them, they looked at each other and were suddenly at a loss for words. Words that had flowed on paper hung between them as they dealt with the reality of their surroundings and feasted on each other with their eyes.

She reached for him first.

"In one of your letters," she said, softly, touching his lips with a fingertip, "you wondered what we would say when we found ourselves together and alone in a room. Right now all I can tell you is that I lost my breath at the first sight of you as you came through the airport. We've been together since then and I still can't breathe." She lifted her face to his. "I need you to help me. If you don't know what to do you can start where you left off a few months ago."

"I know what to do," he said, his mouth close to hers, "but I don't want to start anything I can't finish. I'm supposed to be working."

She kissed him, at first a self conscious kiss that effectively stopped any further words. He kissed her the same way. As they stepped apart and looked at each other they reached for each other again. He took the pins from her upswept hair to let it fall to her shoulders.

"You sent me a photograph like this," he murmured, desire stirring in his voice. "It's one of my favorites. I named it Gipsy."

She kissed him again, this time a more passionate kiss as he dealt with the buttons of her blouse to find her breasts. She helped him when he fumbled. They fell on the bed.

He was fully clothed. With her blouse open and her bra loosened she was already half dressed.

He kissed her again then stopped and pulled away. He seemed uncertain. She was suddenly unsure of herself. "David?"

She had stepped out of his sexual fantasies and imagination to a flesh and blood passionate reality that he didn't really understand. English reserve or lifelong denial?

"I can't," he whispered. "I have to get back to the station." As he stood up he leaned over the bed to kiss her again. "I must get back to work."

"But, David..."

"Julie, you must be tired."

"Yes, but..."

"Get some rest," he said. "You can settle in after you wake up. I should be back with food by then. Just remember I love you." He grinned at her half clothed form on the bed. "If I can wait, you can, too, my darling."

Before he left he added a P.S. to the letter she had written to her children while she had been waiting at the airport.

"Look after yourselves," he wrote. "I will take good care of your mother. She's a very special person, an absolute darling, and very beautiful! We're going to try and see a little of London, buildings and such. I'm afraid though, that I won't make much of a tourist guide. David"

He'd post the letter for her from work.

Julie *was* tired, but she felt somewhat abandoned when David left. She didn't know where she was or how to get anywhere on her own. She looked around. There was no phone to call anyone, not even David. She didn't know how to use the stove to make a cup of coffee or tea. The small fridge held nothing she could use. What little was there belonged to the real tenants. She'd never seen water tanks so she didn't know what to do heat the water in the tanks to get hot water in the tub or the kitchen. The flat was cold and getting colder as night fell. She closed off drafts from the other rooms by closing all the doors in the flat.

Whatever else it lacked the bedroom was the best room in the flat. A closet had blankets for the bed. An electric heater was near a wall and a small bedside table with a little lamp cast a dim light in the room as night fell. A small radio was on the bureau. This would be the room she would call home. The cold dark bathroom was close enough.

It was dark when she woke. She had packed a couple of silky and see through things to wear or lounge in at night but, when David wrote it would be cold, she had added a long, high necked, long sleeved, red flannel nightgown almost in jest.

That's how David found her when he came through the door with an order of fish and chips, a bag of tea, and some biscuits.

"Unless you're planning to get under the blanket with me," she said, "don't you dare take these covers off."

"Aren't you hungry?"

"Starving," she answered, making room for him under the covers.

The room was in semi-darkness from the

light of the little lamp. She saw his form and his shadowed body as he undressed. She reached over to touch him and he collapsed on top of her.

He kissed her, gently, lovingly as he fumbled to find the opening on the flannel nightgown.. He groaned, feeling for her under the red flannel.

"Is this a chastity belt?"

"It is until you find the zipper," she said, guiding his hand.

She wrapped her arms around his neck to pull his lips to hers again when he held the zipper tab. She devoured him, first his lips and his mustache, then his neck, and his strong, muscular chest as he pulled the zipper down.

The flannel parted to let him in. He watched her face as he stroked her. He rested his head between her breasts as he fondled them, With gentle movements he found the warmth of her body waiting for him.

"Oh, my darling," he whispered.

Her passion at a peak she wrapped her self around him to move with him. He was anything but savage. .He was a gentle lover, a sweet lover loving with love to bring her to a climax and she took him with her when she melted. When his pulsing movements stopped he leaned up on one arm and looked down at her.

"We made magic, Julie Martine."

"And it felt so natural."

"As if we belonged together?" he asked,

"Yes. Oh, yes, David," she whispered.

Minutes later, after a trip to clean up in the bathroom, he was dressed and ready to leave.

"Please, not tonight, David.."

"I must go home, darling. I have to put in an appearance."

"Oh, David."

"I know you're disappointed, but we'll have other nights. Just relax and eat the fish and chips." He kissed her lightly before he turned away.

"I hope they're still warm. There's some biscuits, too. I'm sorry I didn't make the tea but, darling, I have to go."

Some Journal Entries
My Irene Dunne Flat

With the radio playing and pen in hand, Julie took a notebook from her carry-on bag and started a journal of her trip to England. The first entry was titled, "My Irene Dunne Flat." David would be her John Boles. Time would tell the ending of her own clandestine back street. Magic moment aside it had not been an auspicious start.

She prayed for a happier ending.

She wrote in her journal when she was alone. David's work and his obligations at home took so much of his time that she was often alone, and lonely. In one of her first journal entries she wrote: I think its Thursday the 27th but with the time change I'm not certain.

In spite of my fears I've managed to leave the flat on my own. David brings some things but

I've found a couple of stores where I can buy food that doesn't require cooking. I bought bread, cheese and fruit the first time. When I said I wanted bottled water he fixed tea to teach me how to brew and make it British style.

"You can always boil the water and put it in the fridge," he said, "But tea does that, too, and it doesn't need ice cubes."

He has his own key so I don't have to run down the stairs to let him in. He's found me in bed, buried under blankets, more than once, morning or evening. I don't need the blankets long after he joins me.

He showed me where the chains were for the overhead lights when I want light in a room. I was looking for electrical outlets. He has been here every day to help me with the hot water tanks over the tub and the kitchen sink. It's probably simple enough but I'm afraid of causing a fire. Once the water is hot it flows from the spigot.

He had to buy bath towels before I could take a bath. In the evening, or on a free afternoon, we bathe together in the old fashioned bathtub in the shivery bathroom of my Irene Dunne flat. He likes playing with my hair and one night he washed it himself under the kitchen spigot. That makes it romantic, but I feel very helpless sometimes and that's not like me.

Richard and Emma told me about the cold rooms and the drafts in them, but they didn't say enough, no matter what they said. Nothing could prepare me to walk in rooms all damp with cold and then try to live in them that way! It feels better outdoors!

When I step out of the magic circle of the heater, even for a minute, the blast of cold air makes me jump and hop back like a rabbit. Cuddling and making love helps but not enough, and with David's horrendous daily schedule that's not often enough.

I don't know my way around yet but I'm trying to learn so that I can get around during the long hours David works. He showed me how to use the subway (tube here) but I prefer the little red double-decker buses that run everywhere. I can see more that way.

The traffic in this area is terrible. Hundreds of little cars and double deck buses all drive on the wrong side of the street. I know there are traffic controls but since I don't know them it seems that autos, buses, and 'lorries' go barging helter skelter from every direction. There are pedestrian crossings that everyone must use and, according to David, the most enforced rule is that a driver must halt whenever anyone is attempting to cross the street. We have the same rule at home but enforcing it makes it sound civilized!

So far, David's help makes a difference, but I've found most people helpful when I'm on my own as well. What I find amusing is that each person tells me to beware of the other fellow and, so far, they've all been very nice.

As far as "swinging London" is concerned, I haven't noticed it around here. I have the feeling I'm in the wrong place anyway.

You should see me trying to make a simple phone call from a public pay phone. No wonder David had trouble in America.

The money here is the most confusing even though David tries to teach me. He has warned me of pickpockets so often that I wonder if they're everywhere. With the way I handle the money they could rob me blind and I'd never know it.

Free time together is wonderful but David has very little spare time. He has to be a nervous wreck trying to fit me into his daily life. He takes my breath away whenever I see him and my joy at seeing him is infectious for his reaction to me is much the same. But sometimes I think he misses my letters, just as I miss his for, even in only a few days, words fail us when we try to speak about what has happened to us, and what will happen later. Reality intrudes and sadness attaches itself to whatever magic we feel for each other now.

I wrote a letter for him today.

Oct 29th. London A letter to David. Darling, Here I sit, alone in my Irene Dunne flat, on a Saturday night, pen in hand, writing to you again. Earlier today you said you find yourself looking for a letter at the office for the hours drag by until we're together again. I know exactly what you mean. Did we need the letters more than the reality that I brought with me, my love? I don't like being alone but I try to understand when you must leave me. My loneliness is tempered by the joy I feel when we're together, no matter what we do.

Elizabeth R. Lawrence

Seeing Buckingham Palace with you, having you tell me about the Plague grounds, holding your hand near the river Thames, walking with you past the Houses of Parliament, makes any history lesson I've ever had and any book I've ever read pale by comparison.

If we should part, for any reason, please don't reduce the love we've shared to a Christmas card a year. It deserves more than that. You once wrote, "Think and think again before you allow my influence to complicate your life…" I am saying the same thing to you now. I love you very much but I am prepared to walk away with my cherished memories when these three weeks end. Don't convince yourself or me that we have a chance for more without weighing the consequences first. That would destroy both of us. I came to you with love, wanting only your love and happiness. That's all I will ever want.

Please, darling, want only that for me."

She sent that one to his office.

"It's a beautiful letter, my darling," he said after he'd read it. "But it made me sad."

Another time she wrote a letter but gave it to him to read when he arrived.. He read it while she distracted him with kisses. By the time he finished they were making love. He asked her her nationality just after they'd made love one day. He already knew she was American so she knew what he meant.

"Italian," she said.

"I knew it," he answered.

"Why?"

"Your warmth," he answered.

"In bed?"

"Everywhere," he said. "In bed you're my own ball of fire."

"I'm certainly spontaneous and you know I want you. Does that please you, my darling?"

"The question is do I please you?"

"On sight," she told him. "You're not the cold reserved English policeman who is sitting on my bed. I must have known it the day we met."

"What amazes me," he said, "is that I'm the recipient of such ardor and passion from a woman like you. Surely you know you're beautiful, Julie, a hot house cultured beauty. What are you doing with a man like me?"

"Don't you know how I see you? You're a good and decent man, David. You're also a handsome man, my love, and you ooze sex appeal. I'll never have enough of you. Why? I don't know. I just know I love you. What I don't understand is why you underestimate yourself. That's part of our problem."

"What are we going to do, Gipsy?"

"I don't know. I'm not ready to know."

"Neither am I," he said.

Gradually, words from his letters, some he'd left unwritten, became part of their rapture. There was a naturalness to their lovemaking that surprised both of them. They loved with their eyes as well as their senses and their bodies. She was inflamed by the sight of him. The beauty he saw in her overwhelmed him.

He whispered words of love when she responded and she purred in his arms.

"Oh, Julie," he said, moaning softly when she kissed him everywhere as he had kissed her. "Love me, Julie. Don't stop loving me."

When he had to leave to get back to work he watched her dress. "You gorgeous woman. I'll never get out of here if I keep looking at you."

"You're not making it easy for me either," she said when he had his shirt on again.

He took her to a Pub where she met many of his colleagues. He was quietly, but obviously, showing her off a bit. She felt a little strange, even somewhat embarrassed but she kept it to herself. David seemed a bit uncomfortable as well. He took her with him when he stopped to see an older, heavyset, man either in an office or flat somewhere. He may have been the Commissioner of his station but, even after an introduction, she still didn't know. Except for a nod in her direction the man didn't say anything to her. She just sat quietly on the side while he and David talked.

It rained that day and David, who managed to get a full day off from work, changed earlier plans and took her for a drive in the country. The areas of Kent and Surrey were lovely and the homes were inviting, but none had central heating and few had modern conveniences. But there were open spaces. A lot like home. It would be an adjustment but she could see herself living there.

Historical areas aside the England she was seeing reminded her of America more than thirty

In a London Fog

years ago. Most homes, even the nicer ones, were without central heating and rooms were warmed with little electric burners. Newer places offered heat and hot water (as luxuries!) but they were prohibitively expensive.

The travel posters hid the reality there just as those of New York city were hidden. But there was much to see and learn.

She was getting an education as she wandered around on her own. She bought three different newspapers a day, not only to relieve her loneliness, but to get a cross section of viewpoints. So far her favorites were The Evening Standard, The Guardian and the London Times. Others seemed little more than scandal sheets, full of gossip and horoscopes.

Even the radio station speaks of horoscopes of the day. In her journal she wrote: TV goes off at midnight. There are only two channels, the BBC, which does not carry commercials, and the ITV, which does. Most of the commercials seem to be about candy, cookies and cakes. They call them sweets or biscuits. The songs I hear on the radio seem to be either rock and roll or sentimental old English or American tunes that we seldom hear at home unless on an FM station. Stores close at 5PM and, except for vending machines here and there, you can't buy anything after that hour. How spoiled we are with our 24 hour convenience stores everywhere.

The prices may be lower for some things (though you can't prove it by me) and there are a number of worthwhile social programs, but it's still hard to understand how people manage on what they earn.

David says a family with a car is considered fairly well off and not every family owns one. (And there we are running around in a country of two and three family cars and taking it all for granted!) Many people ride bicycles but again, according to my dear English guide, not as many as in previous years. The cars, by our standards, are small, but after a while you don't notice the size. You only notice how many there are careening around the streets.

London, like New York, is indeed an international city, but on a smaller scale. It has a charming difference from New York. In another flat, and a nicer area, if it had central heating, it would be very easy to live here. I am delighted by the many accents I hear. Waitresses, bus drivers and clerks in shops all sound, to me, as if they stepped from the pages of Shakespeare. I think of Dickens when I hear the children in the street. The double deck red busses seem out of Walt Disney. Piccadilly Circus is a miniature Broadway and Times Square in New York.

We had lunch today at a restaurant called Dick Turpin's Place. (Dick Turpin, the infamous highwayman.) My eighth grade class did a skit on him at graduation. Very nice. Very old. Full of atmosphere. There were men with monocles and men with bowler hats. I had the only foreign accent in the place! That tickled David who "loves" my voice. He says I'm a 'soft American.' I'm surprised at even a little culture shock when I experience it for I didn't expect it at all. It's mainly in the differences in the customs and language that point out my foreign status. I can't help thinking of my parents who came to America from Italy with a completely foreign language and had to learn another.

David was amused at her journal descriptions even when she said she had the feeling there was a mixture of God and superstition blended into the traditions of England.

"I do get that feeling," she told him.

She didn't share everything she wrote in her journal. He goes home every night, she wrote, holding back tears, so that leaves me to shiver alone in this cold room. She was sometimes fearful of sounds around her.. She accepted things as they were without complaint, but she'd cried into her pillow a few times. After all, she told herself, I knew (or thought I knew) what I was getting into. She just hadn't expected the discomfort or the loneliness.

Seeing him in his own backyard made the words in his letters real. As he said, and as she saw it now, his world revolved around his work. She could only wonder about his home life. He said he got married because he wanted to come home to a warm house after working all day. At the time she thought he'd meant something romantic. Now she knew that he meant that literally.. A woman not only provides the comforts of home but she keeps the home fires burning while a man is working.

Elizabeth R. Lawrence

David explained British things when they were together but many things were still new and strange to her: the landscape, the names of places and things, the lack of heat and running hot water and the lack of telephones. Even electrical outlets seemed different from those she knew. She couldn't figure out how much she weighed in pounds or stones, but she knew she'd lost weight.

When she'd been there a few days David helped her buy a very nice tailored brown suede coat to wear outdoors. She rolled the silver coat in tissue and packed it away in her carryon bag. With the brown coat she wore a soft beige furry hat she'd brought with her. When she was alone and too cold she sometimes added the coat over her flannel nightgown which she already covered with a sweater and blankets.

What she found most shocking was that she seemed to be the only person in the country who felt the cold indoors! At that very minute, as she made notes in her journal, with an electric burner scorching one leg and the drafts hitting her from the other side of the room, she was freezing! I'm a prime candidate for pneumonia," she wrote.

Most people came into their flats, took off their coats, and proceeded to do whatever it is that anyone did at home. She walked into the flat and added a blanket over her sweater, or she wore two sweaters at once. Sweaters are called woolies, she wrote. She liked that.

David was concerned but more often amused at the goose bumps she got in the cold rooms. He didn't seem to mind the cold at all. He even took a leisurely bath. She had given up trying to use the tub unless he was there with her. There was no shower. Now she wore her robe over her nightclothes, and an Indian style blanket over all that, and she got washed in stages so that she wouldn't turn into a shivering, soap covered icycle!

She even got undressed under the covers. David laughed as he helped, but sometimes, caught up in the moment, he fell under the covers with her and they undressed each other.

She'd imagined them lounging around in cozy comfort while David sipped a glass of wine and soft music filled the room. Yet, strangely, in spite of the limitations imposed by the flat it was still a little honeymoon island for them, an amusing one to be sure, but a very sweet one. At least that's the way it was when they were together.

She'd sent cards with little notes to everyone from home and some, not just her family, responded. Her mother, who saw David briefly during his poolside visit told her to be careful. Lee's wife wrote that Lee was in the hospital dealing with cardiac problems. Before she left she told him she'd share her trip with him if she had time. She had more than enough time now. She'd also told him to tell anyone who asked that she was out of town without going into detail. She certainly didn't want Cora to pop up now.

It was late the evening David arrived to take her out to dinner. She hadn't seen much of England at night, but there wasn't much to see as he drove from the neighborhood to a more wooded area. She saw a sign saying Ipswich but wasn't sure where they were when he stopped.

The restaurant was pleasant with tables in white covers, dimly lit lights and soft music.

"You haven't had a decent meal since you've been here," David said, as she gave him the menu to order for her. "Fish and chips or a sandwich from a Pub isn't good enough."

"I have fruit and cheese and some biscuits at the flat and sometimes, when you light the stove, I can heat something."

David wasn't eating. He would eat at home. He had a cup of tea and watched her eat when a plate with curried chicken and vegetables was put before her.

Finally, he leaned toward her. "Julie, you know how much I love you, don't you?"

"I think you love me," she said, quietly, "but I don't know how much. Sometimes I think its more lust than love."

"That's what brought us together, darling, but it's more than that now."

"I like to think so." She paused, "I haven't asked you to change anything for me, but I'm still alone every night, David."

"I know, darling, and you've been very patient with me. I'm trying to do the right thing, Julie. I don't want to hurt anyone."

"Someone always gets hurt, David."

"Time is running out on us, Julie," he said, gently. "You'll have to leave the flat soon. I don't know where to start looking, but I've got to get you another place to stay where we can be together. I don't want you to leave me."

"I'm not leaving yet," she said.

He took a ring from his finger. "I don't want to lose you, Julie. I want you to have this, my darling, until I can put a proper ring on your finger."

"Oh, David. I wish I could take it but you're not ready for this."

He put the ring on her finger. It was much too large. "I can get it sized," he said.

"No, my love, not until you know what you're doing."

He moved her hand back when she held it out to him. "I want you to have it," he said.

"If it pleases you I'll wear it on a chain for now. But.."

"If you can stay until Christmas," he said, "I'll have some leave and enough money to make the trip back with you."

"You have more things to consider than that," she said, quietly. "Right now I think you're dreaming."

He knew and she knew what they were saying. It's a bit premature, she thought, and he certainly can't do anything about it yet, nor had she asked him to. Time has not been with us from the start and I don't think it will be with us now.

Three weeks, two almost gone.

Neither of them was very good at the idea of being in a back street affair. The thought that their love would hurt anyone was always with them.

Under all of their words, and in all their loving time together, they were conscious of an undercurrent of sadness. But how to say goodbye now? If this was supposed to be the cure, they weren't getting any better.

He tore himself away from her when they returned to the flat.

"I have to go, darling," he said.

"I know." She said, quietly

He had been juggling his schedule in order to have time for her, but when he was around and they tried to talk she heard only with her heart and eyes, and she didn't really hear a thing. Then they'd kiss and talking stopped. Each knew what the other was feeling, what the other was facing even when they couldn't speak the words.

I may love David and he may love me, Julie thought, but I'm appalled at the reality of being alone in a strange country, hidden away and alone every night, alone and knowing that the only person for whose sake I am hiding must necessarily leave me alone like this. It isn't easy to accept the thought that I've traveled 3000 miles to find such a sad and bittersweet loneliness on the other end.

Addie is set in her ways, David told himself, but she looks after me and takes care of our home, and we have a daughter. I work too many hours but I'm used to it and so is she. . The only thing we have of any value is our house. If I turn away from Addie I could lose it all. Without money how would I start over? Where?

David had tried to warn her in some of his letters, and, at times, she knew he was aware of her reality. At that time it became his and she saw his torment, but sometimes it seemed that the male ego of having her waiting superceded his innate wish to do everything right.

The thought was painful.

On the morning that pain became real David had found her half dressed sitting on the edge of the bed covered with blankets. She had spent the night shivering. David had spent the night at home. He smiled when he saw her.

"Poor darling," he said. "I wish I could stay and cuddle now, but I'm off to work and," as if he was sharing happy news, with the male ego of a proud rooster crowing aloud, he said, "I think she was testing me but Addie wanted me to make love to her last night, and I did."

Julie's stricken face and the tears that flooded her eyes spoke for her even before she said a word. She stood up, letting the blankets fall from her. He was standing, still in his jacket, at the end of the bed near the window. She walked toward him, putting a finger on his lips as she looked at him.

In a quavering voice that was almost a whisper, she said, "Isn't it enough that I'm alone like this? I never told you what to do at home. Did you have to tell me what I already knew? I know what you mean by what you're saying but it hurts that you're so proud of yourself. Go away. Please go away."

There was no anger in her voice but, deserved or not, she couldn't hide the pain.

He had to get to work. He was anything but proud of himself as he walked away.

She wanted him to find her gone when he returned. She packed and unpacked her suitcase before she finally left the flat and walked through the neighborhood. She found a cinema and bought a ticket, then sat through the same film twice without knowing what was showing.

David had been to the flat a couple of times in her absence. His relief was evident when he found her there later. He put his arms around her and held her.

"I thought I'd lost you," he said.

"You almost did," she answered.

The neighborhood in which she found herself, though near David's station, didn't help for, like some of the less desirable neighborhoods at home, it frightened her, especially at night. This was his country. This was his working area. He didn't live there. He had described his house in a letter and she could imagine it; he now said he wished he could take her there. But he'd seen her townhouse home; he'd been in it, and he knew her lifestyle. This wasn't where she belonged. He knew that, too.

With things as they were already, even if unspoken, she was concerned that David, who seemed to be riding a fence now, could muddle them into a situation neither of them was yet prepared to handle for, if he found himself measuring a way of life against the background of their affair, disaster was sure to follow.

If it comes to that we will both be hurt, she thought, for, even though a physical attraction brought us together, there's a fine line we crossed long ago that should allow us to retain enough respect for each other to remain friends later. At this point Julie had only an overflowing and very fragile heart at stake. Why had she put it on the line this way?

Perhaps if they were less sensitive, less romantic, less tuned in to each other, less mature, or even more experienced it would have been easier. As it was they were strangely in love and they were lost in the heartbreak of what they were doing. If this be ecstasy it hides a mighty sharp thorn.

"...but women's ways are witless ways..."

"If anything were to separate us," he said, when they were drinking tea in the kitchen area of the Irene Dunne flat, "what would you do?"

"I'm not sure," she said. "Maybe what I'd thought of doing before we met. I'd probably go back to school." He was quiet.

"Why are you asking, David?"

"Because we're running out of time, Julie, and I need to know you'll be all right if.."

"I can't say how I'll be," she said, slowly, as tears filled her eyes, "but I'll survive."

Elizabeth R. Lawrence

With David trying to find a place for her at the end of the two weeks, Julie tried looking around on her own. She even thought of finding a job, but not knowing where she was or where to locate places she found in the newspapers made it difficult. All she'd brought with her was her plane ticket and enough to buy a few things. David said he'd take care of the roof over her head and would be sure she had food..."Excuses are mine," he'd written.

She would have brought more money with her; her job paid her more in one week than David earned in a month, but she'd left an emergency fund at home and there were bills to pay there as well.

When she returned from her fruitless trips on the red buses she waited for David in the tea shop or near the phone booth outside his station. Afterwards he took her to Pubs where he had business, and they had something to eat. She didn't care where she was when they were together. If anyone in the Pubs knew anything where David was concerned, they kept it to themselves. She was seen as an American woman visiting friends in England.

When the television was on in a Pub she saw old American films long gone at home. Most seemed to be replays of old American shows. Imagine traveling 3000 miles to see "The Beverly Hillbillies" or "Felony Squad?"

With her interest in British journalism David took her to visit a reporter friend on Fleet Street with the thought that it might have a job opportunity. They were given a tour but there was no mention of a job.

In a London Fog

David, who has just come in, thinks this dull journal/letter entry is very amusing, and sent hello to Tina and Jason. "Keep the home fires burning," he said. That was no joke now.

She'd sent a Get Well letter to Lee, salutation to Tin Man, Straw Man Lion. (whichever one was looking for a heart) and signed it Dorothy. David wanted to know about Lee. She liked that he was a bit jealous though he'd have nothing to worry about if he knew the nice, short, pudgy man himself.

He understood after she explained and let him read the letter she was sending. To wit:

News from the hinterlands of London: A lot of people I've met are very curious about what I'm doing in this offbeat neck of the woods of London. (So am I.) I'm certainly seeing a London seldom seen by tourists. Makes for interesting, sometimes scary, viewing but mighty lonely this way.

I'm spending my own money as I go but, at the same time, even without trying, I'm costing David a few pounds and for him, right now, that's a fortune. The trouble is I'm not aware of the amount because I still can't figure it out and that does upset me. I converted $30.00 in American money the other day and was given ten pounds in British money. I walked away feeling cheated. David laughed when I told him that if I was robbed it wasn't by any pickpocket, it was by a well dressed, pompous, bank official.

Time was running out and David was going through a private hell about being all things to all people, and with his schedule it was hard for him, too. They laughed a lot to hide tears. Whenever he got to the flat it was always as if they were meeting for the first time. There was urgency and passion and then the sadness came.

She was tempted to turn away and say goodbye now, not because she didn't care for him but because she did. Maybe her experiences with the problems she'd had in her own marriage gave her the insight, but she knew, maybe more than he did, that he didn't have the resources, financial or emotional, to cope with what could be ahead.

He couldn't afford to lose anything. He had nothing. Less than nothing. But it made up his world. In spite of his role in their affair he was an innocent, even in the murky world around him, a good and decent man without guile who played cops and robbers for a living. Was it that or his sex appeal that stopped her in her tracks? Was it that combination?

She didn't know, and she didn't know what he'd do if she just turned away but she didn't want to hurt him or see him hurt himself for her sake. When she'd tried to say it he put his arms around her and took the words away. What he had, in spite of what they were doing, was what she wanted. He was everything her husband had not been. Still, she was trying to hold some of herself in reserve, if only for her own sake, for if ever she believed in the promise of a tomorrow with him, and if it then fell apart she didn't know what she would do either.

He once wrote that she should think and think again "because you could be hurt, my darling," *Et tu,* my beloved? Would I hurt you or save your life if I walked away now?

Guy Fawkes Day

The Friday night before she moved away from the flat she wrote David a letter.

Darling David. I miss you. You promised to spend "…days and days and NIGHTS and NIGHTS with me. So far you only have time to run to me and run away. I love you . I do try to understand. But " She didn't send the letter.

He gave her a letter to take with her when she boarded the train to where she would stay for the weekend in Sussex.

"Darling Julie, So, now you are on a train and leaving me or, at least, you will be when you read this. Darling, I shall miss you so much even if you are only away from me for a day. Even now I keep glancing out of the window to see if you are outside waiting for me. I know you won't be but I must look.

How shall I face Nov 14th?

Surely something must turn up before long. Our luck can't be all bad. I only hope this chap comes up with something good. I am waiting for him now and I feel it will make me late in seeing you at 1PM. I shall be seeing you only to send you away. What a terrible thought! Darling Julie, how can I let you go?

You will be on my mind from the second you leave until you return. Think of me while you are away, just once in a while, and keep your fingers crossed that I solve this one problem. Please telephone me (and pay the woman for the call). If in desperate trouble call my home. Don't say a word. Just <u>SIGH</u>.

I think you know how much I love you. You said it yourself last night. I make "love with love," remember? The only thing I can say is I LOVE YOU! Who would think that three little words would mean so much? I love you, sweet Julie, and can't think of life without you now."

From Julie on Sat. Nov, 6th. Crawley, Sussex. "My darling David, My eyes were so flooded with tears as I read your letter I could barely see the words. I'm sure you know how this hurts. I miss you constantly.

Although I didn't think I'd need it it was thoughtful of Richard and Emma to give me Brenda's address when I was leaving to come to you in a foreign land. "For an emergency," they said. Being a homeless alien seemed emergency enough so I was glad to have an address even though we'd never met. It was a somewhat tie to home and still a tie to keep me near you.

Brenda said, on the phone, to look for a pair of look-alikes at the station when I got off the train. She was so right. He's a miniature Charles Laughton who looks like his "Mum." On first observation it appears her description of her life style is right also. It appears helter skelter but it's comfortable for them. (I'm the only cold person in all of England.) Donny, an energetic child, takes a lot of her time but Brenda has amazing patience with him. In the short time I've been here I have yet to see her too busy to answer one of his many questions. She obviously fits her job as a teacher.

It is now late at night and I'm in a small bedroom with an electric heater casting glowing, but weak, rays toward my bed. I can hear Brenda (the woman here) trying to get her seven year old son, Donny, back in bed. He's so excited about meeting an American that he keeps popping into my room just to look at me.

When they met me at their train station his first reaction was to turn to his mother and remark, in a very surprised voice, "But, Mummy, she's pink! I thought all Ameddicans were black!" (He sees Michael Jordan, the basketball player, on TV.")The laughter broke the ice and relieved me, if only temporarily, of some sadness.

After I was settled Brenda took me for a drive through the area to show me the suburban sprawl that is becoming the new Crawley, where Richard and Emma still have their home. We drove on the M1 and off to Furnace Green to see it. It's a world apart from the London flat near your office. It reminded me of home.

When we returned we had dinner, a real English dinner of steak and kidney pie. For a lovesick woman I ate very well. We spent the early evening visiting her friends, among them a number of people who know Richard and Emma. Later, we went to Brenda's family home for the Guy Fawkes celebration.

Elizabeth R. Lawrence

Guy Fawkes Day! In London, on Friday, as I went about my futile search for a job (futile because I don't know what I'm doing) I found myself stopped at every turn by small children who held out their hands saying, "Penny for the Guy?" They were such darlings that I gave them my pennies (I recognize them!) without knowing why. It wasn't until you explained the holiday (and why we couldn't be together) that I understood. The fireworks reminded me of the 4th of July at home. But it was disconcerting to realize that fireworks were being set off from the backyards of homes all over England! (We're not permitted to do that anymore. Fireworks displays at home are supervised by firemen and police.) But, honestly, setting that bonfire and burning that poor man in effigy every year is a strange thing to do, isn't it? Especially when he was drawn and quartered for his crime four centuries ago! I think I've met a couple of them and I have been warned but, oh, what mad people these English be!

As I watched the men of the family lighting the bonfires and setting off the fireworks I knew that's what you were doing. I had to force myself to put all thoughts of you aside or I would have ruined the evening for everyone by bursting into tears. They were all so pleasant to this visiting American that, in the end, the evening was fine.

Donny woke me in the morning with a sweet, sloppy, kiss. The antique auto race to Brighton was to come through Crawley later and he wanted me to see it. In the morning we went to the village, stopped at a small Pub where I met some of Brenda and Emma's fellow teachers, then went to see a church called St. Margaret's which Brenda explained was over a thousand years old! Very impressive. What stories those massive stone walls and worn stone floors contain cannot be imagined I met the Vicar in passing. After lunch, we went to the side of the M1 to watch the cars go by. The titled and the untitled famous waved and smiled as the onlookers cheered them on.

Afterwards I visited the school and met some of the other teachers on hand and, in the evening one of them, a man called Brian, took me to a Pub near Gatwick Airport. He was very pleasant and, though he didn't ask a direct question it was obvious he was curious about the reason for my trip to England. (or maybe he had been told already,) so I told him I had come to see the man I love. One little old man, sitting nearby, leaned over and said, "If I was that bloke I'd follow you to America. He's a fool if he don't." I had to laugh. What could I say?"

Miss me. Love you. Julie

She returned to London on Monday. The only thing she could do was call David from the public phone outside his station. Even that close, as usual, she had to leave a message because he was out on a job. She was always clearly visible whenever she was there in her nice brown coat and her furry hat. She felt like a camp follower every time. That's how she felt as she stood there with her carryon suitcase and waited. There was no place to sit but she didn't want to cause David a problem by walking into the station itself.

The joy on his face at seeing her, and her relief when he finally appeared were obviously mutually heartfelt. He disappeared into the station after taking her to the small tea shop.

"You can have a cup of tea and a biscuit while I see what I can do to get the rest of the day off," he said. "I'll be right back."

When he returned he wanted to see her Passport picture. It was a simple and typical black and white head shot of an attractive woman with long dark hair and a slight smile on her lips. He looked at it as if to memorize it.

"No one looks good in these pictures," he said, quietly. "Why do you look so lovely?"

"Because I was coming to you," she said.

"And now you're leaving me."

"I don't want to go, not without you."

"Let's get out of here."

He put her carryon suitcase in the trunk of his car with the bath towels they'd put there on Saturday. They got in the car.

"I want you to know," he said, as he drove, "that I was a blubbering idiot when I had to leave you on that train with your suitcase and walk away. I love you, Julie. I have got to find a place for us. I don't want to lose you."

By days end they'd had dinner in a restaurant close to Victoria Station, and David had checked her into a small hostel like hotel not far from there. She would not have chosen anything like it at home but it was a fairly clean place with steps leading up to a third floor vacancy. The bathroom was in the hall. A public phone was available on the first floor and breakfast came with the room. Like every other place she had been in it was cold. When David brought her carryon from the car it was at least a roof over her head.

His presence made it a palace. The sexual tension between them was almost palpable by the time they came together. His arms kept her from freezing, and the desire in his voice lit the longing flame in her. Together they were passionate and loving. It was hunger feeding on fear and desperation. He couldn't get enough of her nor she of him. Only when they were both spent did they look up for air.

"I can't lose you, darling," he said.

But he couldn't spend the night, and she couldn't stop her tears when he left.

He came for her the following day.

"I'm working today, Julie, but I'll drop you off at the tea room. I'll meet you there when I can get away. Can you keep yourself busy?"

"Of course," she answered. "I'll read the newspapers and maybe write out some cards. Or I'll wander around a bit."

"With the help of one of the men at the station," he said, as he drove, "I've arranged for you to meet a single woman called Penelope who has a flat nearby. She has an extra room where you might stay. It won't be available for another day but we can have the hotel tonight. I thought you should meet first anyway."

Julie kept busy. She read and she wandered. She even took a red bus to Harrod's Department Store. Her wandering brought her back to the tea room time and again until he finally got there. By then, all British reserve gone when she threw her arms around him, he greeted her with a kiss in front of everyone.

They met Penelope at a Pub that evening.

Penelope, called Penny, was a very pleasant, tall, blonde haired, woman. Julie liked her at once. She worked somewhere not far from where she lived in Straetham Hill. She would move in with Penny the following day.

The distance between these cramped city towns all around London were so foreign to Julie that she never understood how near or far they were from where she was at the time, nor did she know the names of the towns. The houses were mostly old buildings jammed together in a cluttered hodgepodge for the many people who dwelled there. Among them were row houses that were called terraced housing.

They ate at the Pub before David took her back to her hotel. There was a chair and a bed in the room where they could sit. They sat on the bed. This time, when they made love, it was gentle and loving and full of despair.

"I'll be with you all day tomorrow," he said, softly. "We'll watch the parade together, and we'll visit some of the buildings again." He wiped tears from her face as he held her.

"Don't cry, darling. Just be patient and wait for me. I'll come to you, my love."

Friday. 8:20 PM. Nov. 11th, 1966. Remembrance Day. "My dear torment," She wrote. "You have just left me looking as if you now carry the weight of the world on your shoulders. I am writing because, for the little time we have left now I don't know how I will speak without tears when I look at you. I need to picture you happy when I am 3000 miles away again. And I'm writing because when our hearts are too full, when our words fail, when the lump in our throats choke the words to silence, too many things are left unsaid.

We do find it hard to talk now, don't we? You stop in the middle of a sentence and I see tears in your eyes as you look away, and tears fill mine that I hide. Then we laugh because we must. Oh, my darling, you told me earlier that there seemed to be a reverent quality to our love. Yes. It does have that feeling. In spite of the bleakness of our surroundings, in spite of all the problems that have faced us, in spite of the way it may be besmirched as sordid „ it was beautiful if only beautifully sad. Nothing anyone can say will change that, not unless we let it.

We've been like children, darling, joyful children, finding such delight in each other, laughing, talking and holding hands. Then, all at once, we're not children and the feeling, the reverence is there and we talk as our eyes meet.

God knows we're not innocent, and we know it. We are suffering each other's pain because we know it. This sadness, this sadness that has been with us almost from the start, is that what the sadness is, David? Are we blaming ourselves for each other's pain, the pain we knew would come? Did we know, in an instant, that time, our time, would not stand still? Is this why we reached across an ocean for each other?

It's not easy to write such painful thoughts, but, oh, how I will miss you."

Penny

Darling David, It isn't any warmer in this flat but Penny is such good company that I don't seem to mind it as much. Besides she keeps the electric fire going and gives me a hot water bottle to warm my sheets before I go to bed. I've also been able to talk to her without pretense, too, and that helps.

After you left me here today she said, with tears in her eyes, that she could see that we "admired" each other. Admired? Talk about British understatement!

(From my bed now.) We watched television this evening and saw the highlights of the Remembrance Day parade. I had tears in my eyes remembering the way you touched me from time to time, just to let me know you were there with me as I watched the parade.

In a London Fog

In Westminster Abbey you took my hand and I saw the way you looked at me. I remember the reverence we felt there, and the way your fingers moved across my cheek as I pinned a little red poppy on your lapel.

Rememberance Day.

How will I ever forget?

I hope the night was quiet for you. You said Addie has confronted you with suspicions recently. How would she have found out anything? What made her know? We've not spent one night together. What have you said in answer to her questions? Please be wise.

Sat. 7PM Nov 12, 1966. Straetham Hill. My sweet, troubled darling, You have again left me to return to problems that now confront you at home, and I am left with the sadness of your smile. The words you spoke as we made love earlier fill me now with tears. Love words. Tender words. Tormented words. And I can't help you. In less than two days I will be far away again. Oh, David, for your sake, please think of what you're saying, of what it will mean to your life as much as mine. I will accept whatever you say. I know that neither of us could be happy long in a prolonged clandestine affair, nor would we be happy if you came to me with your heart and your life in fragments.

(It is after midnight.) I am in bed, wearing a "woolie" over my nightgown with cotton slippers on my feet, writing to you again. The sheets are like ice! Penny forgot the hot water bottle.

We watched the news on TV and chatted

by the electric fire until about 10 PM when I joined her, with her date, for a brief stop at a nearby Pub. Within minutes after we got there I suddenly felt the room spinning away and had to clutch at Penny for support. She said she actually had to help me to a chair or I would have collapsed on the spot. The feeling, a very strange feeling, persisted for about ten minutes then was gone as completely as if it had not happened at all. Penny is convinced it was an omen or a form of ESP. I don't know.

I think I was tired. I am very tired tonight and I'm so lonely I feel lost. Will we have even a little part of tomorrow together, David? Our last day? How will I ever leave you on Monday? How can you let me go?"

Julie gave David her letter when he came to take her to dinner the following evening. He led her into a restaurant on the side of the road. It was a small, dimly lit room with white tablecovers on small tables. He handled the menu and ordered wine and, for a while, they talked about her visit to Crawley. He changed the subject after their food was on the table.

"Do you love me, Julie?"

"You know I do."

"Would you have me if I came to you?"

"You know I would."

Her heart almost stopped as he went on.

"This weekend Addie threatened to go to my office with her suspicions, so I finally admitted I was seeing another woman."

"Oh, David," she gasped. "I wish you had talked to me first."

"Have I lost Julie Martine, too?"

"No, my love. But, this time, you may have just thrown her away."

"What do you mean?"

"You aren't ready for what might happen, David, and I won't be here with you."

"You'll always be with me, darling," he said. "Just don't give up on me. I love you."

"Oh, David," she whispered. "Why?"

"The look on your face as the train pulled away, and the way I felt watching you go was torment. Then Addie's threat. I think she was testing me the night that I -I had no choice, Julie. "

"Oh, my darling," she said.

Sun Nov. 13, 1966 London. My dearest David, When you are reading this I shall be gone, flying from you to a world 3000 miles away. As I write I feel your arms around me. I want you to know, my darling, that, in spite of the complications that were ours from the moment of my arrival I am not sorry I came to you. I am only sorry to be leaving and doubly sorry to be leaving you with the problems you are facing now, problems for which you are not prepared that have come much too soon.

You said you would come to me someday and we let it go at that.. I never asked you to ask Addie for anything. I wish you had talked to me about it first. I love you, David. I didn't want to hurt you; I didn't want to hurt anyone and I didn't want you to do it for me. However wrong we were neither of us wanted this.

You weren't ready for me, David and I was too caught up in our love for each other to see it. I knew how worried you were that you had let me down. I wish there had been a little place for us where we could have found each other in peace. They hurt now but how dear those memories will be someday.

You asked what I will remember when I return to my warm apartment again. I will remember it all. I will remember the stricken look in your eyes as you leaned forward to ask me this question. I will remember the anguish I saw in your face. I will remember that little table in that little tea shop and the way we smiled to hide the mist in our eyes. I will remember you, my darling, in every possible way: your smile, your touch, your laughter, your love, your mustache, the feel of your body.

What will I remember? You, meeting me that first day, tumbling into bed with me that first time as hungry and frightened as I was, my brave lover. I will remember that first flat and the way you laughed when I tied a blue ribbon onto the old fashioned (to me) toilet chain as we said a sentimental farewell to that cold little haven. I remember leaving a bottle of Sherry for the couple that lent us the flat, with a note of apology for spilling a dot of finger nail polish remover on the bureau top. I will remember you, like a Romeo in distress, throwing stones at my window when you couldn't find your key. I will remember the way you took me in your arms after I ran down the stairs to let you in. I will remember your hand in mine.

What will I remember? Curried chicken and fish and chips and the way you laughed when I used my knife and fork European style. I will remember the way you looked coming toward me as you entered a room, and the way I felt when you smiled. You said you felt it, too. As if someone had kicked you in your solar plexus.. Oh, yes, David. I might have said it differently but it was the same thing.

What will I remember? Every single moment, no matter how trivial: your profile beside me as you drove the car, the way you leaned toward me to kiss me and the way you whispered hello again. The way our lips met, the way our bodies joined and melted, Oh, David. I will remember the wonder that was ours and ours alone. I will remember your hand in mine as we walked through Westminster Abbey and the feeling of reverence we shared.

What will you remember, my love?

Our love will be tested now and I crumble at the thought that I will be lost in the torment to come. I don't know and I'm going away not knowing. I've tried to tell myself that we are two different people who came together in a blinding flash of light, two different people who must now put it behind them. But we are not two different people. The problem is that we are so much alike. We've been lost to our responsibilities and to those who depend on us. Neither of us will take lightly a pain we cause others.

Elizabeth R. Lawrence

Neither of us had ever left the ground for the clouds before. Knowing all this frightens me.

Oh, David, please don't say anything you don't mean. "Will I lose Julie Martine?" you asked, after you told me that you had admitted your involvement with another woman when Addie persisted in her threat to go to your office. (How strange that you would tie in the very moment of that admission to the moment of my unexplained weakness at the Pub with Penny!)

Will you lose Julie Martine? That sad and premature admission, though my identity is not yet known, has placed me on the line, my darling. You may have thrown me away. But lose me? Not unless you come to me and tell me yourself that you don't want me , that you don't love me, not until I hear it from your lips as you look in my eyes and tell me that I am meaningless to your life and happiness. For that reason only, and in that way only, will I walk out of your life.

Darling man, now that you have made this admission I will need your words as I wait and wonder about everything from my warm and lonely corner of America. Write as quickly as you can. I'll miss you constantly. Write as we talked, when we could talk at all, and as we loved, openly, no matter what mood prompts you, no matter what words you use to tell me how you feel. Don't make us into strangers by being different than we were together. I love you.

Oh David, words on paper again, words that might bring a smile to your lips, a smile that I

cannot see now... I can close my eyes and see you reading this.. If only I was not flying away from you now. And, please, my darling, when they finally know it is me, and they will, you know, when they use every ruse to come between us and try to hurt you there, and they will.. If you love me, believe in me as I promise to believe in you always.

I hope I did not behave badly at the airport. I hope you were able to take a small, happy part of me with you as you drove away. Remember me. Remember us.

Be wise, my darling. Take care of yourself. I can't plan but, David, may I dream? One day, won't it be wonderful to have all the TIME we want, to be able to laugh just because we're happy? I love you very much.

Chapter Four

**Half a World Away
USA & London
Letters**

Tues. Nov, 15 New Jersey USA
  Darling David. I don't remember the flight. I don't remember seeing anyone around me. I felt empty. At one o'clock today (6PM there) I pictured you opening the car door and leaning over to kiss me and I finally broke down and cried. I'm not really here, you know. I haven't even unpacked.
  Jason and Tina met me at the airport full of questions about England and you. And what a surprise they had in store. They didn't know if you'd be coming back with me but they redecorated the apartment anyway. It looks so nice. If only we could be here together right now.
My children have adult lives of their own now. I will be alone most of the time. What good is it to me without you?
  I find myself in tears as even the most insignificant memory comes to life. I knew it wouldn't be easy but I didn't count on how it would hurt I have brought home the sadness that haunted us at every turn, David. Now I'm alone with it. I need you, my darling. I hope you've had a chance to write.
  I took your ring off the chain around my neck and tried wrapping the back of it so I could wear it on my finger, but it was still too large. I put

it back on the chain but I worry about losing it if the chain breaks. It's really all I have that belongs to you. The pictures in my bedroom welcomed me home. I see them differently now. I think that's because I knew them as flesh and blood men and I long for them to come to life. Oh, David. Think of me. Miss me. Love me. Talk to me.

 A tormenting memory right this minute: The night before I left, when you sat in the chair near the electric fire and I sat on the floor at your feet, when your hands caressed my face so gently and only our eyes spoke. I want you like that now. "

 Wed, 4PM Nov 16 USA ."My darling, I probably shouldn't tell you but I can't stop crying. Saying goodbye to someone you love is a kind of death, isn't it? Especially this way, when so much is uncertain. Please be patient with me as I find my feet again. I want to write cheerful letters and I will soon.

 I saw Richard and Emma for a few minutes this afternoon and I cried on their shoulders a bit. They were very gentle. I suppose Cora will soon learn I'm back from my business trip so I'm sure to hear from her. I hope she ignores me.

 Oh, David, at the airport, when I turned and saw you in that last second, I wanted to run back. But I knew, if I did that, I would break down completely and there would have been no way to get me on that plane again. I'm sorry now. I wish I had." I love you."

Elizabeth R. Lawrence

London Nov 14, 1966. 1:30PM on a black day. (You have stood outside many times.) As usual I did it all wrong and went to the wrong end of the balcony. When I got to the other end your plane had already begun to taxi to the runway, ready for take off. and all I could do was stand with my hands in my pockets and watch. I stood there until all that was left of you was a puff of smoke in the sky. I felt so empty. I don't remember the drive back.

What hit me most was when you blew me a kiss before you walked off. God, I felt terrible and could have rushed after you. Oh, Julie, please don't cry because it won't be long before we're together. Love me, darling, for I adore you and feel so lost. I love you so! It may only be for a little while but I shall miss my little animal with such a sweet face and body. Have no fear, I shall always have you on my mind until the day when I can hold you again. And that won't be too long, I can tell you.

I have just read your letter and I am not ashamed to say that I sat in the office and cried. I suppose it is a delayed reaction together with the fact that I know you have finally left me. I feel so choked up inside. I can't write much at the moment. I just want you to get this as soon as possible after your arrival home.

I can't write to you. Like a kid I am so choked up with emotion that I can't think straight and somebody will persist in talking to me while I am trying to think. I'm going out to buy that record now and hope to post it the same time as this Listen to it. If my memory of the words is right, it tells you how I feel and will feel until the day my plane lands in Philadelphia. I do love you so much.

Love me always, please, for if this is how I am going to feel I don't want it. It is hell! I do so want to touch you! I know I haven't put this well but you know what I mean. I love you."

Wed. Nov 16 7PM – USA

My darling David, Your letter has made me cry, happy tears as well as sad, all at once. (I'll look like a prune if I don't stop!) Yes, my love, this is hell! We should never have met, never have loved, if we weren't meant to mean everything to each other.

Do you know what hit me at the airport? When we stood at the doorway to customs, after they announced my flight, and you told me you could not go any further with me. If I could only tell you what that did to me. I said, "NOW?"That word came straight from my soul and the lost feeling it contained cannot be imagined. I had to walk away and I blew you that kiss, my darling, trying hard to smile but my eyes were brimming with tears. My last sight of you was through those tears. It hurts to remember even now.

I have all kinds of memories but the one that seems the most constant is that of me waiting for you at the station, in the car, or at the tea shop. I actually get homesick at the memory. I felt that way even in London. No matter where I wandered, (I was doing quite well on those buses.)as the bus brought me back to you I felt I was coming home.

Oh, David, in all the times we were together you never saw me function as a whole person. I never had the chance. I worry about that. I'm not helpless. I want so much to have you see me and know me in a more complete way, outside of a bedroom as well as in it.. We must cheer up but these tears get in the way. I miss you so very much. I wish I was sitting in your car this minute, freezing, waiting for you again."

Thurs. Nov. 17 8PM USA Darling David, Today I forced myself to unpack but it made me cry again. It felt so final. But with that finality came determination to pull myself together. If I can't do anything else I can at least try to be ready and helpful when you come or send for me. I made a few calls and stopped to see Lee, who is recuperating at home now.. He wants to get back to work. We had a good long talk about the office and when I'd get back to work. We talked about you, too.

Police work takes all your time now, but you're also a carpenter. Many opportunities would be open to you here in both areas.

My work includes real estate. I could help if you needed it, but do you know what you could do between what you know and what this country has to offer? With the building boom that's going on you could have a home in both countries with or without central heating. Or you could work for an American firm in London to at least earn more money. You wouldn't have to give up anything, but then, like the snowbirds, you could have more free time to fly back and forth from one warm house to another.

As I drove through the area, seeing it all with new eyes, I found myself making comparisons. It is very beautiful in this area just as many places were there, but I do have a better, more comfortable, more convenient life style here. I do like the creature comforts that I've taken for granted.

But, darling, what is this without you?

I brought home a pocket full of coins that can't be spent here. I probably should send them to you but I want to keep them. My little London collection: your cigarette lighter, an empty box of Embassy cigarettes (you really should stop smoking), a stub from a cinema, your letters, your ring, your pictures.

I wish you were here with me. But darling, darling, please think of what you're doing. Don't be cruel for me. I haven't asked anything of you except to love me as I love you. What might happen now, as a result of that admission, frightens me. And I wonder how Addie learned you were involved with another woman, even before your admission. I can only wonder if Cora is at the bottom of it. If so Addie must already assume I am that woman. Please let me know if and when you find out.

Want me near you so we can grow old together. Want me near you so we can stay young together."

London. Mon night. Nov. 14. (a long, long day). Darling, by now you are at home, and WARM with your children. How I wish I was with you. Thank Jason and Tina for me, for everything. Without their help I would not have had a wonderful three weeks of happiness. I have been happy, you know. Forget the worries, for I have enjoyed the favours of the most beautiful treasure I have ever set my eyes on. I have just reread your letter. How I wish I could put my feelings on paper in a similar manner. Darling, don't doubt that I know of your love. I am just amazed at it. That I should be on the receiving end of such fire and intensity from a woman of your beauty; from a woman like you I shall never understand. (Badly put but you will know what I mean.)

Dear, dear Julie Martine, love me for I am eating my heart out for you already. I have just stopped to dream a little and imagine myself with you. If only I could be NOW. Darling, I love you so. To be able to put my hands on your hips as you walk upstairs, to be able to touch you. What will I do? I feel so empty. Part of me has gone with you.

Sweet Julie, I love you and I am happy that you are comfortable even if you are so far away because I know you won't be there alone long. Keep those memories alive! Think it happened yesterday and the time will fly to bring us together again. Don't worry. I shall never forget. ... I have no paper or envelopes, (I gave them to you , remember?) so will get some in the morning and complete this during the day. Meanwhile, I shall go to my place of abode, (crazy), but it doesn't seem like home, and think. I want you and I am going to have you. Goodnight, sweetheart, till tomorrow.

(My time 8PM. Your time 3PM) You know where I am going. What are you doing?

....Tuesday. 15th. Darling, darling Julie. Another night has passed. I don't want to count the days but this is the way I feel I shall look on every day until I can touch you again. In a way I'm glad you're not here for I feel that, if you were, I would tend to put things off, knowing that I could expect my 'camp follower' (your words not mine) to be outside waiting for me. Do you know I still keep glancing out of the window to see if you are there?

Still, I am not depressed, just sad. I know for a fact that we won't be apart very long. But it is most important to me to get things sorted out correctly. With your influence I can't even think.

When I got home last night the family, (Addies's) complete with "my" grandchildren were there. GRANDAD! Don't laugh. They don't know a thing. The only way I can describe the atmosphere, at the moment, is to say I am tolerated at home. But things must come to a head soon. This is when I will make my demands. I have decided on a course of action which I feel should be acceptable. I only need time to implement it.

You know, by now, that I cannot put into words my feelings for you for even while you were here I could only transmit a little of my love for you. Even so, you must know what you mean to me. I am, at last, <u>AWAKE</u>! I am, you know. In fact, I find it hard to sit still for five minutes. I love you and I miss you like blazes!

It is now very late for I had to dash out and get some work done this afternoon. Has been a rather dreary day, I can tell you. Since I have been back in the office I have sat with my face in my hands, dreaming. When I do this you might as well be with me for the picture of your sweet face haunts me' particularly as I remember you at the airport with your mascara smudged all over your eyelids.

Darling, I love you. "O.K?" I can still hear you say it. What a sentimental fool I am! How right you were to go back. I want you so much I can't wait to get to you. Each time I feel that the world is getting on top of me I shall read the letter you left for me. I can feel every word.

Please give my regards to Richard and Emma Phillips. Tell Richard I am not now "alright" In fact, I am far from being "up the ladder." I need you so much, my darling. Love me always. Face up to Cora (Lita) and he proud. Tell her nothing and giggle up your sleeve. Remember WE are in love and owe <u>them</u> nothing. Love me, my darling, for I worship you.
And wait for me, my beautiful bitch. Don't you know how much I love you? No Christmas card. I love you."

Fri 5PM Nov. 18 USA.. Dear Granddad, Sorry about that. I didn't laugh. It isn't funny. It makes me sad. As for the fire and intensity you find in my love? I'm just a real woman in love with a real man, a man who has been growing prematurely old.

(Your words, not mine) Stay awake for me now, my love. Your camp follower loves you very much.

Yes, it is warm in my apartment. I've been sleeping without covers in flimsy night things (not a red flannel nightgown) and lounging around in comfort. But I miss your arms. I miss your love. I love your love. I love you. I miss you so much it hurts.

But, darling, whenever I write a sad letter, one that I'm sure to regret, wait for the next one. You know me now. All the feelings show, don't they? Remember the day you had a speech prepared for me because you thought I was unhappy? Then, when I saw you and flew in your arms, how that speech was forgotten? That's what's missing now. So send no noble speeches across the sea or I might panic and jump on the next plane! You "have decided on a course of action.." Like what???

On your envelope you wrote Mrs. Julie (in Luv) Martine! You are a dare-devil, aren't you? I'm a sentimental fool, too, for that will now be added to my treasured souviners. And, my darling, may I thank you again for my lovely London brown coat? I pretend your arms are around me each time I wear it. (It doesn't work but it does bring a glow to my heart.) How sweetly you smiled at me that day.

Emma stopped by earlier to invite me to go along with her to bid farewell to one of the English couples who are reversing the brain drain and going back to the Isle of Wight. They said they were sure I'd return from England with my ardor dampened once I realized I had fallen in love with a working class man. My only problem with you is that you're a married man.

I know what they mean and I suppose that's flattery, of sorts, for me, but that's not very American, you know. This country is made up of the working class all striving for more. We even have a Labor Day holiday to celebrate it.

Class snobs who come here soon find they have to earn their piece of the pie or they're welcome to go back where they belong. I come from a good, upwardly mobile Italian-American family with ambition and a work ethic that will take them wherever they want to go. Some, like Cora and Kitty, who never worked at real jobs anywhere, latch onto men with money and think that gives them class. Most people see right through them.

I haven't seen or heard from Cora yet but her words are filtering back to me. I quote: "Julie thinks she's fooling me, but I know what she's up to, only it won't work. She should realize there are plenty of single men around without chasing after a married man!" (Is she really a witch?) My mother told me, too, that while I was away, she received a call from a woman with an English accent who, calling through an operator, changed her mind and broke off. That would have to be Cora or Kitty acting as her cohort, or even Addie, herself, checking on me. My poor mother. She isn't well. I hope they don't bother her again. Tina said she saw Cora one day and that Cora, smiling sweetly, asked, "How was your mother's flight?"

David, she may only be guessing but she's not going to stop until she knows. I know, as you said, this only concerns Addie, you and me, But when the time comes try telling that to Cora, Russ or Kitty. You will hear their screams in England. The thing that will compound their fury will be, not only that we eluded them, but that it was me! The fireworks will BOOM! And, if I'm lucky, an effigy of Julie Martine will join Guy Fawkes on that bonfire!

You may think I'm placing too much importance on Cora and I hope you're right. But I can't help feeling that whatever pain lies in store will come through Cora and, when the smoke clears Cora's veined hand will be found on the dagger just as she (and possibly Addie) were found on the first dozen roses. She may be addled but she's wicked as well.

A triangle across the sea! She's right about one thing. There are single men here and married men and richer men. There are smarter men, English or American. As Edna St. Millay wrote: *"I know a man that's a braver man and twenty men as kind. So what are you that you should be the one man on my mind?"* There are all kinds of men. And I had to trip over you right on my doorstep at that!

I love you, David but that's it for tonight, darling. Your head was sitting in my lap as we "chatted" (without tears) in this letter. You're asleep now, snoring away and my leg, where your heads was resting, has needles and pins in it but I'm afraid to move lest I disturb you. (That's what happened the night you did fall asleep like that. My leg was numb but I memorized every line on your face and tried to count every hair in your mustache. I stopped at a hundred and kissed you awake.) I would have kept you like that all night but you had to go home. Now, off to a warm shower, a lonely, warm bed, and the framed images of my faraway lover. Yours always.."

London. Wed. noon. Nov 16th.. Darling, Life seems so humdrum and dreary without you. I want you back so much. It seems strange not to worry about whether you are standing outside or whether you have eaten, where I am going to see you and when, and for how long. I want to feel you close to me.

I hope I get a letter from you in the morning. It now seems such a long time. Remember, as far as mail goes, the time difference is an advantage to you and not me. Please write, darling. I want to know what is happening. What has Cora had to say? What do Richard and Emma have to say about your exploits in London? Most of all I want to know how you are.

I am taking a childish delight in the thought that I will walk in on you when you least expect it. Talk about a dream situation. It will shake you out of your shoes!

Last night was my toughest test for Addie made such a fuss of me. How she must have felt when I rebuffed her, I don't know. Anyway, I did, and felt terrible about it. She cried and sobbed and told me she wanted to help me, asked all sorts of questions; were you pregnant, making trouble, did you work with me, were you in love with me, etc., etc., She tells me she wants to help me and make things easy.

When I told her what I wanted this wasn't accepted. Anyway, tonight I will try to sit down and have a frank chat about things. Whether things will work out as I want them I don't know. I think, as you do, it would have been better had a little more time gone by but how can you be faithful to two women?

Remember, I love you, my darling. Don't let me become hard and brutal with my family and above all, love me for without you now I don't know what I would do. If you are unfaithful to me.. I had better not say because it is a felony to send a threat to kill by post!! I love you so.. Love me, my darling, and when you are despondent, close your eyes and imagine I am near you, reaching out to touch and caress you. How I wish I could!

The record I want to send is a new issue so I had to order it. I will pick it up in the morning and send it with this letter. I will have the film developed after I use the remainder on scenes that will twist your heart with memories.

Love me, Julie. I love you always."

Sat. 3PM Nov 19th. USA My beloved David, I have just come out of the shower and am sitting here in a terry cloth robe, with a hair dryer in my hand. Not a very romantic picture, is it? But it conjures up the memory of our baths together. Funny but, in this memory, the glow outweighs the pain. How "young" we were!

I can still see you, with that soap dish between us, as we played like children in the bath water, then ran around in towels until I let you catch me. (And I was freezing!)

The most elusive memory is that of my two nights at that little hotel. Very strange. I have to stop and think to remember it at all. All I remember is how we felt and how we held each other. I didn't tell you what happened that night because I felt so foolish. After you left I turned on what I thought was another electric heater, then I got into bed and settled down with the "London Times" The "Evening Standard," and the "Manchester Guardiaan." I read for quite a while until I realized gas fumes were wafting toward me. Can you imagine the headlines if I had fallen asleep? "AMERICAN WOMAN SUICIDE IN HOTEL LOVE NEST!" Ye Gads! Everyone would surely believe I had killed myself for love of you. And you, poor darling, would have had such a scandal on your hands!

Stopped there to fix my hair and put on my face. I feel tingly and perfumed and my hair is shining. (I am just struck with the memory of you washing my hair in the kitchen sink because you wanted to do it when I was afraid of the hot water tank.) I would love to be flirting with you right now. What a waste of good time, to be all this ready for you, and you so far away.

Instead I will be taking my parents to the movies to see an Italian film, *Cinema Paradisio.* You could come. Has subtitles in English. Afterwards I will go to the convenience store (where you used the phone one night) to buy the Sunday papers. Then I will go home to a warm, but lonely, apartment. (My children will be out doing what young people do.)

I will think of you (and wonder what you're doing) this evening. Love always Julie"

Sun. 4:30PM Nov 20th. USA.. My darling, I forgot to tell you that we had been invited to a party in Crawley last night because I was already in America. I did remember in time to send our regrets. They were all so kind to their lovelorn visitor. They called me a "soft American" as you do. I'm going to send a gift to Donny and a thank you letter to Brenda..

I shall keep in touch with Penny and plan to send her a gift in gratitude so you need not feel obligated on that score. (You have other obligations far more pressing.) Penny was really very sweet to me. One day (you were working) she took me to Kings Row in Chelsea to show me the mod shops there. Another day we went for a walk in the commons near her flat and, on my last Sunday, just before you arrived, she prepared a roast beef dinner complete with Yorkshire pudding. And wasn't she thoughtful to leave us alone in the flat as she did? She couldn't have had that many errands to run.

Oh, darling, wait until it's my turn to show you this part of the world. Wait until I can show you off to all my friends. They will love you. (But not as much as I do.) Do you know how much I love you? Do you know how much I miss you? Do you care? Or are you sitting back grinning like a Cheshire cat?

Some men need a chase to make life interesting. I don't think you're one of them and I'm glad. But if you do, you still have one. Overcome the Atlantic Ocean and chase me here. I want to hear your words, not just read them. That's another thing I miss about all this letter writing now. All the sounds and all the action is missing. Of course, a letter is better than nothing at all so please write. I need to read what you say no matter how I get the words.

Oh, how I love you, David Gregory!.

Christmas decorations are all over the stores here as they were when I left. What a sad and lonely Christmas this will be without you."

Fri. Nov. 18th London: Darling, Almost time for me to creep home and report once more. I am afraid I have no interest at all at the moment. I weighed myself yesterday and find I have lost a stone (14 lbs), and look haggard with it, too. See what you've done to me? I love it, really, so take no notice of me.

Today I was elated to receive your first two letters. It was a wonderful start to the day. Did you feel me in bed with you this morning? As I came into the office I thought of you so snug and warm in bed and wished I was there. I do think of you at 6PM (as we promised) In fact, I think of you all through the day. I wonder what you are doing, how you have managed for cash, etc. Please tell me as soon as you're back to work. I shall worry till then. I love you so much.

How nice of your children to fix your place up like that. I bet you were thrilled. I can just imagine your face when you walked in and saw it. Still, its nothing to what you will do when I send you the surprise I have in store.! Did you get the record? What do you think of it? When I picked it up I had someone with me so I couldn't play it. Anyway, I think you will get the general idea. I would love to have heard the words. You can play it for me before long.

London seems so dull without you; dull and uninteresting . I won't be happy until you are back again. I give you permission to look pretty, my beautiful one, but remember I will arrive, very unexpectedly, and woe and betide you if you are playing around! I can't help it, but I am not there to keep an eye on you.

I have just heard that the Police Federation are going to Toronto and New York soon for conferences in both places. I'd go with them but I haven't any leave to take.

Please don't be sad. I love you very much. You wouldn't be unhappy if you could see the celibate life I am leading at the moment. How long I can hang on I don't know, but you can be sure you'll have a maniac on your hands before long. I promise the fiasco of the bathtub will not be repeated.

(Sat. 19th now.) Sorry about the delay. Please cheer up. I had two letters from you again this morning and I do feel upset when I know you are sad. I love you so much and feel terrible to know you have cried and cried since you arrived home. I told you I would make you cry just for the hell of it but I didn't want it like this. I want to be there to see you. So hang on. Save those tears for me.

Don't underrate yourself and worry about the things you didn't do while you were here. Save a little of yourself for me when I come to you. Anyway, I saw enough of you to get hooked for life. Don't you know what an impatient wreck you have left behind in little ole London? If only I could tell you what an impression you made on me. You are the most beautiful and sweet person in my life and I won't be satisfied until I can wrap you in my arms again. You really are a very beautiful woman, Julie. Inside and out. With and without your makeup. I love you very much.

The view outside of a busy road junction seems to be empty without that darling figure standing by the telephone booth. Why aren't you there to meet me? What an impossible situation! Don't, please don't be unhappy. We won't be separated long. Let's fight to get at each other.

Things seem to be at a standstill at home. Mutual tolerance would be the best way to describe it. This is just how I want it at the moment for it must eventually lead to the situation I want, one where no one gets hurt. D'you still want me for keeps?

Addie is about to take a part time job or, at least, is trying to get one. What do you think that means? And last night, in front of me, Addie asked Janet if she would like to go to the States for a holiday next year. What do you make of that? I don't mind, providing I go to "Canada" first. How would you feel about that? No. Let me be serious and get my plans on a more solid footing.

What a crazy idiot I am. I suddenly got up and used up the last two photographs on that film. I set the camera up on my desk, presssd the button, then ran like blazes to sit in a chair. I bet it looks terrible. The reason I smoke too much is, I think, due to the fact that I look for an excuse to get close to you by taking my cigarette case out (the one you gave me.) I must cut it down by being content with touching it now and again. You must think I am daft. I keep jumping from one thing to another. How I hate the necessity to write. As you say, we should be together talking.

I don't know why but, when making up my Diary yesterday, I wrote March instead of November no less than three times. See what you have done to me? March is the end of the annual leave period! I love you.

You will lose that ring if you don't have it made the right size or wear it on a chain. It can't look very decorative anyway. Take it to a jeweler and have it done now.

Darling, I hope you liked the record. Give my regards to anyone who is interested. Forget the rest. I love you, my darling. I want to touch you and be close to you so much. I want you back in my arms. Remember the happy, intimate moments and fall back on them when you are sad. Most of all remember YOUR Englishman."

The Record

Mon. 9AM Nov 21ˢᵗ. USA Darling, darling, David, What a wonderful record! Oh, my love, thank you. It is very beautiful and very comforting. An echo of my own feelings.

I remember you saying something about 'Half a world away.' to a comment of mine at the airport. I'll put the whole thing on tape for you soon, but for now, here are the words:

Though you're half a world away, How close you seem to be....Every moment, every day, You're still here with me. ...We can't be separated.. Even though we're far apart,..Fate may tear you from my arms..But never from my heart...Even half a world away,..Love brings you close and then I can hear the things you say,...See you smile again...I promise I'll be waiting..Till that happy day..When you're not..Half a world away.. You're in my arms to stay!"

It is playing now, for the third time, so its anyone's guess what mood I'll be in by the time I finish this letter. The melody is wonderful. It is playing now, for the third time, so it's anyone's guess what mood I'll be in by the time I finish this letter. The melody is wonderful. The male singer is good. It's like hearing you saying those heartfelt words. You can be sure I'll have the music and the words memorized and saved in my heart by the time I finish writing. Memorize them with me so you won't forget.

If they write songs like this, my darling, it says we're not the only lovesick lovers around the world. I'm so glad. It's nice to know we have company. But I'll bet this was written by someone young and free for someone else young and free. I feel those words in my heart and soul.

I will hear them forever.

A letter came with the record and, as I've been writing, another letter was put in the door. This is my lucky day. All I need now is you. (One week, darling, since we parted.)

I'm sorry my letters take so long to reach you. I write every day and hope you get them that way. With our investment in postage we should be permitted to find out what goes wrong. Oh well, slow mail is better than no mail and, when I think about it, it isn't so bad.

The record is playing again as I read the new letter and reread the earlier one. Maybe now I can make sense of them.

Yes, I do want you for keeps! Cash in the bank is fine and food is on the table. I only wish I'd had more loose cash to bring with me. As for going back to work? The only question now is whether I should stay in the local office (my preference right now) or go to Trenton or Philadelphia.

What is your surprise, darling? You? That's all I want so don't go mad and buy anything. No, I won't lose the ring. It looks fine just the way it is. Don't worry too much when I'm sad. It passes. I promise I'll have more than enough tears left for your sadistic pleasure. As to dream situations? What would you do if I surprised you?

In one of these letters you say "it's a felony to threaten to kill by post," and in the other you say "woe betide you if you are playing around." Haven't you guessed by now that I truly love you and love you truly?? As for looking pretty if you do drop in from the sky unannounced? I'd be ready for you whether I'd been the belle of a ball or digging in a garden. . But another man? Oh, I see them looking at times but put that out of your mind. No matter what our inventive Cora dreams up don't you know you have me tied up in knots?

As to Addie? It upset me to read that she is looking for work. I'm not indifferent to how she must feel, and I'm not cruel, nor do I want you to be hard or brutal to your family, just the opposite. It isn't easy for anyone in these situations whatever their age. I can't imagine you as less than considerate and kind. I love you for it, but it also frightens me because one of us is going to live with that pain.

We should never have met, David, or we should have looked the other way when we did. But how do we put the genie back in the bottle?

As to why Addie mentioned a trip to the States in front of you? I think she was telling you something, probably about me. But there is no way I can tell you what to do.

However painful the thought, knowing your circumstances, I know that I am the one who must go. I'm better able to take care of myself; I'm healthy, and I'm years younger than Addie. But it would break my heart and, in a way, I think it will hurt you as well. I hear the cry and the need in your heart, too. A cry like mine, a need like mine. This beautiful thing between us should have died aborning, you know. But here we are.

We are caught on the horns of a financial dilemma, you know, even more than a moral one. Richard summed it up the other day when he said, "Now all you need is money." Getting started here would not be easy, but it would be financially beneficial faster than you can imagine from where you are now. I know enough to help and I earn enough to keep home and hearth going while you got your feet wet. But, for now, let's say I want Utopia and I worry about you. I love you always." Julie.

Nov 23rd. Wed. 7PM. USA My sweet David, By now you've received my card with my medical news. Did you laugh? Among the questions the doctor asked was, "Have you been in extreme cold lately?" I thought of those ice cold sheets and said, "Yes." Other questions led me to tell him of our recent activity. As he laughed he said, "Doctors often refer to this as honeymoon cystitis!"

I met Lee for lunch today (I did not tell him what you said about breaking his arm!) and, though I'm not half ready to go back to work, I'm back in the schedule. Lee had questions about England and the man who was able to get me there. Some talk of what you could do here if you want to work here. Opportunities abound.

The consensus of opinion among those who have heard the record is , "Don't worry, Julie. The man loves you., Everything will be all right." Everyone is telling me I look younger, even radiant, etc., when the record plays. I think it's the improvement in my honeymoon problem.

Oh, my darling, I miss you. I can't bear this distance between us. Can you still see me as you read my letters? Can you add the sound of my voice to the words now? If only one of my pictures would come to life and speak for me. Miss me, darling, as I miss you. This is not going to get any better so I'll close and go back to reading the book you gave me on the British Police. Very interesting. Maybe I'm easy to please but I have treasures in my souvenir drawer.

Thurs. 1PM Nov 24th USA My darling David, 6PM in England. Thanksgiving Day in America. Missing you amidst televised parades in Philadelphia, New York and points east, west, north and south. Football (not soccer) games everywhere. I love you. Weather brisk and sunny. Cheeks glow and tingle. Warm inside. I need you. I want you. Honeymoon problem continues.. Are you thinking of me at 6PM..our connected memory hour? Our Santa Claus, the round, jolly old fellow, is now on television. How come your Father Christmas is such a skinny fellow?All I need is you. Always.

In a London Fog

Thurs. 1PM Nov 24th USA My darling David, **6PM in England.** Thanksgiving Day in America. Missing you amidst televised parades in Philadelphia, New York and points east, west, north and south. Football (not soccer) games everywhere.

I love you. Weather brisk and sunny. Cheeks glow and tingle. Warm inside. I need you. I want you. Honeymoon problem continues.. Are you thinking of me at 6PM..our connected memory hour? Our Santa Claus, the round, jolly old fellow, is now on television. How come your Father Christmas is such a skinny fellow?

Thanksgiving. I am running in and out of the kitchen while writing this letter. My parents, one brother and two sisters complete with families will be here for dinner today. Two other brothers are with in-laws. Tina is eating with her boyfriend's family and Jason is at an old school football game. He'll be home in time to eat.

Now you know what I am doing today, wanting you. What are you doing?

I'm sure I don't have to tell you much about Thanksgiving. We are having the traditional turkey with all the trimmings but, since we are an Italian family something Italian is part of the meal as well. Today it will be Lasagne, from my mother for my father, plus other treats. Jason's gift to the day is a couple of bottles of wine. I wish you were here. We could eat here or go out to eat. We could substitute ham (gammon to you) or roast beef or curried chicken or fish and chips if you don't like turkey.

I am so lonely for you I'm rambling.

No matter what I've said everything begins and ends with I love you. This is a stop and go letter anyway.

Richard and Emma stopped in for coffee and dessert. They send regards to you. Richard laughed when I told him what you said about "not now being up the ladder," but he didn't explain. Why do I get the feeling it has something to do with sex?

I'm tired now, darling, so I shall close, take my medicine, (yes, honeymoon afterglow continues but less painfully) go to bed, and in lonely creature comfort, I will return to my reading of the British Police. There's a commercial on TV right now showing a man teaching his bride to make coffee. I thought of you teaching me about English tea, teapot and all. I love you my sweet Englishman. Julie

Mon. Nov. 21st. London: Tonight it must be just a few words to let you know I love you for it is very late and I have been so busy today.

During the day I received a post card and no less than three letters. Quite something, I can tell you. I am so pleased that you feel a little better. I was rather upset to think you were weeping in a corner somewhere where I couldn't do much about it. It would, of course, be a shock to my pride if I thought you were happy about it.

Developments? None really. Addie and I had a gigantic row yesterday over my lack of interest in the family. (I can't get my mind off you.) She told me she would find out the address of "that girl" if it was the last thing she did. I thought it was rather funny and giggled which didn't help much.

The only thing which upset me was that Janet burst into tears and went to her bedroom crying, just because we had a row. If it wasn't for her I would have moved out ages ago. Not to worry. Things will work out.

You! You are a sweet, adorable darling who I want so much my mind and body are making me a nervous wreck. It is only the thought of my past satisfaction that is keeping me alive now. Why the hell aren't you outside waiting for me now? Good Lord, you sure would have a rough time if you were. (Boasting again!) I did think of you at 6PM. In fact, I saved your letters to read until then. I had a rather funny sensation in the loins. Seriously, I love you and desire you so much, even more, now we are apart like this.

Curse the time lapse between us! I would dearly love to know what you thought of the record. You must have it by now but, of course, I won't get your reaction for several days. The photographs are being developed and should be ready next week. A friend of mine is doing them, any decent ones I'll have blown up. I'm sorry if this doesn't seem to make much sense but this is rather a rushed effort. You know what a mad, daredevil fool of a lover you have!

Change the subject yet again. Addie wrote a letter to Cora and Russ, and also to Richard and Emma yesterday. I didn't get a chance to peruse them as I normally do, however, I should have no fear of a bombshell dropping in your lap for the last person she suspects of my corruption is you!

Remember, I love you very much. More than you can imagine! And I want you and need you more than you can imagine! Have just had a look through your photographs. Not one of them does you justice. You are a beautiful woman. Your David.

Tues. Nov 22$^{nd.}$ London: Hello, my love, For once alone and, with a bit of luck, will stay that way for some time. I have had quite a busy day dashing about and now deserve some rest. Received a letter from you this morning which brightened my day and am now looking forward to the next one. I hope to hear news about your job soon as I worry to think about you starving and I can't do anything about it.

There isn't much news. In fact, none at all. I think I told you about the letters Addie had written to the folks out there. I notice the envelopes are still on the sideboard but I can't find the letters to have a peek at them. Things are a little more pleasant on the home front so perhaps none of her suspicions will be conveyed to them. Anyway, I can't wait to hear what happens when you and Cora meet again. From her attitude it would appear that she already has some idea of what has been going on. (or has she?) If she has, I don't think the information has come from this end. Good luck, anyway. If she reacts the way I think she will it will be rather funny. (For me.)

I telephoned John today to make sure of Penny's address. It is the great day tomorrow when my monthly cheque is paid into the bank. Hoorah! I'm solvent again! What I intend to do is send her a few pounds with a letter of thanks and suggest she buy something for the flat..

Now for us! Once I get Christmas over with I intend to start looking around for somewhere for us to live. In the months after Christmas I am going to save my pennies and get over there for a holiday. And, perhaps, you may like to come back with me. Yes? This sort of thinking is the only thing that helps me tolerate the life I am leading.

I am so bored and miserable without you. Why aren't you here to brighten up the dull streets outside? I know it' my fault. What an ass I've been. I love you and miss you so much that, I can assure you, if I had some leave due, it wouldn't be many days before I was knocking at your door. I'm sorry, a photograph is no substitute for the real you. I look at your pictures and, as I said before, they don't do you justice. I love you, my darling. I'm sure you know you are a very pretty woman.

Now read about a certain woman I know and who I think rather a lot of...

She is about -?--years of age. Approx 5'7" tall. Weight? (just right) Has soft black hair, rather wavy if she lets it be, nice and shiny, Very attractive. Rather prone to add bits and pieces when wishing to look smart. Succeeds. Wonderful dark brown eyes which flash in every direction and beam love and warmth now and again. (Rather like that bit.) Nose straight, nostrils inclined to twitch under certain kinds of tension (and on sight of a white shirt) (on me.) Mouth, full, well shaped, hungry and definitely kissable Chin, round with faint cleft. Ears. Small.

Elizabeth R. Lawrence

Wears Gipsy type earrings well. Shoulders, nice, plenty of flesh. Bears recent vaccination scar on right arm. Breast. Plenty! Full. Well rounded. Very tempting. Stomach. Have nestled there and feel well satisfied. Now..hold it a minute.. Careful what you say. Stick to very nice or wonderful or WOW! In fact, leave this bit out! Legs. Well shaped, sturdy, rather beautiful. Overall picture.. A very beautiful, attractive female fancied by a quiet English rozer who, since meeting her, has slowly gone mad with love and desire and who, at the moment, feels like jumping in the river Thames in desperation!

Recognize her? Darling I love you so much. I want to touch your beautiful body. I want to taste it. I want to feel it. I want to see what it is I desire most in this world. If only you were pressed tightly against me now. My biggest regret is that Addie didn't find out sooner. We would then have had the excuse to take to a hotel as man and wife. I hope you realize how much I want to hold you. I feel absolutely savage with desire at the moment.

Six o'clock. What a time to be thinking about sex. I wonder what your thoughts are in the middle of the day for you? I bet, at the moment, your thoughts are so sweet and gentle I feel that way, too, but at the same time permit me to want you like hell. At the moment your body is against mine, all the way down, and my fingers are fumbling with your bra, and any minute you will be thrown to the floor and raped and raped. What the hell have you done to me, Julie? I feel like a boy at his first sex experience, veins throbbing an'all. I had better leave the subject. I feel too randy! WOW!

Love me, dear Julie. If I don't crack under the strain of waiting I think I can hang on until April or May. If not, watch your back door for a babbling lunatic will come rushing in to have you forever. "David.

Fri. 4PM. Nov 25th. USA-Hi, my dare devil lover, Your reaction to my tearful letters was so full of male ego that I'm not sure I should speak to you again. But I do wish I could kiss you and go on with your corruption. Corruption? Who corrupted who? (Or is that whom?)All I did, if I did anything at all, was to shake you , (and it didn't take much shaking) out of that premature rocker! You looked at me and I looked at you and you leapt of that euphoria of mothballs like a man jolted out of storage!

Your problems didn't begin with me, David. They were built into your life years ago. Now you have a matronly wife, a darling child and clean white shirts. And because you are the man you are, they have your love (yes, love) your sense of responsibility and, until you made that admission they had your loyalty. Whatever excitement or reward you need seems to be supplied by your work.

Maybe that's enough for you. Maybe, in the end, it will have to be. But I know you now, my darling, and I know that I could never have happened to you, in this way, if your life had been complete. You are not a man who has casual affairs. I also know that if I am not the disease I am, most certainly, the symptom. Whether I'm the disease or not, I'm part of the problem now and I love you. My love is not a mothering (or smothering) kind of love. I want your complete love and I want to give you all of mine. If that translates to the fire and intensity you find in my love, so be it.

Put my voice into these paper words, my darling. Don't be angry with me for saying them. You started to talk about it yourself when you held me close in that little hotel. But the words were lost to a kiss as desire filled us. Oh, David, if only we could be like that now.   As to Addie's comment about locating "that girl's" address, I notice, by her letters over here, that her search is starting right in my backyard. Whether you think a bombshell is to fall or not, I have the feeling it's on the way if only because it will take no genius to add up the facts. We were so obvious, David. And, least important, but significant, Addie did not write to me. Logical conclusion? Julie Martine.

David, I thought you were the detective in the family. That bomb is due, my darling. Very soon we are going to be confronted by a screaming coven of witches out for blood. They will do all they can to paint me purple and you a fool. They will do all they can to paint our love sordid, ugly and demeaning to us both. But, most of all, they will do whatever they can to add to the guilt you feel already. At the risk of cutting my own throat, I am trying to say that in these circumstances, we were inevitable, and you have nothing to feel guilty about.

I love you. I don't want to lose you. But, no matter what happens, for your sake and mine, I don't want you to feel guilty or ashamed for having loved me.

As to my feelings? Now that I've said all that I feel sick and hurt and lonely, and confused and empty. How I wish we were left to solve our own problems.

Perhaps the circumstances of your life, clearer to me now that the pieces have fallen in place, would part us anyway but, oh, my darling, we would at least keep the memory true without these complications. Don't let them hurt us, please.

From the home front I learn, through Emma, that Cora read her a letter from James Haines (?), "dear, old family friend," in which he mentions again that you and Addie are definitely thinking of emigrating to America. Richard, bless his heart, took off his horn rimmed glasses, rubbed his beard, (quite a growth now), and kissed my hand up to my elbow. "But for now," he said, "Julie is all mine."

Emma also said that Cora and Kitty had stopped over and discussed me "at length" recently. In the end the visiting ladies decided that I was single because I was too proud (possibly), too foolish, (maybe) too selfish (if only that were true!) holding out for too much (probably) or that my standards were too high (true enough.)That, my darling, is the news of the day from my part of America in the usually green, prosperous area ten miles outside Philadelphia, and 3000 miles from you. Think you can find me? I love you. Julie"

Sat. 12 PM. Nov 26th USA: My darling David, What a wonderful letter! And this, from the fellow who said he couldn't spell or express himself? You're an English major and don't know it. What a marvelous (and funny) description of the woman you love! You, sweet darling, are quite an observer. Now, let me see what portrait I can draw of the man I love, who has now been among the missing for 12 days and 12 nights.

He says he is exactly 40 years of age. (I'm a year older.) Approx,<u>?? perfect..</u>-weight.. Hair, golden, thick and delightful to run fingers through. Has fabulous blue eyes trained to hide a rather soft and gentle soul, but they smoulder with invitation to sex, sex, and more sex. Covers them with spectacles when reading. Nose, straight. Kissing tip tends to start more serious kissing. Mustache, masculine, sexy. Mouth, soft, kissable, devouring.. Chin. Strong with faint cleft (like mine?) Has tendency to jut when wishing to look fierce. Ears. Nice. Responds well to nibbling. Shoulders, wide, wonderful, muscular. Arms, strong, gentle, loving when holding woman he loves, Hands. Large, strong,, gentle, electrifying.. Can't do this bit justice. Body, A young British lion, gorgeous.. Male parts (won't leave this bit out) Size: Perfect. Satisfying. Fits well but can cause cystitis on cold sheets. Legs. Strong. Sturdy. Feet (Didn't notice them.) Flat??

Overall picture.. A very handsome, virile Viking warrior, who is also a rather quiet, sensitive man.. Comes to life when it's important. Desired by a rather sensitive, earthier American woman who, since meeting him, has gone mad with love and desire and who, at this minute, feels like jumping on a plane to get to him.

I love you and lust for you constantly.

Thank you for saying I look nicer than my photos. So do you. Oh, my darling, may we both wear those rose colored glasses for life. Your ring flashes on the chain as I type and I wish you were here to smudge my lipstick. Can you see me? Flesh and blood lonely, hungry me? Always? All ways? I love you. Julie.

Thurs. Nov 24th. London: Dear sweet Julie, I am so sorry. I didn't. mean to miss a day but, owing to pressure of work yesterday, I was unable to write to you. I know what its like when there is nothing in the post; one is left high and dry and wondering what has happened. I promise to try and see that it doesn't happen again but, just in case, things are getting a bit hectic.

I have loved your most recent letters and I am so pleased you got the record at long last. It's not much but at least is says some of the things I want to say. Tomorrow's mail should bring me news about your job. I do hope it went O.K. It must seem terrible to cool your heels at home now.

There isn't much news at the moment. No developments at all, in fact,. Life just grinds on. I am determined about one thing. I shall see you in the spring. I hope that things are all arranged so I can bring you back with me. I had better not say too much about my plans. That only leads to disappointment. (off again. Will come back later.)

Now you have gone all the sparkle seems to have gone from the month of November. Its quite foggy now and a bit dismal. Did you feel my thoughts today? I hope you were on your own because I was choked full of desire tonight. If only you knew how much I miss you!

Darling, this is madness.! I must make some enquiries Now I have some experience I don't think it will be too difficult to find somewhere to live. Anyway, there's plenty of time for that. Do you know, when I am low, I sit back and imagine your face when I surprise you! I have pictured all sorts of situations although, when the time comes, I won't have the cheek to do it and will write you first.

I now have a confession to make. When you were here I didn't know, although I thought I did, how much I love you. I didn't know how much I wanted you. Oh, I loved you then, to be sure, but now? I was such a fool! The hours we have missed. Why the hell did I leave you alone like that? Why didn't I sleep with you? I know it's no good to regret things that have passed but I do.

Why couldn't I be evil and grab what I want so much? I despise myself for trying to be a man, for trying to do the right thing. I love you. By that I mean really love. I love you to desperation. Not only are you beautiful; you are everything I want. I torture myself when I think of how our bodies were when we were close. You feel so right when you are against me when my hands touch your back. ..I want to hold you so close to me, desire, yes, but also love. Oh, darling, I long for you so much.

Dear, dear Julie, don't let anything change us particularly you. I can keep you alive and dream of you. Can you hang on for me until I can come to you? I love you so. I want you so much it hurts like hell. Please love me always. Yours, my darling. David

Mon, 1PM. Nov. 28th USA Dear Faraway Lover,,, Our witching hour. (6 PM to you, darling) I love you, but after waiting all week I did feel as if I'd been left high and dry and I thought, "Aha! He had our film developed and his rose colored glasses shattered!" (I won't tell you what my other thoughts were.) Then, voila! As if you knew, your letter arrived this morning. It is a day of rain but my heart could light up the world.

Happiness, thy name is David Gregory! (Are you sure your name wasn't once David Gregorio for the Italian Viking ancestor in your handsome, romantic genes?)

As to your confession? Noted. But no surprise. I slept alone in those Irene Dunne rooms, you know. Though neither of us has ever really spoken these doubts aloud, whenever you have one, know in your heart, my darling, that I have probably had the same one, about you, about me, about the changes in my life, about the changes in yours. But, David, if we could see each other as we should, every day, these things would be spoken, dealt with and put aside because we would have the reality of daily life to weigh our doubts against. And we would have time. Time, closely followed by money as well as proximity, is one of our most important words.

As it is, I am here alone, working again, clinging to the promise of your love and falling apart when my fears overwhelm me. You are there, not so alone, without me. Don't you know where my doubts lie? Don't you know the sadness between us, the sadness I brought home is partly rooted in those feelings?

Why do you think I came to you, David, instead of urging you to come to me? I didn't want to fall at your feet. I wanted you to slay a dragon for me but I came to you because I didn't want you to jeopardize anything in your life. For what? A glance? An instinct? Hormones?

Maybe one night was all we needed but now? Why do you think I was so dismayed when you told me about that admission? You were not ready for the consequences then. I'm not sure you are now. I almost cried at the table as you told me. I did later,

We found each other, David, as we dealt with our physical attraction to each other. It wasn't just desire. I am no more inclined to a casual affair than you. That may account for our wonder. We weren't ready for reality yet.

Of course, I'll wait till spring if I must, and I'll go back with you if you wish (although I still think you could do better here, at least to save money to do whatever you want to do) but I should be with you now, my darling.

I want you to want me so much that you'll move heaven and earth to get to me. I want you to slay that dragon for me. I won't change us, David. I love you ." Julie.

Bombshells

Mon. 9:30PM Nov. 28th USA – Darling, the first bomb just dropped in my lap! I'll write it as a script to make it easier to follow.
First Player: Russ.. Time 7:30 PM
Setting: My apartment Opens with knock at back door.
Me: Hello Russ. Would you like to come in?
Russ: Ah, No..I I just stopped over to find out why you haven't been around. (He walks in)
Me: I've been working.
Russ: Is your phone out of order?
Me: I don't think so.
Russ (Getting to the point) I received a letter from David at my office on Friday in which he told me there is a definite possibility of a separation between he and Addie.
Me: But why would he write to you?
Russ: David and I are very close and he is turning to me for help.
Me: But why are you telling me?
Russ: (Looks away) Cora received a letter in which Addie says she is looking for a job in order to earn the fare for a trip to America for herself and Janet. Cora was so upset that we placed a call to Addie and spoke to her. (Pause) Addie asked us to check with Julie Martine (that's how he said it) to see where she has spent the past few weeks and to find out if she

has made a recent trip to England! (Not waiting for an answer: Russ raises his voice another notch and, in a higher pitched, somewhat threatening tone) I will be getting to the bottom of this!

Me: This isn't something you should be discussing with me.

Russ: (No longer hiding his thoughts) David is probably infatuated with you and doesn't know what he is doing. If I find out there is any truth to these letters, and if you are involved, I will not wait for Addie to earn her fare. I'll send for them myself in a day or two.

Me: Aren't you interfering in..?

Russ: It's my job to interfere! (Then staring right at me) Julie, is anything going on between you and David?

Me: I don't know what you mean..

Russ: Have you been in touch with him?

Me: I'm busy, Russ. I'm..

Russ: (His voice as high as his pencil mustache is thin) Where have you been for the past few weeks?

Me: I beg your pardon?

Russ: I want to know. I can find out, you know.

Me: What I do is none of your business.

Russ: It is when it concerns my family. (Then) Julie I don't believe you've been away on business. Addie knows something but she couldn't talk with David on the extension..

Me: This is really none of my business..

Russ: Are you claiming to be the innocent victim in this?

Me: (Staring right at him) I'm not claiming anything.
Russ: I intend to talk to David. Men never know what they're doing in a situation like this and I can put some sense in his head before everybody gets hurt. (Then, looking at me) I know you, Julie. You don't want just an affair. You want to accomplish more in life. You're used to more than David can offer you.
Me: I don't know if you know me or not but..
Russ: Oh, yes. You've probably led him on. You're probably used to these little flirtations..
Me: You've contradicted yourself.
Russ: You haven't used your head. You've been using your emotions instead. You know, if they do break up David will lose Janet because Addie will bring her here and stay with us. (Pause) Are you in love with David?
Me: I was certainly attracted to him and he did send me roses. I'm sure I'd probably feel the same way if I saw him again.
Russ on back step as I close the door.

That was it. I later saw Richard and Emma who said that while Russ was with me Cora had them on the phone. They feigned surprise. She told them she intends to contact James Haines (don't know who this is) and Kitty's mother to have them drop in on you for a "friendly little chat," and to see if they can put some sense in you. Richard was annoyed for my sake and yours. Said he would "boot" them out for interfering at all.

Under different circumstances, so would I.

That won't be easy with this group. I'm dealing with a very strange woman (or two or three, counting Russ.) I suppose Cora and Kitty will soon make an appearance in tandem. (Cora won't come alone, I'm sure.)

God only knows what I can expect. I will bite my tongue for your sake but it won't be easy. I wish you were here with me. If I could only tell you how much I hate the thought of what they'll put us through because we're apart like this Don't be intimidated, David Love always. Julie

Sat. Nov 26th London. Darling, I am so sorry. Another day missed. What will make it worse is the fact that apparently my letters are arriving together, which will give you gaps in the mail. Yesterday, I had nothing other than a postcard from you. Today, a card with two letters . Do the letters I send express take a shorter time? I love you. I do, you know.

I do want you back so much, so on 17th December I am going to the Café Royale for dinner (stag) to meet someone who may well provide the answer to our problem. At least for a job for you, possibly one you want, to get backward and forward to the States. Don't get your hopes up too high though I know it looks good at the moment but, until I meet this chap, I won't know much. I can only say it looks good.

Your complaint? Yes, I giggled. I know what it is. Too much love at one time! Hang on to the pills though. Second honeymoon coming up! Darling, I love you. Glad you liked the record. I gave you the title at the airport to see if you listened to what I say. Obviously, you do.

Although it would be nice to send for you what I most look forward to is a holiday with you out there; not so much in Canada. I was thinking of an apartment with you there.

At home? Tolerant, or, I should say, tolerable. Miss you like hell! Getting a bit desperate.! Have not been able to get along to see Penny or even write. Just not got the time.

Bolting down with rain at the moment. Since you left, nothing. I am fed up and wishing you were here with me. I want to say all the things I didn't say and do all the things I should have done. This is hell. Why aren't you outside? Don't say it.

As you have gathered I am a bit depressed today. I have just glanced through your last letters to try to cheer myself up. No good. Will keep busy doing a bit of decorating this weekend, if I can muster up the energy. Love me, my darling, and forgive me this horrible mess. I don't know how long I shall be able to keep it up. Being away from you is torture! Those eyes have just smiled at me from the drawer and told me to cheer up. Perhaps I will if I don't go mad first. I want you near me. I can't go through life like this. Richard has hit the nail on the head when he talks about money. This is the root of our problem. We have everything else. Money. Oh, what's the use? I haven't got it.

I love you, Mrs. Julie Gregory. Over here you would be Mrs David Gregory. You assume the name of your husband. It does sound rather nice, doesn't it? Love me, my darling, for at this moment I need you like hell. I can almost feel the skin of you under my fingertips. I wish I hadn't gone so mad with you. I want to savour every delicious moment with you.

Time is passing. I want to get this in the post so that you don't wait too long. Love me always, Julie. I adore you and I am racking my brain to get you back to me. Don't worry, my love can't change. Remember the words of that song. That's how I feel although I don't feel like singing about it. Yours, David.

Tues. 9PM. Nov 29th. USA Dear, dear David. Cheer up. Please cheer up. That letter made me want to take the next plane! Let me set your mind at ease about things here. Obviously, my mail has been mixed up again. I am back to work, David. I am not starving and neither are my children (when they get home.) And I'm saving every extra penny! As for companies in England? A cosmetic company, looks promising. I've had two local interviews and have been asked to go to New York for a third after the holidays when the company will make their selection. (Pray!)

The only good thing about any of this is, with or without a job lined up in England, if I can take the pace, I will be able, out of my present earnings, to save a lot more than pennies.

By spring (if spring it is) I should have a decent nest egg to tide us over until I locate something there. With you for moral support while I pound the pavements I will do well. But paychecks in England are so meager I don't know if that's much of a solution. I want American wages from an American company branch in England. That means the best of both worlds for both of us. My goodness, are we coming down to earth!

I haven't told you I love you yet, have I? Well, I do. I surely do!

Now to the problems with Cora and friends! Character assassination is probably the best way to define what's going on here. There are veiled threats in the form of obscene hone calls and little notes such as the one that follows. (Found in my door today):

"Julie, I would appreciate it if you would come to see me tonight. It is a matter of principle. I know everything and many more people will know it before the weekend. Such as your children and your family! Everyone you know! All of them! Signed, Cora."

(That was one of the nicer notes.) Have no fear. I have no intention of answering such notes or reporting to Cora's house. She probably wants to tape record my answers. (She has done these things.) She has already translated threats into action for, among other things, she phoned Jason at work and told him, "Your mother has been in London and she is not going to get away with it. I will stop at nothing to end this thing. Those roses he sent her were just a joke ..etc." She neglected to add that she had played the joke.

I decided I'd better visit some of the people she plans to see and prepare them for her visit.

Most are amused and all are shocked that I'm even involved with "such a character." Lee's wife was furious with me for letting her get away with what she's doing. She said, "If that female shows up here and upsets Lee I will take action myself if you don't." Cora doesn't know these people. She knows Lee's title and where the office is because that's where she was interviewed (and basically rejected). Anyway, wanting to prevent any action by Lee's wife, I phoned Cora's house.

Russ answered. I was very polite but I told him it was not only ridiculous but it was illegal to harass me and annoy other people with these stories." Russ said, "It is my right to do what I'm doing. As for legal action I've already spoken to my lawyer." That struck me funny and I laughed. "It's not a laughing matter," Russ shouted into the phone and continued, saying, "You lied to me about going to England. We know and soon Addie will know, too. You think you can get away with this?" He was still shouting when I told him he was a stupid man. I heard him say, "I'll show you who'se stupid." His high pitched voice almost squeaked. "You owe Cora an explanation!" "Nonsense," I said. "Cora is caught in her own trap." He said, among other things, that he had called your office today (Nov 29th) but had not been able to reach you. That was the end of the conversation.

David, I only hope you're prepared for the things they say. They will come at you from all sides. If it will make it easier for you just tell them our affair has ended and you'd like them to stay out of your personal affairs.

But, if you do this, please, please, tell me or I'll fall apart as the words filter back to me. Even so, I won't believe a thing until I hear it from your lips, so don't worry. Of course, I'd rather have you fly right over and carry me off right under their noses.

Tina just came home. Cora actually went to see her at her office. Among other things she said, in front of the entire staff, "With your mother's history of married men ..." Tina was furious. She has, so far, called my office and former associates, Sometimes she uses an alias, but her accent give her away. Other times she says she once worked for me and actually gives her name. She never worked for me. She wasn't actually hired. In every instance she is seeking information on my whereabouts for that last month or so. That's Lady Coralita in action.

I had hoped to write a happy letter in response to yours but our mail should soon catch up, and your letters should soon let me know what you think of what is going on. Oh, David, please don't let them get to you. And please write. I'll need your letters more than ever now. The gaps in the mail will have me hanging by my thumbs. I feel a little sick already. I love you, David. Always Julie.

Nov 28th, 1966 London –Darling,
Disregard the last letter I sent you. At the time I wasn't in the mood for anything but self pity. I feel a bit better now mainly because I'm a little tight. Thank you for the letter I received today. It cheered

me up no end although it gave me a sharp nudge. You know what I mean. I shall never understand how women can be so subtle yet have so much drive. I love you, Julie Martine. D'you know how much?

This must be a short letter, I'm afraid. I'm so busy at the moment I don't know which way to turn for a minute's respite.

Darling, I am so high. I have taken a few moments before I drive home so that you won't have to wait too long for a decent letter. Do you know how I feel? I bet you don't and I can't explain. I am so lost. There is nothing here for me. Addie keeps asking me if I am worried about anything. (I think she thinks you are pregnant!) I suppose it's because I daydream about you. Is it that obvious?

I'm not worried. I just sit and think and wait until I can get near to you. I am afraid that is all I exist for now. I imagine you amongst your friends; how very nice it must be, without me. I mustn't get bitter. You know what you have done, don't you? I just can't live without you. I am so far away. I kid myself that it won't be long before I am with you, but have you thought how long it is? It isn't right that we're separated like this.. Hell, I'm working myself up to the same sort of mood, which isn't right either. Sober down, boy! Will continue in the morning. Goodnight, sweetheart, I love you.

Tuesday, 29th. Now the fur has started to fly! At a quarter to midnight last night the telephone rang. Who do you think? I listened on the extension. The conversation went something like this:

In a London Fog

U know hoo, herinafter referred to as C or L. "I am sending a letter off tonight. I have been so worried since I received your letter I had to ring you. Is everything alright now? " (Ans. Trivial rubbish then…) "Yes, David is on the extension so I will write to you and send you a letter in the morning. Don't worry about me. How are you, etc.,etc.." (Talk about the dog, house, then…) A. Have you seen Richard and Emma? L aka C. Yes. They are being rather funny. We were at a party a little while ago and they walked out on me." A. What about Julie. Have you seen her?" L. "She has been away on a job for about five weeks and I haven't heard a word from her. Her phone has been out of order." A. That doesn't stop her from using a phone box. L. "No. I can't understand it. " A. HAS SHE BEEN IN ENGLAND, DO YOU KNOW?"(Me, hand over mouthpiece: Titter, titter, guffaw.) L. I don't know where she's been. She was supposed to have been to (Forget where) Sbe hasn't sent a card or anything." A. "I think she has been over here." L. (Gabbled something, couldn't hear). A. I will write and let you know." Then, "Say something to Russ, David." Me: (jerking on the end of the strings, and in a puppet like voice), "Hello, Russ, how ya been keeping?" He: "Hello, David. (I wish I could imitate his voice on paper.) How are you, brother-in-law?" Me: Very well. When are you coming over to see us?" He: (Long story about company plans etc.) Won't be free till about July."

Me: "Ah, pity, etc." A. (Interrupts with) "I wish I could come over and keep L. company while you were away. I would love to come over again." L. "Yes, I wish you would. This is one reason why I haven't been in touch. I have felt so terrible since you went back. I have missed you so much, (then yap, yap, yap then all) "Cheerlo, etc etc for about twenty minutes.

After this thrilling episode Addie said, :"It was Julie, wasn't it?" Me. Why keep on about it? She: Well, it was, wasn't it? All I want is a yes or no." Me: "If you are going to keep on about it I may as well pack my bags now." She. "No, I'm being sensible. I'm not upset. It is you that is getting excited. All I want is a yes or no." Me: "Leave the subject alone." End of conversation.

Carry on, dear reader.

This morning I received a cable by phone. I don't know when you sent it. I should think last night AFTER the phone call. Am I right? What happened? I suppose that I'll hear in the next letter. I can't wait to hear. I hope you told them that family wrangles are no concern of yours and kept yourself out of it. If you are pestered too much let me know. I shall do something about it from this end. Be sure to tell them to mind their own damn business! Blasted sauce! This is now getting too funny for words! Now, what about us?

First, I must apologize for my last letter' so very foolish. I suppose I was frustrated at the time. I'm sorry to inflict that on you. I love you very much, you know. Don't get involved that end for no one will get anything out of me which will implicate you. I don't want things to get unpleasant for you.

If they pester Richard and Emma I would be much obliged if you would let me know. Why the hell they have to involve everybody in sight, I don't know.

I am busy making plans at the moment which may bring me over earlier than I thought so watch what you're doing. Hey, do you know that you're beautiful and that I want you?

I must get this off now as I expect to be going out and working until midnight tonight so love me. I want you, understand? I will love you forever, sweet Julie. Yours, David."

Thurs. 10AM. Dec 1st. USA –My darling English Viking, "Titter, titter, titter, guffaw?" What are you laughing about? The roof is crashing in around us and I'm climbing the walls with worry about you, and there you are all boozed up laughing about it. It does have a comic side, but it isn't funny.

Cora's trick of the roses has turned on her in a way that has surprised, and I must admit, delighted me. She seems to think she triggered the start of things between us because of those roses. She still seems unaware that I know she sent them (in your name) but she does seem to be wriggling in the thorns now.

As for keeping myself out of it? Too late. I'm in over my head , darling. Besides, what's the point now? I've admitted nothing but they're already sharpening their claws with which to draw and quarter me. I'm guilty by deduction at this point and the torture chamber is being readied with or without proof. I told you the facts would point to me. Our attraction to each other wasn't much of a secret, was it?

Yes. Money is our problem. Yours, even more than mine. I can help solve some of our problems. I'd just like to find a way to transfer what I do and still be able to go back and forth if I'm needed at home. You're locked into your job. I'm not. (However much you enjoy what you do, you're working too hard for too little!) And with your obligations, sadly. I'm the expendable expense. Oh, David. Why did you ever walk in my door?

One day, if we ever have time to talk, I will tell you how I was living when I first met Cora and Russ. That's why Russ thinks he knows what I want out of life. We may need dollars and cents (or pounds and pence) but I don't measure love that way. I'd like you here, if only to start, so you can see the real me, (not at a pool or lost and freezing in a new country.)

–I want you to see me in a 24 hour day in a 24 hour way. I want to cook you a meal . Measured against English cooking I'm practically a chef, of both Italian and American cuisine.

And FYI, my darling, a woman takes her husband's name in America, too. I use my maiden name in business and it has carried over to my personal life, but I prefer it for now. I may pronounce it with an Italian flair but I'll be happy to take yours someday.

As for picturing me with my friends? Actually, I am often alone. I see those I know infrequently and, usually in a few rushed minutes .

In a London Fog

I see Richard and Emma more than anyone else lately. On occasion I socialize with those from the office, mainly during lunch hours or at special events. I also have a large family around here who pop in once in a while, but mostly they're busy with their own families. I'm the only one with any sort of freedom. I was the child bride, you know. Tina is dating someone she likes and Jason has a very active social life. I don't go to clubs very often; I enjoy good films but don't like to go alone, I see plays at the community theater and I read a lot. You could give me a test on the British Police now. I think I'd pass with flying colors.

I do artsy craftsy things, too, (You should see the watercolor I've done of you using Detective Hardface as my model. He's so gorgeous I could eat him up alive.) I'll give it to you someday.) I watch some television. Every so often I play our record. I don't really need to hear it now. Music and all I know it by heart. Then you fell into this quiet life and look at all the trouble I'm in now!

In spite of the news I enjoyed your writing of the phone call, very entertaining. If you knew how much I enjoy your letters, when they finally arrive, you'd never apologize again. I love you. I'm lost without you, too. You've taken over my life more than you know. The thought that we're 3000 miles apart in the midst of this furor accounts for much of my worry. I want to be with you. I want to kiss you everywhere. I want to touch you and have you touch me the same way. And we could share all the other problems with at least this one, solved!

Always yours. Love Julie
Fri. 3PM. Dec. 2nd. USA.—Dearest David,
A quiet day so far. I love you. As I came up my walk to my front door earlier, a neighbor said a gentleman had stopped by. She described him as being a nice looking fellow with a mustache. I know many men fitting that description, except for nice looking, even Russ, but my knees turned to jelly. I was sure it was you. A card in the door identified a salesman. I wanted to cry.

Emma spent part of the time with me. (Her apartment is being painted.) We went for a walk through the park and came back with red cheeks ready for a 'spot of tea.' She told me to be careful around Cora. It seems that she is now threatening to disfigure me! Unbelievable! Russ would probably hold me while she did it, too! Emma thinks Cora enjoys "fishing in troubled waters," that "this will "probably put the bloom of the rose in her empty life."

Richard, usually with a funny bone, has had his fill of Russ as well as Cora. It seems, while I was in England, they were all at a party and Russ took it upon himself to speak to them as if they were a couple of children. When Emma found insult in his attitude Russ turned to Richard and made a snide remark about Emma. Richard was furious. He said he didn't want to cause a fuss and he couldn't sit still for it so he simply told Emma to get her coat and they left the party. (That should refer you to Cora's line in that call to your house, "they walked out on me.") They sure did. But it doesn't stop Cora from calling them. Now they're going through the torment of trying to get her off the phone.

Oh, darling, you won't let them hurt us, will you? If only we could do it all over. If only those three weeks were just beginning. My memories, my sad and beautiful memories, torment me. I need you very much, my love.

Always yours, Julie"
P.S. Yes. Express letters do reach me faster. J

Sat. 2PM. Dec 3rd. USA. My darling, No letter from you for days. Is everything all right? Has my news caught up with you? Do you love me? Tell me again. At this moment I'm haunted by your voice asking me, "Will I lose Julie Martine" (for that admission). Will I lose David Gregory, my darling?

Snow flurries. Darkening skies. And suddenly a new memory" <u>La Place Chantilly</u> where we sat at the table and tried to eat and couldn't swallow when we caught a glimpse of ourselves in a mirror. Your surprise when I gave you that cigarette case. The way our eyes met and held. The way we held hands catching another glimpse of ourselves walking down the stairs. I miss you very much right now.

Darling, darling, right this second your face is looking up at me from the photograph I carry, and all I can see is that last moment at the airport when I had to turn and walk away from you. I love you. Love me. Always.. Julie.

Sun. 1PM. Dec 4th USA. Dear love, No

mail again. I know the holiday is making it harder for you now but I miss you. Are you thinking of me at 6PM your time on a Sunday night in England? Or is that now Monday there? Oh, David, right now I can't figure out the day or the time between us.

I feel as if I'm standing on the edge of a cliff! And all because of days and days without mail from you. And days and nights of being bombarded on all sides by the feedback of Cora's visits to people I know. If only you knew what she's saying. Or do you?

She's already called most of my family. I saw my father last night. He looked at me from under his brows and said, "Juliana, watch out for that English woman. " He may not have heard from her but he's become aware of the problem. God help her if she should bring my problems, or her tales, to his doorstep. His roar alone will frighten her.

She has gone to the rental agent at this complex. It only makes me an object of gossip and curiosity which I simply ignore. But I am furious and feel trapped, not by my guilt any longer, but by my concern for you. I need to know you're all right. I need you.

I hope you let the story of the roses remain as it is. They can torture themselves forever at the thought that they brought us together by interfering in the first place. (Sometimes, the Indians win, after all!)

Enough said, my darling man. I am now going to the shopping center. Perhaps I can browse away this longing for you.

Siempre en cora (Italian: Always in my heart) J'taime (Short cut French: I love you) Julie

Thurs. Dec. 1st. 5PM. London. –Darling, Received your letter this morning. "Express." Had a good laugh at the attitude adopted by my 'friends.' Instructions!

DON'T bother to tell them anything other than to go to hell and mind their own business!!

DON'T let them pester you. If they intend to adopt that attitude tell them to leave.

DON'T worry about correspondence this end. If you want to number them, 1-2-3, etc. in the top left hand corner. I shall soon see if one is missing!

DON'T worry about me. I am OK and enjoying this. (Sorry that you're involved though.)

DON'T be unhappy.

DO love me.

DO write to me.

Loved your letter. Will get this off to put your mind at rest. I love you. <u>O.K</u>? Sorry about delays. Hectic life. Will write in the morning. You are beautiful.

Have not been in touch with Russ by any means or at any place! James Haines and Kitty's mother wouldn't dare to speak to ME about this. Nor would anyone there so don't stand for any nonsense. If Lita and Kitty throw their weight around kick them out.

To me this is all a big laugh. Please don't get too serious about what is going on. We expected this, didn't we? Actually, they have all played into our hands. We can now stand back and listen to them scream. So, please, don't worry about anything, particularly me. I'm OK. D'you understand? I would prefer it if you were close to me and making love right this minute though.

It is now 10PM. I have been in and out in the midst of this little lot so I'm afraid this has been delayed a little. Will post Express first thing in the morning and will answer your letter in full during the day. DON'T worry. I love you and am pleased that things are moving at a faster pace. I want you like blazes!! D'you feel you could sleep with me tonight? Not a care in the world, except money. Yours David.

Mon. 1PM. Dec 5th. USA My darling David, If only you could see what that letter has done to me. I could fly to England, on my own power this minute. I wish we were together today. I'm home alone. (Half day at work) Soft, romantic music is coming from the stereo. There's a grey sky filtering through the windows making the room a bit shadowy but so perfect. I want to kiss you.

The other day I read something about creativity having its source in adversity. We qualify. Now where's that great idea that will spring us into each other's arms?

David, if a motion picture camera had followed us, right from the start, it would have filmed the sweetest, the saddest, and the dearest love story of the 20th Century. It might have won the Academy Award for the love that surprised us both. And maybe we'd stop worrying about money. Oh, darling, I want you so much. I'd better stop. Your loving animal. Julie

Tues. Dec 6th. 5PM. USA My darling David, I love you. And I need you very much.

CoraLita, (whatever her name is) has brewed up quite a clever, diabolic, tale. She is attributing most of the statements to you.

Divide and conquer?

As I've heard it, beloved:

1. I have chased you from the start. All is forgiven at home for, after all, how can any man refuse a woman who drops in his lap from 3000 miles away.
2. You had to force me to leave London.
3. You are no longer writing to me but, so far, have been unable to stop me from writing. But you and Addie, plus Cora and Russ, will soon put a stop to it. I'll soon realize that no man will leave his family for anyone like me, a typical one night stand.
4. You feel no guilt (and have been assured that you should not because of my past.)
5. Cora will fill in the dirty details when she visits you and Addie in January and completes her threat to stop at nothing to destroy me and this thing between us.
6. You said I arrived in a silver coat.
7. You were very much in love with Addie and that all was love and kisses and would remain that way forever.
8. You say that Richard and Emma were aware of everything but they prefer to remain out of it.

If you have said any of this (as per my suggestion for your sake) please let me know. Or does she have psychic power? Read on:

She claims I am not allowed to drive my car into the city because the police are looking for me. (That's a strange one. I drive there two or three times a week on business). That my trip was financed via the boudoir! I am, according to our resident moralist, constantly chasing other women's husbands, but I soon learn no man wants me beyond a quick affair. That my unsavory manner of raising money has existed for a long time. (That's funny. I should introduce her to my Internal Revenue man.) That she has, in the past, painted me and my life as more than it is because she was trying to help me. (God save me!) More? She claims that I not only participated in orgies, wife swapping parties, etc., but I led the pack which, in her words, included negroes. (Her usual reading matter, no doubt.) She claims to have visited all my friends (that's closer to the truth.) and they all feel sorry for her, agree that I am evil, etc. (They've asked me where I found that reject from a courtesan's club in England.)

She seems to have lost sight of her original outrage and now the rage is feeding on itself. She says she has just begun. (Gad!) her campaign to destroy me. She will show me that I have not only lost my lover but that I will lose much more before she is finished with me!

I'm getting all this in bits and pieces from those she corners. It makes me sick at my stomach.

Richard and Emma are trying to shake her but she is haunting them.

David, I could stop Cora in a minute, but I worry about what this might do to you, and to you and me. When I was with you I was happy whenever you were there and you knew it. Can you close your eyes and see me sitting at your feet in a cold room, sleeping alone in a strange country, holding your hand? Do you think I had to come to England for a man, for that? I'm trying so hard from this distance to hold myself together, but I need your shoulder. I love you. Always, Julie.

Dec. 2nd. 1966. London – Darling Julie, I haven't much news . I should think everything is going on your end at the moment.

I love you very much. If only you knew how much I want you this minute. Just after lunch, too! I shall begin with the first thing first and kiss you and kiss you and kiss you. Oh.. I get so little free time. At the moment I have not got time to say anything. Care to move in with me? I am still waiting for those photographs. A pal of mine was going to get them done on the hurry-up but, of course, it is taking longer than normal.

I just broke off to look out of the window. The street outside looks so bare. This has become a habit, you know. I know you won't be there but I still look for you. Oh, darling, I want you back so much! (Out again, back later. I love you. Love me.)

6PM and thinking of you. Have just returned and am thinking of you. Am standing by to go out again. What a time I have! Work all day and booze most evenings.

The nights? Empty.

I was amused by the last letter I received from you. At times you are so serious it makes me laugh, not because you are serious, but it's the way you put things. I can picture your face as you talked to me while you were here.. The thought has just crossed my mind,, How wonderful you are to make love to...the thought is so real I can almost feel you.

Darling, I want you. I mustn't get like this but I must tell you that I love you and want you and won't be satisfied until I have you again! My plans? Leave them for a little while. I mustn't say too much at the moment, not until after the 17th anyway. So hang on just a little longer, please. I love you.

Will leave this until morning and try to complete then. Goodnight, my darling. Huh? It's late afternoon for you. LOVE ME always!

Now, it is Saturday afternoon 5PM. Dec 3rd! I don't know where the day has gone. What I intended to be a long letter has turned out to be a big nothing. I have a sudden, shocking cold with all the usual signs. Why aren't you here to nurse me? Will come back refreshed after the weekend. Received your letters OK. I got the message in the last one. Have no fear. No one will intimidate me. Don't you realize all this is turning on them?

Love me. I feel terrible and am going home to bed with a hot whiskey and a couple of tablets (in lieu of you) I love you. Yours David.

Tues. 11AM. Dec 6th. USA.-Darling David,

In a London Fog

How do I miss thee?? Do you know? The suspense of this separation and the gaps in the mail, unbearable of its own accord, has been heightened in view of the deadly drama going on around me. And since I know the news in your letters is four to eight days, sometimes longer, behind news from me. I am literally holding my emotional breath until we catch up.

You once said love by post did not suit you one bit. I couldn't agree with you more. As it is just remember I love you. A sudden thought.. What have you done with those towels? Are you still driving around with them in the boot? That's at least one domestic bond between us, a set of bath towels! Love me as I love you and miss me as I miss you. Always. Julie

Wed. Dec. 7th, 6PM. USA –My darlng, my love. A letter! I cried when it came. (five days of waiting) then I glowed, and then I panicked because I'm still waiting for you to catch up with news from here. Oh, David, what torment! I'm not this serious all the time. (You should know that.) That's the problem. Yes, I do love you. Yes, I would love to live with you, here or there! And, yes, I hope you're right when you say this is all turning against them. I tell myself that Cora, et al, will be destroyed by the tail of their own monster, but sitting it out alone "ain't" easy, my darling.

I'm not used to this, you know. I usually cope with problems well. Throughout my life, I've been told I have a happy face. I hope the smile still shows. But my silence seems to be encouraging her.

I'm now getting calls from people who are no longer amused telling me to keep her away from them. How?

Richard says "Cora seems to go about adopting people into the family then hangs on any words said, weighing them in the balance for further use to verify against other actions or further words!" (That's a mouthful!) I hope I've quoted him correctly. Emma describes her as "The would be Lady Cora with undercurrents of malice shining through the silk lady in her eyes like a volcano constantly waiting to pick at something so she can erupt.!" (Another mouthful Whew!)

The newest reason for the trick of the roses? "Addie sent Julie those roses through me to thank her for the flowers she sent to Janet."

Darling, I am alone here. I'm not a celebrity with public relations people at my command to handle yellow journalism type scandal. \ I have a family and children who will live here no matter where I go. I can't just keep turning the other cheek to the fact that she's disturbing everyone like this. But what do I do? I love you. Always, Julie,

Mon. 7PM Dec. 5th. London. My darling, The BOMB bounce back! This morning a letter arrived, to us both, from Lita. Cora. As expected it contained a number of innuendos and a blatant attack on your character, together with a load of mush about nothing in particular. The part of the letter I was <u>permitted</u> to read was rather pointed. It didn't make much of an impression on me but boy! did it get Addie steamed up! We had a heck of a row before I left for work this morning during which she told me she would divorce me. I won't tell you what she called you or what she said, but I would expect a letter from her soon.

It is obvious that Cora put something in the letter for Addie's eyes only for she is sure it is you who I am <u>involved</u> with! The fact that I won't tell her who it is annoys her more than anything. Anyway, I am just preparing myself for another verbal battle when I get home.

What a life!

I won't go into detail about the whole conversation or, in fact, the letter. The idea of a slanging match over this sickens me. I can manage without all this nonsense, thank you.

I dread the thought of what will transpire tonight. I think what Addie wants is a full and frank confession which I am not prepared to make. If I do I will leave nothing for her mind to work on, and things will go back to the former stodgy routine. This won't be good. Ah, well, let us wait and see!

What a weekend I had. I got home late on Saturday evening and felt terrible, went to bed with a whiskey and pills and shivered for hours. I stayed there until this morning and don't feel much better for it. I don't know if I was delirious but, at one time, I woke up with my head between your breasts! It was very nice.

To your letter this morning. Facts about my job? Will do that when I have time. Rozer means policeman, cop, Bobby, etc.. Well, I must call it a day now, go home, and see what's in store for me. If possible I will scribble a few words on here before posting in the morning. Keep healthy and contain yourself. I love you. (I expect you were wondering when I would get around to that.)

Tuesday. A silent nothing on my arrival home and since. Received your letter about the troubles your end. So sorry. But don't worry too much. There is nothing they can do, legal or otherwise, only issue threats which are worth nothing! Keep happy and don't worry.

Fri. 10AM. Dec 9th USA.-David, my sweet darling.. I love you. Cold and all. In the midst of our Greek tragedy how could you go and get yourself anything as simple as a common cold?! I hope you're feeling better. I'd love to nurse you.. Right now I'm going to send you a cheery scene for your amusement. I hope I can do it justice. Call it a news flash from the new American battlefront.
Title: The Saga of the Bouncing Bomb!
Setting: My apartment. (Last night) Open with knock at my back door at midnight. Me Opening door to two mink clad witches with large brimmed black hats over silver hair. (honestly, I didn't make that up!) Me: (agape, standing there in robe over night clothes, hair brush in hand, hair falling down , They walked in as I stood there.)
Kitty: "Well! The femme fatale! (Pause for effect) You are rotten to the core! Even my husband, Stan (does she have any at all?) said you were only good for a quick motel job."
Me: (Politely) I don't remember inviting you in. Please leave.

In a London Fog

Kitty: (Cora watching) We have spoken to David, you know. And he is laughing at you. He told me he used you like a lavatory (great expression, that) and that his life at home is everything he wants. He said he knows he was a fool and is very sorry it happened at all, especially with a woman like you.

Cora (getting started) He said you arrived looking like a Christmas tree in a silver coat. (Pause and raise voice.) I am going to ruin you, I've already seen everyone you know and I'm not through yet. When anyone hurts my family I'll do anything and say anything <u>even if I have to make it all up.</u> If the man was anyone outside the family I would be the first one to help you. (Would I even think of going to her for help?) (Me, still standing quietly, waiting for them to leave. Door ajar. They ignore me and door. They appear to be talking to, and entertaining, themselves as they talk.)

Cora: "It must have cost you a fortune to stay somewhere. David has nothing. What do you want with him? Did you think he would come with you to America?"

Kitty: "Rawlly, Lita, please! Not the way he spoke to us on Saturday. (Turns to me) You know David is completely forgiven at home, don't you? Men are roving animals anyway. It takes a woman like you to turn them into beasts. Do you think he respects you? Do you think Addie had to force him to stay with her? If he loved you he wouldn't have sent you away, you know. He could have gone with you if he loved you."

Me: (Polite but cold.) "I think you've said enough. I've already asked you to leave. Now, please, go."
Kitty: (Ignoring me) "All you have, Julie, are a pair of breasts, a pretty face and a can. (no comment) Do you think they can hold a man? They might at first but it takes more.
(Me" (Sweetly sarcastic) Tell me more, Kitty. I like professional advice.
Kitty: (Blinking with surprise) I wouldn't cross the street for a man for nothing. Certainly not at my own expense. And not if I didn't expect to get something out of it."
Me. (Coldly) "Yes, I know."
Cora: "She wouldn't make good prostitute. She did it for nothing."
Kitty: I wouldn't cross the street but you flew 3000 miles across an ocean. What did you hope to gain?"
Me: (Exasperated and repeating myself in another way) "Ladies (for want of a better word) "This meeting is over." (I open the door all the way.)
Kitty (Ignoring the now wide open door) "He used her, Lita, that's all. He just used her." (Cora: "She can't get a single man."
Kitty: "He would never leave Addie for her."
Cora: "I saw Lee today."
Kitty and Cora in huddle. Words muffled.
Kitty: "Tell me, Julie, Have you heard from David since you returned?"
Cora: "He probably sent her a card for a wonderful time."
Kitty: "Have you written to him since your return?"

In a London Fog

Cora: "She probably sent him a card to announce her safe arrival and he was glad to be rid of her."
Kitty: "Julie, do you know how low his opinion is of you? He thinks you're rotten, too. How can you feel to know you've been used?"
Me: I asked you to leave. (Shivering as much from cold coming in door as from anger.. Hoping Jason comes home to throw them out for me.)
Cora: "He's not in love with you, you know."
Me: This is none of your business. I can't speak for David but I'm certainly not going to speak against him.
Cora: "Why not? He's speaking against you.
Kitty: It's obvious, Lita. Julie is in love with David. All he did was take advantage of it. He's not in love with her." (They laugh together.)
Cora: (still giggling) "If he had come to America with her Julie would have to keep him. (sounded okay to me.) They continue to laugh.)
Me: (Not a very polite voice)_ "If you don't leave now I will get someone to help you out." (They walk to back door which is still wide open)
Cora (From back step now) "Now I'm going to see your parents!"
Me? (Quiet fury) "At 12:30 in the morning? To tell them about their little girl or to disturb their sleep, " (Tina, who has awakend to hear the end of this comes to back door, pokes out her head and says, "My mother asked you to leave. Now leave." (Brooms lift to sound of muttering as they descend steps. Jason's car pulls in. Cora speaks to him but words indistinct.) Jason's response loud and clear:

"Cora, if you told me there was thunder and lightning outside, and I could see and hear it, I would still have to check it for myself. I don't care what you say or what you think. Stay away from my mother!"

Scene changes as they fly toward my parents' apartment not far away.

They didn't unnerve me, David. It was pathetic. I only feel sorry for those being disturbed with this nonsense. In the main they're defeating their purpose this way. Comments that follow their visits vary but something like this: "They're a couple of oddball.s," "With friends like these you don't need any enemies." "What did you have in common with them in the first place?" "We'd have to be out of our minds to believe anything they say." "They look like a couple of reformed whores who think they've made good in America." And from Richard? "They sit on their brains." From a co-worker, "They don't do much to advance the cause of Anglo-American relations." From those who know they have American men in their lives (husbands or not) "What kind of men are they?"

David, my darling, my poor sick man over there who should be nursed in comfort with healthy doses of love, the plain truth is that your notorious woman from America, is notorious, to the Coras and Kittys of the world, for standing on her own two feet, for not twisting love into a springboard for financial gain, and for conducting her social life out in the open. In spite of what we've done, illicit or not, it can be seen in the light of day.

If that damns me, I am damned.

I need no defense, nor would I offer any. As your own Disraeli said, and I paraphrase, "To those who love me no defense is necessary. To those who do not none is possible."

You, my darling, have been my only secret (and forbidden) love. You've been my secret, my surprise and my torment. All my life, or most of it, has been spent right around here and the life I've led is an open book. When did they drop in? From what? They don't come across as Polly Pure Breds, that's for sure.

If we had been together today I would have made your breakfast and stayed home from work to nurse you. I love you, David. I wouldn't love you any less if you had a million pounds, but I sure couldn't love you any more. Just more often. Yours always. Julie.

Wed. Dec. 7th. London - During a short break thought I must scribble a few lines to let you know all is well except that I am living in a brittle silence, the like of which I have never experienced. I certainly do not feel welcome in my own home to say the least.

As I left for work this morning an airmail letter was delivered which Addie crept away with. The contents? Anybody's guess. I must wait and see what sort of reception I get when I get home. I hope the pressure isn't too bad your end and that you have managed to cope. I do think the least they could do was to leave your children out of this but, still, there you are!

My cold still hangs on and I haven't had a letter today which hasn't lifted my temporary depression. I miss you. Will write soon when I can wheedle the time. Enclosing some photos at last. Remember, I love you very much. David.

Sat. 10PM. Dec. 10th USA – Dearest David, What wonderful pictures! What a nice, gentle mood the camera captured between us. What a handsome man you are, David. There had to be more than that but I loved you on sight and I still love the sight of you. The one taken from your office window does twist my heart with memories, but I didn't need any help. That picture is in my memory album. How lonely that little red phone booth looks now. I can picture myself standing there waiting for you, even wondering what in the world I was doing there and hating myself, and you a little, for placing myself in that position. Then you'd come through the station door and smile at me and nothing else mattered. As you said this must be a form of insanity. It felt as natural as breathing. Why must it hurt like this?

I love you so much that if you can't feel it coming through even over the Atlantic ocean, something is wrong. Our "love lit hour," my darling, is now five months old. What a tiny part of that time has been ours together.

You're depressed? It isn't easy to sit alone night after night now, knowing that the man you love is so far away, not only far away but with another woman, (deep freeze or not) knowing he is married to that other woman and knowing, though he begs you to "hang on just a little longer, please" that anything can happen. I cope as best I can but.. I'm happy to have the pictures but oh, David, I miss you.

I stopped there to run errands and do my grocery shopping. The mundane does go one but I thought of you as I went along. It is now 8PM. My children are out for the evening. The television set is on but I've only seen part of the news. The Sunday papers are unopened on a nearby table. A book from the library is near them. I'm here with the London photographs, my memories, and a portable typewriter on which to write to you. From my window, as I write, I can see Christmas lights twinkling from windows and doors outside. Tina and Jason did the decorating. Looks very nice but

My mother just came in. Her face bears a worried look so will stop for now. Sleep well, my darling. I hope you dream of me.

(Next day) Sunday. 1:30PM. Dec. 11th Darling, would you believe those idiots actually went to see my parents the night they left me? My father was already asleep so they missed the consequences of his wrath but my mother was half awake in the living room. She opened the door when they knocked.

My mother, dear little, gentle, soul that she is, was subjected to their idiocy. She told me what she said to them before they left. Would that all had been as intelligent. She said, "My Juliana is a grown woman. She's a good woman and she's had a hard life. Why are you trying to make trouble for her? What do you think I should do? Turn her over my knee and spank her? She is a woman. This David is a man, If he wants my daughter and my daughter wants him nothing you can do will stop them. It happens all the time in this world. Leave them alone. Do you think you are doing any good for anybody like this? All you're doing is making enemies. When love comes no one comes between."

My mother is not well, David. She must have been unnerved by their midnight visit, doubly so because if my father had heard them and come downstairs, all hell would have broken loose. What am I to do, darling?

I saw Richard and Emma this morning and showed them the London pictures. They said we looked like a honeymoon couple. We do. Richard put his arms around me when Emma told me that Cora had called there to warn her to keep a eye on Richard "...or Julie will have him, too." Emma giggled. Cora also told them "If Russ hadn't realized what Julie was from the beginning she might have had him, too." We all laughed at that.

I don't want to be completely alone this afternoon so I will be going to a little theatre production of "You Can't Take it With You" at the college Arts center. (I've taken some of their art classes.) I wish we were going together. I miss you. On this cold and sunny Sunday afternoon I love you. Maybe I do believe in fairy tales, but someday, soon, I want our love story to read, ""and they lived happily ever after!" Always, Julie."

Mon. 10PM. Dec. 12th. USA My darling,

I have just had a violent complaint re; Cora from Lee's wife and now I have a real problem. Lee, who had returned to work too soon, had a heart attack, but he was making slow, but steady progress. He talked his wife into taking him for a drive to the Philadelphia office on Friday. She reluctantly drove him there, walked him through the lobby to the elevator, and then a short walk to his office. No strain. No stairs. She left him there for an hour's visit with the staff while she ran an errand. She returned to find him deathly ill!

In that hour Cora entered the office. (She knew where it was because that's where she filled out her job application.) I can only imagine what she said but he was in no condition to deal with her. His wife got him home, and called me. She was furious. Before she hung up she told me that if I didn't act to put a stop to Cora's repulsive behavior she would do it even if she had to go to court. I promised to see that Cora did not trouble them again. I didn't want any court action but while I was trying to decide what to do Lee had a second heart attack on Saturday. He may have had that attack even without Cora's visit, but I've let her get away with malicious slander for too long.

You've said "not to worry," or "tell them to go to hell." That's fine if it was just me, but she's causing problems for other people and I feel responsible. I love you but you're not in a position to help me so I am now faced with the very action I've wanted to avoid if only for your sake. I've been trying to reach Cora by phone but her line has been busy for over an hour. If I can't get through to her and get her to listen to reason I will have to take legal action myself. I'd rather do it before Lee's wife does so I can, at least, try to keep it out of open court.

I wish you would tell me what to do first. I don't want to do it. I just want to stop her. What she says about me to anyone who wants to listen doesn't matter. This does matter.

Oh, darling, maybe the problems here have intensified my longing but I need to feel you beside me. You once told me not to let you down, to hang on. I'm hanging. Help. I love you. Julie

Fri. Dec.9th. London – Darling, It is only time that keeps me from writing you. I had four letters from you today, and to stop you from worrying, listen to this: I have taken no notice of <u>scandal</u> pushed across the Atlantic by our friends, so don't worry.

How did she know about the silver coat?

Will write as soon as I have a chance to read your letters. I think I shall have to creep back here at night to write to you.

Have not and will not write or communicate with the Russell Dents. "O.K."
I love you. Don't forget it. I love you!
Ditto! Ditto! David.

Tues. 8PM Dec 13th. USA- Dearest David, Lee died last night. I have just returned from his house where I spent time with his family while they dealt with funeral arrangements. The funeral will be tomorrow and many of the people from the company will be there. The thought that one of Cora's tales could crop up there sickens me.

I hope, with all my heart, that we will survive this, David, but if things should ever change between us, I hope and pray that it will never be a change brought about by such a woman. I love you, Remember us. Always. Julie.

Sat. 3PM. Dec. 17th USA My dear David, It has been four days since my last letter. These have been very lonely and sad days.

The funeral was complicated (for me) as I thought it might be, by the attitude of the people from the office. They feel, and rightly I'm afraid, that I should have stopped Cora long ago. I was grateful for the support of Lee's family.

I have since filed an informal charge of harassment and criminal slander against Cora. The hearing, scheduled for Dec. 21st will serve as a warning to advise her that she is in violation of the law. I received a copy of her summons in today's mail so I imagine she has her summons now. I don't know if she's aware of Lee's death, or if she is resting up for another attack, but I do know she is not answering her door or her phone. If she is aware of his death she probably expects retribution from the grave!

The only positive note to emerge from this is that Lee's Uncle Victor, a business man with overseas clients, has promised to see what he can do on my behalf to get me back to England and you. I didn't know, unfortunately, that he was in England when I was there. He said he would have helped us on the spot. At the very least, he said, he would have put me in a room at the Dorchester, where his family was staying.

You! Do you know how much I love you? Do you know how much I miss you? Do you really? I know you're busy but the days without a word from you are so much longer, so much emptier. I need your hand in mine. I want your arms around me. I want to come home to you. Always. Julie

Sat. Dec. 10th London: Darling Julie, Please don't worry too much about lack of mail from me. I can assure you that it is for no other reason than lack of time. As you can well imagine we are pretty busy as far as business is concerned and that, combined with the fact that I can't write from home, should help you see how difficult it is. Do you know that, at this time, I just have not had time to read your letters. Will do so now. ..

The eight points alleged to be my quotes are untrue!! How did they know about the silver coat? I asked you that before, didn't I? I don't think I need explain anything like this as you know I haven't been in touch with them.

Yes! I love you! Need you ask?

Yes, the towels are still in the hoot! Do you know I can smell you on this paper? It sure does bring back memories..

Well, I have read them at last. All I can say is I love you. Isn't that stupid? Will pop some more photographs in with this on Monday. Must dash off. I love you. D.

In a London Fog

Monday. Dec. 12th. Received your card this morning and a letter this evening. The tale of the conversation at your home was very entertaining! So, Kitty is now involved? How nice for you. Enough to make you sick, isn't it? The only thing I can warn you against is letting them know we are still corresponding. I would hate to have any obstacle put in the way of us keeping in touch. I would advise you to send your letters together, once a week. I won't like waiting for the week to go by but it would be safer.

I am expecting to dash off out in a minute so I am afraid this is a little hurried. I don't seem to have time to give you any news. These letters must bore you. Will endorse some more photographs. They will cheer you up.

It is now Tuesday, 13th. 2PM!! I will try and settle down to give you some news tonight, if I'm lucky.

You have figured in my dreams of late. I won't tell you how but, boy, did you feel nice!! How about the pretty girl in the endorsed photograph? You look sweet. I love you very much. Keep your chin up and smile. David

Sun, 7PM. Dec. 18th USA-Darling, Have just returned from an afternoon's drive to Atlantic City with Richard, Emma and family. We walked on the boardwalk, looked at the sea, (I wanted to swim across!) took some photos, stopped for hot chocolate, (cold, brisk, sunny day), and sang Christmas carols on the way home. It helped me. I just wish you were with us.

At home I found that Jason had finished decorating the apartment for Christmas. He's rushing it a bit. It looks very nice, very festive. I just wish you were here to share it with me.

The problems of the last week seem a bit eased at the moment. I've received a number of party invitations for the holiday. Not sure I'll go, but I don't want to sit here alone either. You know what I need right now, don't you? You! In the flesh! A fat, juicy letter that says something specific wouldn't hurt either. I love you and I miss you very much. Always..Julie.

Wed. Dec. 14th London – Darling, Another full day and it is only 2PM. I suppose you are getting used to these short, sharp notes. I received three letters from you yesterday and enjoyed them very much. I only wish I could make enough time to sit down and write something in a similar vein.

I love you, sweet Julie.

At home things have settled down a little, mainly because of Janet. I told you she is very sensitive and the atmosphere was so strained that she felt it and came out in a rash all over her head. For this reason Addie has become a little less bitter and I a little less hard. It would be a shame to inflict my troubles on Janet.

However, I still need you badly. I had the most real dream the other night in which you played a most important role. Oh, it was beautiful. The feel of you was so real it wakened the most tantalizing memories . I won't tell you what we were doing except that we were both naked at the time! Wonderful! You ARE beautiful, you know.

It is this Saturday when I must meet the people about the job. I hope it comes out O,K, I'm glad you like the photographs. We do look nice. I hope it takes your mind back to some pleasant thoughts. When I think about how little time we had together.. It was wonderful though, wasn't it?

Don't think I get mad with you over things you say. The last thing you must worry about is saying what you feel. I don't want you to think I dwell on every word and look for hidden meaning, I take what you say as it comes. The trouble is that I don't get the time to express myself properly. I love you! and I want you so very much, Behave or else! David.

Mon. 10AM. Dec. 19th – USA – My sweet David A letter. A sweet letter! But, oh, how I hate this time lapse between our letters. Waiting for your letters to reflect current events in mine is maddening.

Yes, the problems have sickened me. You seemed surprised that Kitty would become involved. I wasn't. She is Cora's protector. Her moral outrage, in view of the things that have filtered through her whispers and giggles with Cora, is a bit strange though. I know Stan isn't her first husband. He may not even be her husband. I also know she was paid quite a sum of money by another man's family to avoid a scandal of some kind, but I've never cared enough to wonder about the details.

Christmas! I won't even get a present to you for Christmas now. I'd like to send a flight ticket to bring you to Cherry Hill, NJ., USA. And an oversized flight bag. Return trip optional. Just to see you, just to talk to you, would be gift enough for me. I love you. Always. Julie.

Sat. Dec. 17th London. –Darling Julie, I should think by now you think I have completely deserted you. Not true! Life now is so hectic I haven't gone off duty one night this week before 10:30PM.

Your letters have been arriving O.K.and the news absorbed. I am sorry about all the troubles you have had.

Legal action? I shall have to leave that to you. Please don't send me anything for Christmas. <u>No Christmas cards, please. You know what we said about that!!</u>

Too much drink, lack of sleep and food is not making me a very nice person at the moment but things are OK at home, so don't worry. A couple of letters have been sent from your end addressed to us both. I won't bother to try and give the contents. Would make you sick!

I can't stand the pace here at the moment and will be glad when Christmas is over so that I can find time to sit down and give you some news.

Now, don't worry about lack of mail! Will do my best when I can make some time. You know how things are. You've been here!!

Please give my regards to Richard and Emma. Will write to them when things die down a bit. The last of the photographs enclosed. D'you remember taking them?

I love you. Don't forget. David.

Tues. 10PM, Dec, 20th USA-Snow. Snow. Snow. All over the place. Those who like a white Christmas will be happy. Children will flop on Christmas sleds . I will hope for ice free roads! End of weather report.

I love you, David Gregory!

Have you heard the words from the song, "Somewhere, My Love"? I thought of us when I heard it. I hope there will be songs to sing someday. In the movie Dr. Zhivago is telling Lara why he must go back to his wife and he asks if she understands. Tears are running down her cheeks as she says "Yes" and shakes her head "No." I cried with her. It hit too close to home where I was sitting by myself.

Now to your letter. I do cling to our pleasant memories. I do try to be understanding and patient when you don't write. But when I wait for a response to a letter that begs an answer I go through an emotional wringer. I still face that court hearing tomorrow night and you haven't read or received my letter regarding that yet. I know you're busy, and I know the postal service doesn't care about the gaps as our letters cross so I'm not blaming you. I just miss having you with me, if only in words of support now.

Christmas in the midst of it all! Tina is sitting here wrapping her presents and making out her cards and Jason just walked in with packages covered with snow. How beautiful and lonely Christmas can be. It's 3:30AM (your time) so you are probably asleep. I love you. Dream sweet dreams, my darling. Julie

Wed. 10PM. Dec 21st USA My darling David, I love you is all I want to say but please sit back and read carefully I will attempt as clear a picture of the court proceeding as possible. I want you to have all the facts to weigh against anything that follows. I'm also enclosing my copy of the complaint which shows address, date and time of hearing. This, too, is so that you may, at any time, verify the facts yourself.

Darling, let me say again how sorry I am that such a step was necessary. I would have given anything to avoid it.

I love you very much, David.

The hearing took place at 8PM this evening and was held, at my request, in the Judge's chambers rather than in a public open court. Present with Cora was Russ, Kitty, and a local attorney called Mr. Weitz. Tina was with me. I did not use an attorney. (Richard and Emma, among others, had offered to go with me but I felt it best to leave them out of it.) Judge Klein was seated behind his desk, the rest of us in chairs to the front or side of that desk.

Judge Klein opened the hearing with an explanation of what the hearing was meant to accomplish. "The first purpose of this hearing," he said, "is to establish the validity of the charges. The second is to advise all parties of their rights."

(Words to that effect.) He then explained the meaning of harassment and criminal slander as defined in law and explained that such charges, if proven, could mean large fines, possible civil suit for damages, criminal charges or even prison.

Throughout his explanation the gruesome, threesome (Cora, Russ and Kitty) were turning to one another and giggling. The Judge frowned. Their attorney spoke to them and the hearing proceeded.

I was then given the oath. The questions posed were to explain my relationship to the person charged in the complaint and to explain my reason for filing the charges. I simply told how and when I met Cora, my relationship with her since, her attitude toward me prior to any meeting with you, the trick of the roses after you left, and the subsequent harassment of family and friends, including a visit to a critically ill man who died only days later. (Cora and Kitty giggled. The Judge had to admonish them.) . I continued to explain that this behavior was part of their announced intention to destroy me for whatever interest I had shown in you. (Your name was never mentioned. You were referred to as a member of the family or her brother in law.) I then repeated the statements she has been making about me. The Judge stopped me after about ten sickening quotes. (I had the feeling he had heard enough.)

He then asked Mr. Weitz if he wanted to cross examine me. Mr. Weitz said, "No, your Honor. I believe Mrs. Martine has sufficient grounds to bring charges." Mr. Weitz then asked the Judge to explain this to his clients for he couldn't get their cooperation and he didn't want them to think he was misrepresenting them.

More explanation from the Judge. They grinned, looked at one another and ignored him.

The Judge was now openly annoyed with their behavior. "This is not a laughing matter," he said. "Mrs. Dint, you are damaging your own testimony by this behavior and..."(Cora interrupted him and, in her most sarcastic tone corrected his pronunciation of her name.)"My name is Dent not Dint," she said. The Judge's face flushed with anger at her nitpicking and Mr. Weitz looked embarrassed.

Tina was then given the oath. She was asked what she had heard, where, when, in the presence of how many people, what people, etc..

When she had completed her testimony Mr. Weitz was asked if he wanted to cross examine her. He smiled at Tina and said, "No questions, you Honor."

Cora was then given the oath. "Now, Mrs. Dent," said the Judge, "will you explain your actions to this court?" Cora, a small grin on her face, murmured , "Hmmmm, I, yes, I did say those things. Julie is breaking up my sister's home and I am going to put a stop to it." She went on to say she believed I had gone to see you in England, etc..

"Mrs. Dent," said an exasperated Judge, "You have broken the law. You have no right to interfere in the private lives of other people, but especially when you do it in a way that breaks the law." (Cora grins and turns away from him. Russ came to life from his knee crossed position in the corner chair.) "WE will stop this if she leaves MY brother-in law alone."

"You will stop this," shouted a now angry Judge, "no matter what she does. This is none of your business!" The Judge shook his head and looked at Mr. Weitz in disbelief.

He then said, "Mrs. Martine has notified this court that she wants this court to be lenient, and asked that this hearing serve only as a warning. However, in light of what I have seen and heard here, I am advising Mrs. Martine to institute further action and to sue for damages. If I was her attorney I would strongly press for her to take this action immediately."

Cora was sputtering but her words seemed strangled so I couldn't hear what she was trying to say. However the Judge turned and looked straight at her. (This part came as a complete surprise to me but it looked as if Cora had been pierced by an arrow! Her eyes narrowed in fury and hatred!)

What the Judge had said was "I understand you have recently remarried!" (???)

He went on. "How would you like it if your new husband (Russ??) has to spend thousands of dollars to defend those charges only to find that the court has found in Mrs. Martine's favor and places a judgement against you that could amount to more thousands of dollars?"

Russ was getting the message but, big shot that he sees himself, retorted, "You mean_I_have no recourse to stop her? That there is nothing we can do?" He lit a cigarette. (The policeman nearest him, there were two in the room,) tapped him on the shoulder to put it out.

Kitty, who until now had been giggling and giving Cora moral support, then asked, "Is it illegal in England?"

"It is," said the Judge, "And it's none of your business in either country. However I have no jurisdiction in England. I am concerned with what is going on here. I am advising you to get together with your attorney and come to some understanding of the laws in this country.."

Cora interrupted him three times as he attempted to make that statement, and he spoke firmly. "Mrs. Dent," he said, "I believe you are a vain and foolish woman who is nothing more than a troublemaker within her own family. And you are causing trouble here. Can't I make you understand that you are in violation of the law and, in this room now, that you are in a court of law? I will charge you with contempt if you interrupt these proceedings again!"

Kitty interrupted this time and, in a tone meant to comfort Cora, said, "You can write to England and say whatever you want."

The Judge looked at me and said I should have filed against all three of them, and if I took further action to make sure I did.

Their behavior was damaging to them and embarrassing to observe. The "ladies," bedecked in furs and jewels, had painted a very unflattering portrait of themselves. And Russ's stupidity was evident. At one point he interrupted.

"But she saw MY brother-in-law!"

"That is not illegal," said the Judge.

"She went to England," Russ said.

"That is not illegal either," the Judge said.

"She had an affair with my brother-in-law," hissed Cora.

"That is none of <u>your</u> business," retorted the Judge.

That's about it, my darling. I'm sick to death of them. As I was putting on my coat, my London brown coat, one of the policemen came over and asked, "How in the world did a woman like you get mixed up with that crowd?" What could I say? She was a neighbor who had once come to me for a job? That she kept coming in and out of my life from that point? That we had so little in common that I kept her at arm's length but I was polite? I didn't have to answer so I said nothing.

In the chambers I spoke when I was spoken to and left when I was dismissed. I didn't find one thing amusing about any of it. Maybe tomorrow. Maybe later. Maybe someday. I don't know. But I can tell you one thing, I feel a lot better for having taken a stand. David, the hearing was nothing more than a legal warning, a slap on the wrist. For your sake alone I tried to avoid even that but the choice was no longer mine. The problem was mine. The responsibility was mine. When they had been advised of the folly of their actions the hearing was adjourned., I'm not so sure they got the message.

As we were leaving the chamber a negro man was entering an adjoining courtoom and, as he passed me, Kitty looked at me and said, clearly, so that everyone could hear, "There goes one of Julie's boyfriends now!" Mr. Weitz looked at me, raised his eyes to the ceiling and ran after her to shut her up before the Judge heard her. He really had his hands full with clients like them.

By the way, what's this about Cora being recently remarried? She's led everyone to believe they've been married for over 20 years! I don't care one way or another but she sure wanted to kill when the judge mentioned her new marriage. Her response was, "Yes, a few years ago." She looked as though she had been struck by lightning. (as if being exposed?) I'd also make a bet that their backgrounds couldn't stand the courtroom scrutiny that mine could. Just how many skeletons do the dear outraged ladies have hidden between them? Americans aren't fooled. They're called a couple of courtesans anyway.

Darling, it will be your turn next. I can only guess how they will get to you but be careful.

Oh, David! Why weren't we left to work out our own problems without all this idiocy? Between us we would have found a way to be gentle even with ourselves. Now? Please write, even a short note, upon receipt of this letter, and send it express because of the holiday mail.

I was very tired when I started this letter. I am exhausted now and, all at once, I am filled with an overwhelming sadness that not even tears can relieve.

I love you very much. Have a good Christmas, my darling. Think of me. Julie.

Fri. 2PM. Dec. 23rd. –USA – My darling, I missed a day of writing because I was sent to handle a real estate office. I am writing from that office now. There's a slower pace so it gives me time to schedule interviews for opportunities in London.

Should you drop from the sky while I am here you can take a taxi to the building then take the elevator to the ninth floor. Or, if you want to phone me dial O for operator and get them to connect you. What am I expecting? I don't know but I don't want to take any chances. I want you to find me at all times.

I miss you. I need your shoulder. I love you. Always. Julie.

Sat. 1PM. Dec 24th. USA – Dear sweet David, The world must be coming to an end and it is starting here in America in my corner of the world! Why? Did you ever hear of thunder and lightening and snow all at the same time? That's what's happening here this minute. When I heard that first clap of thunder I almost collapsed! I'm still a little shaken.

And it's our witching hour. Is anything happening to you? Are you thinking of me?

It is now 7PM and the heavens are still rumbling. I don't know why; I'm usually awed by the elements, but I am frightened.. My hands are actually trembling. Yet, it is warm as toast in the apartment. I'm sipping wine as I write (not something I usually do). The television is set on the world news. Tina has braved the swirling snow for dinner with her young man (Matt.) I think he will give her an engagement ring tonight. Jason is out trying to find a place open that sells either snow tires or chains for the tires on the car and here I am. At 7PM on the eve of Christmas what are you doing? Am I on your mind just a little this moment?

Earlier today, as I drove home, I saw the pretty Christmas lights filtering through the snow. I saw it all through your eyes, darling. It looked like a picture post card. I wanted to cry remembering our promise never to send a Christmas card to each other as long as we were apart. Why did we make such a promise?

What did Santa bring you for Christmas? Who kissed you under the mistletoe? Why are we still so far apart?

I went to a party last night with Richard and Emma but it was no good without you. I wore a black velvet dress that you've never seen with sparkling white and gold beads and gold earrings. One man latched onto me as if I was his Christmas present. It was no good without you so I left early. It means nothing if I can't look pretty for you. I'm a one man woman. The last thing I needed was to stumble over you.

I've finally solved the riddle of how Cora knew of my silver coat. A woman at the party, who knew Cora, had seen me with it and simply mentioned how much she liked it. Just that little and Cora put words in your mouth that you never uttered!

Where is that longed for letter from you? I feel as though I'm talking to myself. Please talk to me. I miss you very much.

In a little while I will be visiting my parents to help with Christmas cooking and to help wrap presents. It is midnight there for you now. I hope you had a nice day and that you lifted at least one glass of cheer for me.

Christmas day now. 8PM here. Merry Christmas (or) Happy Christmas, my love. A winter wonderland today. Sunny and cold. I spent a brisk couple of hours outdoors today. I shoveled snow from the walk and helped some children build a snowman. I came in to my warm apartment exhilarated and made myself a hot chocolate. Now, as I write, I can see the snowman from the window. How forlorn he looks in the moonlight. He looks like I feel right now. I wonder if snowmen can cry.

It was a quiet (?) family day here today. Dinner with my parents and all the other relatives who dropped in. Jason and Tina lazed around afterwards but are out again. Tina, who is so happy she glows, got a diamond engagement ring last night. . (I'm still wearing your ring on the chain.) I cried. Silly me She gave me a ring, too, a mother's ring set with their birthstones and mine. My father had learned about the court hearing and in a quiet aside he asked if I'd heard from you. When I said not yet, he said, "This man make you for fool, Juliana." "No, Poppa," I said, trying to sound cheerful. "He's a good man but he's very busy."

I don't like this writing (mailing) once a week. It takes too long to catch up. And I miss you. Will continue this tomorrow.

Mon. 11:30AM Dec 26th. Boxer's Day there now, isn't it? Did you have to work or did you have the day off? It's not a holiday here so I'm at work. From my ninth floor window I can see a lovely snow scene with a white wooden church decorated with a large holiday wreath, topped by a high, pointed steeple. It sits right across the street. It looks like a Grandma Moses or a Currier and Ives print in the midst of all the snow. Marring the scene are the stalled automobiles and the tow trucks.

It seems so long since your last letter and, unless you've sent a letter express, there will be no mail from you when I get home for the regular mail will not be delivered today.

Oh, David.

The office is quiet today. Maybe the snow is keeping people away. My paperwork is interrupted by an occasional salesman or a tenant with a problem, or the maintenance men working from a little room nearby. They go about with a breezy hello to me. The elderly doorman stops by to have coffee with me from time to time. He once traveled the world for a large company. Now, retired, he works to fill his days. As you can imagine we discuss England and American companies with jobs over there.

I have found the quiet useful for I have been able to do a more organized search for companies interested in staff for their offices in England. Lee's Uncle Victor has turned up a few people he thinks I should see, and after the new year I also have that appointment with the cosmetic firm. I've had some responses but nothing worth chasing.

I love you, David. I miss you. Julie.

Mon. . Dec. 19th London - Darling Julie, This should reach you on the day before Christmas day so I must first of all wish you a happy Christmas. I am so sorry I can't kiss you and tell you myself what I wish for you. But at this distance?? Just remember I love you. In spite of all the trouble and trials you are having at the moment, enjoy your Christmas and, my darling, <u>MAY THE NEW YEAR BE KIND TO US BOTH!</u> I love you very much.

I am so tired, Julie. I feel as though I have been beaten to my knees and kicked. I don't think I have taxed myself like this for years. 12 midnight! I am just going home to sleep, sleep, sleep! Up again at 7AM.

Please understand that I couldn't write. I have understood the heartcry in your letters, honest! Will get back to normal when all this work is done.

I love you. A Merry Christmas! David
P.S. I could have sent a card!!!

Tues. 12PM. Dec. 27th. – USA- Darling, darling, David, The tiniest dearest little note was delivered just before I left for work. It came after Christmas, my love, and took eight days to reach me. I do try, I try very hard to understand why you have been unable to write. But I am still waiting for a reply to news you must have by now. I only hope you understand why I am so distraught.

How very tired you sound in this note. You DO work too hard. The view I'd had of the British police has changed from one of unfailing respect to outrage at the way they use their own loyal, overworked, police force. Using a man until his body is worn out is cruel. Don't you have some sort of police union to fight for better wages and better hours for the detectives in the mix? I'm fast becoming a banner carrying "suffragette" to start such a union. What else I could do, beyond holding you in my arms, escapes me. I'd love to learn more.

Maybe now, with the holidays behind us, and with a little more peace, we will have time to settle down to solving our own problems. There was no mention of the man you were to see on the 17th. Were you able to see him?

I will move to England if that's what you want or you can choose to move here. It might be more comfortable for me here but I'm adaptable. The choice is yours. Once you got your feet wet it would be easier for you here and probably easier for you to find an American company that will send you back to England with an American paycheck.

My door is open for you, darling, whatever you decide. If we do it right you can have a home in both countries. But we have to do something. No one else will do it for us.

Yes, yes, yes, MAY THE NEW YEAR BE KIND TO US! Yes, I know you could have sent a card. I'm glad you remembered . So did I. May we be together soon. I love you. Always." J.

Wed. 3 PM. Dec. 28th. USA Dearest David, very cold outside today. Comfortable inside. Right this minute I think I'm catching your cold. That's what I get for playing in the snow the other day.

I had the sweetest note from you yesterday but it was written on the 19th. Today is the 28th. You have to have the letter I wrote on the 21st by now. There must have been feedback. Please let me know what is happening.

If they come between us now, darling, it will leave a sadness, along with the pain, that will never go away, at least for me. And, one day, when you take stock and remember a sensitive, perhaps foolish, American woman who dared to cross the sea for you, who responded to the cry in your heart, who was content just to be with you, what would it do to you?

I'm suddenly in tears, David. I feel so alone right now. I feel somewhat hurt and I don't know why. I want to be proud and hide these feelings but I have not dealt in pretense with you from the start and I won't try now.

I need a letter, a real letter, soon.

Continued Thurs. 12 PM Dec 29th. Hello my silent darling. Your picture is looking at me from its position on my desk but I'm living in a painful silence. Am I in love with you by myself now? It isn't like you no matter how busy you are. In view of what has happened this is too abrupt a silence and I am reacting to it like a woman in pain.

I sense that you are making, or have made, a decision and I hope, with all my heart, that you are making the right one because, even now, with tears in my eyes and a very bewildered heart, I want only your happiness.

I hope it is tied to mine. You said it was. Your words, and I heard every one, echo in my heart. The words of your letters fill my heart with tears. I've almost worn out the record even though I hear it without the recording. I cling to them but they hurt in this silence and they confuse me now.

You once wrote, "What would I do if suddenly you were not there?" What would I do?

Friday,. Dec 30th Good morning, beloved. I am talking into silence again, looking at the photographs from London right now. I have them with me at the office. But I have decided that I did, indeed, make it all up. The fact of the pictures? Science fiction. And what an imagination I've had!

In a London Fog

Was there ever a summer night and a tender moment stolen like two children on a dark and lonely road? Was there ever such a kiss as that one? Did letters fly back and forth across the sea full of wonder and longing? And when it seemed impossible were there calls and letters and cables to and from England, full of love and impatient desire urging me to continue to imagine and to dream? Was there ever a plane? A flight? A London? Was there ever a David Gregory who said he loved me?

What was real? The Irene Dunne cold flat where I was alone? Feeling displaced and lost in cold rooms until my imagination gave me David again? The tenderness? The handholding? Eyes that spoke when lips failed? Lips that touched and clung? Bodies that sang? The tears? The loneliness? The reverence? The promises? Was any of it ever real?

I can see English coins in my purse and pictures of a man called David Gregory . If it was only a dream how is it that I can still see them and touch them? There is a ring on a chain . How is it possible that such a ring exists in the silence of this unreal moment? What does it mean? Why did I believe it all real?

Is it possible that I didn't dream at all, that it was all real, after all? Will there ever be another real letter from David Gregory in England? Is there an England? Was there ever the David I loved who loved me, who took words from my heart for his lips? I don't know. It hurts not to know.

Elizabeth R. Lawrence

Why did I think it was real? I'm too old for such foolishness. Why, at this time of my life, did I believe in the tomorrow of such a dream? Why did I believe in the promise it held? Why do I have these memories? And why do they haunt me in this silence? I'm sorry, David. These are my thoughts. I love you. I just don't understand.

Saturday. New Year's Eve. 1966. Again no letter. Two weeks. Fourteen days. An eternity, my love. I tell myself that you are too busy, too tired, even injured or worse but it doesn't help because I don't believe what I'm telling myself. I feel as though I'm falling and there's no one to catch me. I am so lost. If you have reconciled your life there please tell me. If that is truly what you want I wouldn't hurt you. I thought you understood that. Why would you want less for me?

You don't owe me anything, David. You can't owe me your love. I wouldn't want it that way. But, David, I came to you with my heart in my hands asking nothing. You asked that I leave my heart with you. And I've waited as you asked. I haven't let you down. Why then is there all this deathly silence?

What a sad way to end the year, my darling. Yes, still my darling. We shared such a tiny part of it, the smallest moment of autumn. If it means nothing more to you beyond that moment I hope the memory is a lovely one. I hope I'm reading all the signals wrong but this is the week that was mine. I'm sorry. But I'm "in Luv," remember? Julie

In a London Fog

Happy New Year, my silent English rozer.

On New Year's day, in Philadelphia, there is a parade called the Mummer's Parade in which various performing string bands, arrayed in wildly colorful costumes, strut and do a Mummer's Waltz down the main street to a sound of music that is uniquely their own. It started many years ago and, though most people have forgotten the reason and simply accept the custom, there are those who remember that it is done in honor of King Mummos, the Greek God of Ridicule.

I wept.

I have written a number of letters, asked a number of important questions, sent my love and my loneliness for you through the holidays and the problems here, and have had only silence in return. I feel very foolish.

I have loved you, David. I still do. If that is meaningless to you now, please tell me. I have never wanted anything but love and happiness for you or from you. Always. Julie.

Sat. Jan. 7th.1967. 8PM USA – A week since I've written to you, my darling, A new year. Three weeks of silence. Oh, David, why, and why like this? Have I truly been standing as alone ands defenseless as I feel? I told you once that I would not fight for your affection and I won't. No one wins that fight. The only fighting I've done was to protect those around me from those malicious attacks. If there is any fighting to be done the man who loves me, who will stand beside me openly, will do it for me and I know it. That man would slay a dragon to protect me.

The thing that hurts, that will hurt forever, is that you are doing the very thing I asked you not to do. In the letter I gave you at the airport when I was leaving London, I asked you to "please not make us into strangers." We're 3000 miles apart. There's little room for chance meetings. I truly don't deserve this. I wouldn't do that to you and you know it. I love you, David, the way you said it "really love."

If you have reconciled I hope it brings you the happiness I wished for us. But right now, all I can feel is this God awful pain. And I'm left with the tormenting question of why and why like this? How will I live without you now, David? I'm sure I'll get through it but it won't be easy and it won't be overnight. I shall miss you always and think of you far too much for my own happiness. We had a special love, at least for a time, one that blotted out the world and lifted two earthbound forty year olds into the clouds. Even in the bleakest rooms, David, there was something special between us. Maybe it shouldn't have happened but it did, and you know it. When your "family" maligns me now, David, if you cannot or will not defend me, please don't let it tarnish your memory of me. I asked for nothing. I gave you everything. My real self. My real heart. My real love.

Tears are streaming down my face now. It's impossible to go on. Please take care of yourself and remember me, if only at 6PM. Think kind thoughts, my darling.   Oh David, the thought of this. and why?? For what we had it shouldn't end like this.. so cruelly abrupt, so deathly silent…Oh, my darling, I can't say goodbye.. I'll love you always. Julie.

Jan. 1st. 1967 London (Written on the outside of the blue airmail envelope.) Julie, You will not enjoy the contents of this envelope so I suggest that you wait until you are on your own and are in a suitable place to read what I can only describe as unpleasant news. Be brave. D.) (Letter enclosed):

Dear Gipsy,

This is the letter you will not like. You remember I said that you were the one who would get hurt and you accepted it? Well, the time is now. You remember that I said I would do something in person if it had to be done? Well, I have tried. But what has transpired over the last two weeks has made it certain that I shall never visit the U. S. again, so I must resort to the means with which I got to know you: a letter. I hope, as you read this, you are on your own for I know that this will upset you.

As I know you have suspected I have reconciled with Addie. My reasons I will give you later in this letter. What I first want to do is to assure you that what has happened is no fault of yours. The Court case had the most influence on what happened. The subsequent events had such an effect on Addie that I knew that, whatever else I may feel, my duty, and to be truthful, my love, belonged with her and to her.

I know enough of your character to know how you will take this and I hope that as you stride along with your proud nose in the air your heart won't ache too long. I'm not worth it anyway. Now for the reasons for this letter.

As you know Addie took this whole affair very well but subsequent events, particularly as we got the repercussions of the Court case, made her very ill, so ill in fact, that the worry of it made me lose a stone in weight in about a week. I knew that someone had to do something in the situation and it had to be me.

Of course, whatever my own feelings on the subject you, as well as I, know where my first duty lies. Maybe, one day, I will be able to give you an explanation of what has happened, and why, although I hesitate to even suppose it will be over there. But who knows? My biggest regret is that I cannot speak to you in person.

Gipsy, this must be the end for I cannot hurt Addie any more. I don't think you would be very proud of me if I did, knowing how things are. I am so sorry that I have hurt you for this particular letter must be terrible for you.

How do you think I feel at this moment?

I know that what we had (and have possibly still got) takes a lot to get over but what must be must be. I only hope that you don't feel too badly about me for I know that, at some time or other, we are going to meet again and I don't want you to look at me like a piece of dirt.

Just remember what we had going and that I kept my promise to be honest with you even though I couldn't tell you as I wanted to.

Gipsy, I won't trot out the usual trite sayings or even try to explain myself for I, too, find this very hard. I won't even say goodbye for that is too final. Suffice it to use an English expression…"Cheerio" from someone who must remain forever "Half a World Away." David

Tues. Jan. 10 1 PM, USA

My dearest David, Be brave, you said. I am sobbing. If you could hear my incoherent words the pain that you would hear would be much more honest than this. The pain is so many things. As heartbroken as I am with the news I was being destroyed by silence. As it is I know of no words to describe how I've been longing for your letter, even knowing what the news would be, and praying it would be different. I know of no words to describe the leaden sadness inside me now.

"What we had (and have probably still got) takes a lot to get over?" We do still have it. If we could look into each other's eyes now how do you think we'd feel? It's this distance, David, this God awful distance.

You say you're sorry you hurt me. No, David. We share that responsibility. We weren't children, We just ran off and, for a little while, we found NeverNever Land. We knew we couldn't stay. We knew it from the beginning. And from the beginning we both knew what that sadness was between us.

Oh, David, why did we meet at all? I don't know how clearly I'm saying any of this but, even as I cry, even knowing and understanding how things are, I don't know how to stop loving you. Maybe time will help. Right now I am devastated.

I don't know why that court hearing (spelling with a small c) had such consequences. I should have realized, by the look in Cora's eyes when the Judge mentioned her recent marriage, that he'd struck a nerve, that she felt exposed somehow. My only curiosity is why it hurt you and my sorrow is that it did. I can't undo what has been done and, though I don't understand why it has torn us apart, I am not sorry I did it. It had to be done and I was the one who had to do it. (We are alike, you know.)

Should we meet again I would never look at you "like a piece of dirt." With 3000 miles between us there's little chance that I will have a cry on your shoulder, but my joy at seeing you will show even if I shed a tear or two. If I cry now without pride it's because of the helplessness of this distance.

Brave? Right now I'm lost. To know what we had and to turn away like this? Your pictures, still on my bed, your ring still on the chain. The end? I find it unthinkable that we'll never see each other again. Don't let anyone tell you it meant nothing to me. It meant everything. Life without you will be lonely, lonelier than it has ever been before . Yes, I had been hurt in the past but not like this and not with my heart on my sleeve.

I will find my feet again someday and I will cherish our memories as the years pass but right now, this minute, I find it impossible to think about any direction in my life. I may not even stay at this

In a London Fog

address but I'd want you to find me so I don't know. Yes, I am proud, but at 3000 miles pride seems unimportant. I suppose as long as I live I'll be looking over my shoulder for you, hear a knock at my door and wonder if it's you or the post man delivering an express letter. The letters. Oh, God, David.. I want you to be happy but what will I do without a word from you?..How will you find me if I move? I love you. Julie.

Tues. Jan. 17, 1967 –London.

Dear Julie, It must be rough for you. I, too, don't feel too grand about the whole business, as you have no doubt gathered. I write in view of your request although I promised Addie that I wouldn't get in touch with you again. I know it is so dangerous to fan the flames as we would be doing if we continue to correspond so, please, don't expect regular mail from me, will you? Once, now and again won't hurt and PLEASE SEND ME YOUR NEW ADDRESS, PLEASE!!!

I know there are so many things that I should say to you at the moment, things that would be sweet and kind, things that apply only to us and between us, but they would hurt both of us and are far better left unsaid. You know what two people like us can find in each other; you know the sort of MUSIC we made. What could I say to justify what has happened since? It is all best forgotten.

I want you to remember me, of course I do, but please don't set me on fire again. I have been

burnt and it will take a long, long time to get over.
      I loved your letter, so like you. \
            Remember me. David.
      Thurs. Feb 2, 19967 –USA
      Dear David, I have written a dozen letters in the past month that I could not complete or send. It seems like years have passed yet it has only been two months since we saw each other, and only two letters ago when we wished each other a Happy New Year. I miss you.
      I've tried to pack my wounded pride, along with my pen, in a grave called "Might have been," but you said "a letter now and then.." If we were closer, no matter how sad these moments apart, we might have smiled into each other's eyes. Even if our eyes met only in a crowd, David, by now there could be a twinkle there. How I wish I could see you smile.
      It is now March! I didn't get very far, did I? Another month of not knowing if you are happy, if you are safe and well, if you're working too hard, another month of missing you. Oh, David, I hear from so many of the people I met there. Penny writes to me. Brenda (even son, Donny) writes to me. People I met in Crawley write. Everyone but you, the man I crossed an ocean for, the man who pulled me across like a magnet. Oh, my darling, always my darling, my proud, reserved Englishman, who is so dear to me, I miss you so..
      There's no point in telling you my heart has stopped aching because, knowing me, you wouldn't believe me and you'd be right. But I'm trying very

hard to be sensible and, strangely enough, what do you think is helping me most? You. Your pictures! When I wake in the morning or go to bed at night there you are, and there is a gentleness that flows from the break in my heart to yours just at the sight of you. You should see old double chin now. I knew from the start he liked me best. He's the one I love most of all.

The airport photo torments me. I can't even look at the pictures from London. But old double chin? He lets me cry on his shoulder. He tells me that you had no options, but I already knew that. I also knew you didn't understand the options we might have had together.

A lot has changed in the past couple of months. Jason has a job in New York and gets home mostly on weekends. Tina has set her wedding date for June. Richard and Emma will soon be going back to England, and I have picked up the thread of an old dream and may return to school. I remember telling you that when you asked what I would do if anything happened between us. Maybe if I search hard enough through all the books I'll figure out how to help the British police earn more and work less. Anyway, it will be therapy of sorts and will keep me busy after work. Who knows? I may end up with a university degree someday.

Oh, David, why do I continue to dream about anything? I'm hanging onto my sanity but my world without you in it is lonely. Perhaps the Coras of the world are right to survive through cunning and trickery. But I can't be what I'm not even now.

I don't know how to play that game. If I did I'd be on your doorstep or on that corner waiting for you right this minute.

I'd better stop. Tears are rolling down my grown up face again. Rough for me? I wear my brave face but there must be a chink in it now. I smile enough and I am polite but, every so often I'm caught with a mist in my eyes. Richard says the sparkle has gone out. Someone at work said . "Whenever you're nice to Julie she starts to cry." One said, "I don't know what your problem is but you suffer beautifully." David, I am so sorry. I shouldn't tell you any of this but I'm stumbling. It has been hard. Too much has happened too fast.

I miss you constantly. Be well. Be happy. Remember me. I love you. Julie

Mon. Feb. 13, 1967. London

Dear "Pen-Pal," Sounds terrible. There are many reasons why I have not sent you a word for some time, too many to waste time explaining. It does appear though that there is an informant somewhere about for Addie seems to know exactly when I hear from you. It is also obvious that I must watch how I send any sort of communication to you.

As for me? I am happy enough. Working hard as usual. I do at least twelve hours a day now at work and, although I get tired, I still enjoy it. But sometimes, Gipsy, I look out of the window and… Ah, no… No good to go on..

Saw Kitty while she was here for a short visit. Nothing was said about us but, I gather, from what Addie had to say to me, that they both had a good chin wag about the whole business. It does appear that Russ and Cora blame me for the Court case and seem to think I supplied the ammunition to fire. Ah me..I have let the matter drop and, as far as I'm concerned, the whole thing is dead. I hope it is the same for you. Needless to say we haven't heard a word from them since the initial complaint...

It is March, 1967. I have made several attempts to write to you but for many reasons have not sent them. There is no doubt that there is an informant working for our "friends" somewhere so watch your mail.

Make sure you see the film, "The Great Train Robbery," when it is released. You will see some familiar scenes.

Julie, I wish.. Julie, what can I say? I can't write now.

I promise to write before long.

David

Wed. April 1967 USA Dear Pen=Pal..?

Terrible? Yes. But it doesn't matter as long as you are safe and well and happy enough. Informants? That's a foreign word to me, David. Still, I must be getting a bit paranoid for, the other day, a man came up to my office to check on some real estate and the conversation swung to talk of London. Because of what you wrote I was immediately on guard. Turned out he was going there on business. I don't want to become suspicious of everyone I meet. I couldn't live that way.

Oh, my dear David, I received your letter on the 19th of March. It is now the end of April. I, too, find it difficult to write now. But not because of informants or prying eyes. It's because you're doing what you feel you must, and I understand, but I feel like Lara in Dr. Zhivago who said Yes and shook her head No.

Ammunition at that hearing? I am as much in the dark now as ever. Blaming you was clever but ridiculous. Their own attorney probably talked to the Judge about his clients prior to the hearing. If I had had any information before I filed suit, and if I knew it was enough to stop them, I would not have had to take them to court in the first place. I wouldn't worry about them, David. It all turned out as they wished. They will probably spend many an evening consoling themselves with anecdotes about the whole thing.

In a way, whether they know it or not, their interference when we met turned desire into love. Right or wrong, had we been free to do what we wanted we'd have found the remedy on our own and maybe, by now, we'd have been satisfied with the memory. Real love changed everything. Now we're a couple of star crossed lovers trying to deal with what has happened without hurting ourselves anymore. Ties bind you. Distance cripples us.

At times I've felt like a timid child reaching out across the sea and pulling back again. I do understand, but there's a deep sadness in me and, with it, a well of churning mixed emotion. I've cried too much; I've longed for you and wanted to hate you at the same time and I know I can never hate you. I might as well hate myself. We mustn't become strangers. This is hard enough. I am writing as honestly as I've written all my letters, not without tears or pride, so that there will be no misunderstanding between us.

Don't be too proud with me. The ocean has been wall enough. As I said long ago, "when you write, write what you feel and say what you think and don't worry about the English or the spelling." I want you to know, my darling, though we must move in another direction that you, or a letter from you, will always be welcome.

The sadness comes with the thought that our hearts will no longer hear and respond to each other even half a world away.

I love you very much, David. Julie

P.S. It is a beautiful and suuny day this minute in my corner of America. Trees are budding and flowers are beginning to bloom. It is too lovely to keep it all to myself and my heart is overflowing with tenderness and love for you.

Be happy, you beautiful man.. Don't forget me. Forever yours. Julie

Elizabeth R. Lawrence

In a London Fog

Part Two

Elizabeth R. Lawrence

Chapter Five.. To Say Goodbye –

The year was 1992. Her original plan was to visit relatives in Italy. She could have taken Al Italia to Rome then gone on to the Bari Airport, but a long buried memory and a sudden urge to see him again played a part in her decision to add England to her trip. A bit of whimsy took her to British Air instead. The plane would land at Heathrow in London first. *As it did in 1966....*

She didn't know where he was; she didn't even know how he was but she knew, at 67, assuming he was well, he would be at least as old as she was now and had probably retired from the British police. She had already retired as a teacher, but she was working as needed, as a substitute. Free time to do as she pleased was long overdue.

Vanity almost stopped her. *If it's in the eye of the beholder let's see what he sees now.* John Boles look-a-like or not he, too, would have aged. Vanity is not exclusive to a woman.

In 1966 her face and figure were intact and she didn't need anything to keep her hair dark. In 1992 she used Clairol to keep it that way. A flesh like prosthesis had replaced her breasts after a 1975 bilateral mastectomy but the curves were the same and it didn't show. Because of her happy nature as well as her innate dignity few knew she'd had such a problem, and she was still considered attractive. The words gorgeous and beautiful were once used to describe her. David had used them all. Today, people who meant well said, "You're very pretty. You must have been a beauty."

With stirring memories from their old letters she began her search for David..

Even before she found him she wanted to be sure she wouldn't be starting WW3 by just showing up. She first contacted those she knew in England. Neither Penny nor her husband, James, who had also worked for the Metropolitan Police, could help. Julie didn't want to contact Emma, who was now divorced from Richard, if only because she'd become a bit of a flake, and drank too much. But David had been in touch with them years ago and she might be helpful. Emma couldn't help but she invited Julie to stay with her and her second husband, Robert, if she did get to England. Richard, who had also remarried and was now living in Spain with his wife, Maralisa, and their teenage son was just as clueless. But he invited Julie to visit them should she make the trip "over the pond."

Then, in a surreal moment, as if David had put the book in her hand himself, she found his name, home address and phone number simply by looking in a donated British phone directory at her local Cherry Hill library.

There was almost a collective gasp from colleagues who kept up with what she was doing when she said she'd found him. It wasn't enough to tell everyone that she was simply curious. They were sure she had been carrying a 25 year torch for him and, as the tension mounted, by the time she dialed him at home, they were right.

Her eyes misted at the sound of his very British voice on the answering machine. It told her to leave a message. She spoke lightly, even joyfully, as she left her message. "It's so nice to hear you again, David," she said. "This is Julie calling from home in America." She gave him her telephone number. "Please call me."

She was trembling when she hung up.

That evening she wrote a short letter in which she told him she was on her way to Italy.

"I'm really only passing through," she wrote, "I hope we can see each other while I'm in England." She enclosed one of the London photos from her album. It was the one showing them together on the bridge near the river Thames. He is wearing the tan suede shearling jacket; she is wearing the London brown coat and the beige furry hat. David had written "On our honeymoon" on the back with the words "In Luv" beneath it.

She also enclosed a color snapshot showing her at work as a teacher in an elementary school classroom. It showed her standing near a wall calendar that was obviously current. Her dark brown eyes twinkled on a smiling unlined face. It was the face of an attractive, friendly, woman with short, somewhat wind blown, dark wavy hair. On the back she wrote the date and signed it Love, Julie.

A week passed before he returned her call. It felt like forever. *Suddenly it was 1966 again.* She burst into tears as she answered the phone.

"I'm so sorry," she said, trying to stop crying, "I didn't mean to cry. I didn't expect to cry." In a voice choked with tears she said, " I just wanted to talk to you."

His voice was gentle. "I understand, Julie," he said. "I would have called right back but we had been on holiday in Spain and had just returned to find your message. I am so pleased to hear from you."

We. That told her something.

Her letter had been waiting for him, too. His letter followed about a week later. In it he enclosed a color photo from a company brochure. It showed an older, still handsome, man who photographed well. He had sun streaked white hair similar to his once deep golden hair. His mustache, somewhat fuller but still tempting, was also white. His dark blue eyes were smiling. The lines in his face were more pronounced but, on a man, they added maturity, not age.

The handwriting in his letter, however, was markedly changed from that of the man who had written love letters to her years ago when he didn't type them.. This was the shaky hand of a sick or an elderly man.

His letter answered her questions. No. He wasn't married. His wife had died three years earlier. His daughter, Janet, now 34, was expecting a baby and living in a flat in London. He had retired from the Metropolitan Police and now worked for an American marketing security firm in London. He wanted to see her but he was currently involved with someone.

"I've changed," he wrote. "I'm not the same person, Julie. ."

She phoned him after reading his letter.

"We all change," she said, "but I think the important things never change."

"Like your voice," he said, quietly. "It's still the same."

Oh, David, she thought, remembering.

"Even 3000 miles away?"

"Yes," he replied. "Even after 26 years. Time has been kind to you, Julie.

"You've aged well, too, David."

"It was just a good picture," he said.

There was eagerness and some self consciousness in their voices as they spoke about the pictures they'd exchanged.

"I *would* like to see you again, Julie," he said. "When you know where you're staying in England send me a note or ring me, and perhaps we can arrange to have lunch or tea. Or maybe I can take you on a walking tour of London. There are things you didn't see the first time."

The first time. She was glad he couldn't see the tears in her eyes.

The last thing she wanted was to interfere with whatever was going on in his life. She didn't want to cause a problem nor did she want to find herself involved in one.

Once was more than enough.

"The woman you're seeing," she said, "Are you planning to get married?"

"That's what she wants," he said, "But I'll never marry again. We have an understanding."

A few nights later she received two calls at about 8PM a couple of nights apart. No one answered either time when she picked up the receiver, but she knew the caller was still on the phone. Thinking it might be David who had changed his mind about speaking, she spoke into the silence. "Hello, David," she said. "I will phone as soon as I know where I'll be staying." The caller hung up without a word.

May 4th (Mon) Still in USA. She left a message on David's answering machine giving him a phone number where he could reach her when she reached England. She had spent the previous night packing. Among her clothes was her box of souvenirs.. She looked through it once more then closed it and returned it to her new carryon bag. Tina phoned from her home in Chicago to say Bon Voyage. Jason left work early to wave her off as the airport limo drove her away.

England 1992

Her large purse and her drag along helped her avoid the stored baggage area as lines formed near immigration. A young hippie looking American female in front of her ignored signs saying to keep an eye on hand held baggage kicking hers away from her from time to time. Julie didn't like being near her. Security eventually took her from the line.

A warning light triggered a closer inspection of Julie as she was going through customs. She had already removed her jewelry, but the warning light continued to flicker as two young security females did a hand search. In the end it was the metal sutures from her mastectomy years ago, that had triggered the alarm. They gave her a card to help her with Security until she was able to get something from her doctor.

May 5th (Greenwich MeanTime) Emma's husband, Robert, was there to "collect" her as she came through customs. A major mistake. I should have gone to a hotel or a B&B, she thought as she changed $40.00 American Express to British money. She wasn't at all sure what she got back but it didn't seem like much. It was just some colorful paper money with a few thick coins.

David had tried so hard to teach me..

"The dollar isn't doing too well against the pound right now." Robert said as he drove.

Julie held her breath. *Riding on the wrong side of the road, even if you're in the passenger seat takes getting used to, David..*

She thought of Emma's house as belonging to Richard because he'd bought the house with money he'd earned in America when they returned to England. Very nice. Spotlessly clean. Robert, a nice looking man with a head full of silver hair and a mustache to match, didn't talk much but he smiled a lot between sounds like "Mmmm," or "I see."

Somehow, between his monosyllabic responses and Emma's inane patter, she learned that they had been introduced to each other by someone who knew them both. Obviously the matchmaker saw a need and filled it. Robert, divorced and estranged from his five children needed a nest. Emma had the nest and she needed tending. Both got what they needed.

Julie was shown around the house, and shown her room, all very nice, all very polite, but she didn't feel welcome. She assumed it was because she and Richard were still in touch. But why display the oil painting she'd done of her years before? And why ask me here?

First impression was that they seem compatible and appeared happy. Both were busy with their work, which they did in second floor bedrooms that had been converted to his and her offices, fax machines, computers and all. She had been a teacher, but was so off the wall when her marriage broke up that the school let her go citing a "mental breakdown." That information had come from her daughter, Denise. Emma had been losing her grip on reality long ago, so it came as no surprise.

She and Richard had had little more than a night school class in handwriting analysis at the high school, but Emma had used it to her advantage since returning to England. Her office papers, letterhead, business cards and a certificate she'd had printed, and which hung on the wall of her bedroom/office, read "Educated in the United States." She had convinced herself and others, including courts and employers, that she was an expert in handwriting analysis.

Julie saw her activity as little more than entertainment at small parties.

In one of his longest sentences Robert said he was a middle man for people and companies searching for items worldwide. He was also chief cook and bottle washer in the house as Julie learned when he made dinner from already prepared frozen foods. While he did all the work Emma exhausted herself with her handwriting work. She came down to eat.

Julie's conclusion, based on the things they did manage to say, was that Emma got what she wanted because Robert stood to get the house someday. She was making it legal.

David called at eight o'clock that evening. Emma took the call and the message about a car problem, but she didn't bother to ask if Julie wanted to speak to him. She just gave her his message. "The car will be fixed by 7PM tomorrow night."

Julie was so annoyed that she went straight to her room to write in her journal before going to bed. The house was chilly but covers on the bed kept her warm. Had it been colder weather she would have been cold all night for there was no central heating even in this well kept, well appointed, house.

She woke at 2AM to use the bathroom. The hall light was on but she couldn't find the bathroom light. She managed. *Some things hadn't changed.*

In a London Fog

6 May..Wed. 6AM. 6AM. She went to a bathroom on the first floor where she had seen a hand held shower. It took getting used to but it worked. She didn't recall a good cup of coffee from 1966 so she'd put a jar of Instant coffee in her carryon to be safe. She was in the back garden with her coffee when Robert and Emma came downstairs.

They said they were up late discussing a new, potentially important client and, at 4 AM Emma was hurt when a picture fell from a wall and landed on her foot. From what she heard later it seems Emma fell into the picture because she'd had too much to drink.

Julie didn't know what to do with herself. She wanted to leave but the message she'd left on David's answering machine before she'd left home told him where she'd be, and the message Emma had taken told her he got the message. Had she known she was within walking distance or a short taxi ride of a train station she would have left at once and called David again. Maybe I can get him to drive me to a hotel.

She almost laughed at the memory.

After noon Robert invited her to go with them into a Crawley shopping area nearby while they went to a solicitor's office to get him on the deed to the house.

Julie went to the post office. She sent cards to family and friends. "In England. Having a wonderful time." No point in worrying anyone with the truth.

Charging it to her credit card she phoned Penny. They'd been in touch with each other for the past 25 years. She had married and now had two sons. There was no way she could be in England without visiting her.

"I'll ring you tomorrow,," Penny said. "and we can plan some time together."

She hadn't been invited to join Robert and Emma to watch TV in the lounge so she left them alone with their drinks and went to bed.

May 7th Thurs. Jason's 48th birthday. She'd sent him a card from the Philadelphia Airport so it would arrive on his birthday, and she'd send another from Sussex with her first roll of film after she'd seen Penny. He could share the trip as he developed them.

With Robert doing the housekeeping and Emma playing Twiddle Dee and Tweedle Dum with handwriting all day, Julie helped Robert clean up after the next frozen food meal. She'd contributed some of the paper pounds to his shopping trips to Tosca's supermarket earlier. She had no idea how much she gave him, but it seemed to be enough to buy a few things including a couple of bottles of wine. It surprised her that he was able to buy wine in a supermarket.

David called around 9PM. Again Emma took the call and again would not have put her on the phone until David asked to speak to her.

He seemed uncomfortable.

"You sound tired," Julie said.

"I am," he answered. "I go to London every day before 7AM to work a full time job, and I don't get home until quite late."

He didn't say what he did at work.

"I finish work early on Friday," he said. "I will pick you up for dinner so we can talk quietly, if that is all right with you."

He sounded so formal.

"That will be fine," Julie replied. She hesitated, swallowing the lump in her throat. "Do you feel strange talking to me after so long, David?" she asked.

"Yes." he replied. "Don't you?"

"A little," she said, but in truth, she didn't feel strange at all. *She longed to see him.*

"Friday seems a long way off," she said.

"It's only one more day, Julie," he said, gently. "After 26 years that's not so long now, is it?"

She wanted to cry. She wanted to cry out loud. She felt as if she was still holding her breath.

"I need directions to the house," he said.

"Robert will have to give you the directions," she said "I look forward to seeing you on Friday, David."

Robert took the phone.

"The longing in your voice," Emma said, after the call, "must be devastating for him."

The important client arrived. They spoke mysteriously about a Hitler diary. Emma seemed to be assuring him she would be able to ensure its authenticity with her handwriting analysis.

Emma wasn't around when Penny called.

"Whatever longing she heard," she told Penny, "was mixed with a longing to get out of this house. This is the home of the world is flat society."

They laughed, making plans to meet.

That night Julie was invited to watch a show on television that Emma, who was already drinking, was sure they didn't get in America. It was the "Eastenders." She could have told them it was shown at midnight when it was on at home. She had seen a few episodes but she was reminded of the neighborhood of her Irene Dunne flat and she didn't need reminding,

Afterwards they watched home videos of Emma at a spa doing handwriting analysis for guests there which got them a free weekend at the spa. That seemed exactly where she belonged. She worked it like a fortune teller.

Before the evening ended Emma was a loud, foul mouthed drunk, and she made it clear with nasty comments that she didn't particularly like her.

"I didn't think you'd look so good." The tone spoke for her. "Maybe it helps women who chase married men."

Ah, Julie thought. She had certainly done an about turn from the Emma of years ago, but then Richard had married again and Emma never got over it. She's at least ten years younger than I am, but she sprays gold in her dark hair that cheapens her appearance. It may add highlights in photos but up close it's a disaster, and her face is wizened.

She kept her thoughts to herself as Robert

tried to talk around her, changing the subject to David, suggesting places David might take her locally when he picked her up the next day. Emma interjected the thought that they go along. Robert diplomatically talked her out of it. Julie had the feeling he'd had a lot of practice.

Emma left the room only to return moments later completely naked. Julie sat, stunned, smiling and polite, as Emma proceeded to prance around the lounge.

"And I have my own breasts," she said.

Robert made no apologies. He just calmly found a robe and put it on her. Julie made as graceful an exit as possible and went up to bed. She wrote in her journal. *Maybe you had to be there to believe it, but honestly, I couldn't make this up. I couldn't believe my own eyes.*

Years ago, in one of the British newspapers, she had read a quote by a Lady Antonio who said, "You Americans think the English are so civilized because of our British accents and polite manners. But when you get to know us you will find we are really vile creatures."

You are so right, Lady A. Some are.

Their First Meeting

8 May Fri. Julie spent most of the day either in her room or sketching in the garden that Richard had so cherished when he was there.

David phoned around six but spoke only to Emma who again didn't give Julie the phone. The message was that there had been a bomb scare at Victoria Station and he was late getting out of London. He would arrive about eight.

Emma stage managed his arrival. Julie held her tongue wishing she could push her under the wheels of his car that Robert said was a Saab as he pulled up.

The David Julie remembered and the one she'd seen in the photo was, if nothing else, a good looking man. From a distance he looked much the same as he came up the walk toward the house.

Telling Julie to wait in the lounge Emma opened the door to greet him, and to introduce him to Robert. When they finally came in the lounge she came in with him.

Julie could have killed her.

David, very much a proper, dignified, good looking British gentleman, held out his hand and smiled. "It's so nice to see you again after so long," he said, formally.

Julie moved his hand aside to hug him. She was so shocked at his physical appearance she couldn't say anything. In that instant she saw a David she'd never seen.

I can't breathe when I see you, David. Now she wanted to cry and breathe for him.

Instead she smiled handing Robert her camera to take a picture of the two of them before they left the house.

David was thinner, much too thin, and he seemed less vigorous than the David she had loved 25 years ago. He was wearing a nice business suit that fit him well, but his body mass seemed to have shrunk. He actually looked frail. She'd expected an older man, but she hadn't thought beyond that.

"It's a beautiful house," he said, when they were in his car. "Have you known your friends long?"

"You knew them, too, David. That was the house Richard bought when he and Emma returned to England. The house is nice but I'd settle for my Irene Dunne flat to get away." She explained her problem with Emma.

"That's because you're beautiful," he said, "and she's jealous. *Thank you, David.*

He had a vague memory of Richard, none of Emma and "Who is Irene Dunne?"

"Don't you remember?" she asked

"I have memory problems now," he said

"Oh, my dear David," she said, "How could you forget?"

"I never forgot you," he answered.

She caught him glancing at her from time to time as he drove. In his profile she saw the David she had known. His quick glances brought him back. Hello brought him back.

"Hello, Julie," he said, quietly.

"How have you been, David?" The tremor in her voice betrayed her feeling. She spoke with a composure she did not feel but as if she cared and he knew it.

"I'm doing all right," he said, somewhat nervously. "I still work too many hours and," he paused. "I seldom drive anymore."

"Why?"

"I've had four strokes and have been left with a bad left arm."

"Oh, David." *Oh, my darling.*

He had a number of other medical problems, high blood pressure and cardiac problems among them. And he was still smoking. It was, she knew, a nervous habit he could not change so she said nothing. *Once she'd bought him a cigarette case.*

Without seeming embarrassed, though he may have hidden it well, he stopped to urinate in darkened areas on the roadside behind the car from time to time.

"I'm sorry, Julie," he said, when he returned to the car. "My medication causes the problem."

"I understand," she said, remembering her father. "At least men can go in the bushes."

He had to stop for directions more than once. He seemed as lost in his own country as she was. By the time they reached the restaurant she hoped he had someone in his life who cared enough for him to drive him around.

We could have grown old together.

In the restaurant, one with a "Carvery," they waited and watched quietly as meat was cut and put on plates. Afterwards a waitress led them to a table, handled the rest of the meal and took the wine order from David before he went to the men's room.

They were quiet when they finally looked at each other across the table.

"Your picture didn't do you justice," he said, at last. "They never did."

"It's the lighting in here," Julie said. . "You look very nice, as nice as your picture."

He smiled. "If you hadn't sent that honeymoon photo I probably wouldn't be here. But I thought the lines in my face hadn't changed that much." *Ah, sweet vanity.*

"I'm glad you came," she said.

They were silent as their wine was poured.

The silence lingered as they looked at each other. She swallowed the lump in her throat.

Lord Bryon wrote: *"When we were parted in heartache and tears, all broken hearted to sever for years, Faint grew sweet dreams and cold. Colder a kiss, Truly that hour foretold sorrow to this. In silence we met. In silence I grieve that thy heart could so break, Thy spirit deceive. If I should meet thee, After long years, How should I greet thee? With silence and tears."*

David spoke first. "I always wanted to see you again, Julie, but why did you want to come?"

"I don't know," she said, quietly, letting the words come of themselves. "Maybe because I wanted to know how you were and maybe because we never said goodbye."

It was a poignant moment for both of them. She hadn't expected it. He thought he had steeled himself against it. The lump in her throat spilled into tears and, even in the darkened room, she saw tears in his eyes. They were quiet, letting the silence speak first as they dealt with the food and drink before them. Music from somewhere and the buzz of voices around them filled the silence.

"I let you down, Julie," he said, gently.

She wanted to tell him she understood long ago and recriminations weren't necessary, but he had wrestled with words that he had come prepared to say, words that he wanted to say, so she listened as this new David spoke with David's old voice.

"We had a special magic between us," he said. "I knew it and you knew it. No matter what else I say I want you to know it was a mistake to have let you go."

Yes, it was, my darling..

"But it is better forgotten now," he continued. "I caused all the problems that resulted when I tried to do the right thing, but I was too weak to deal with it.

Not weak, my love. Not ready.

She wanted to interrupt.

"No," he said. "Let me finish. I'm a changed person. The years since we parted have changed me to a harder, colder person. I'm a workaholic, working 7AM to 8 or 9PM, and I'm set in my ways now. I don't plan to marry at this point in my life. I meet a disparate group of friends in gaming clubs once a week, and I have a young woman in my life."

He hesitated then added, "She was jealous that I was meeting you after so many years."

She wanted to say something but again he wouldn't let her interrupt.

"No, please let me speak."

He was certainly not "Hmming" and "umming" like Robert. He spoke in sentences.

"I left the police force as a Detective. Constable fourteen years ago, and was offered nine jobs at nine different firms that I had done work for as a police officer. One, before retiring, involved security for works of Art. As a result I met many company executives. Eventually I was offered a job that entailed traveling all over the world. Europe, America, Australia, and I found out I liked it.

Once you came out of mothballs I knew you would. I now work for an American firm in London as their chief executive handling crisis situations here. There's a little less travel involved. I thought of you when I took that job. You were way ahead of me then, Julie."

I just knew the way of America, my love.

Now, his speech finished, he wanted to hear her talk. "But don't talk about the past."

"That might be hard," she said, "but I'll start with your girlfriend. What's her name?"

He hesitated. "I – Her name is Hilda."

"How old is she?"

Another hesitation. "She's a lot younger than I am. She's 45."

At least 17 years younger. As young as Tina.
"Do you have her picture with you?"
"Are you sure you want to see it?"
"It would satisfy my curiosity."

He took a photograph from his wallet and handed it to her. *What happened to my pictures?*

A pretty, blue eyed, blonde haired young woman smiled at her. Julie's reaction was spontaneous and sincere. "She's very pretty," she said. "She has no reason to be jealous."

He smiled, pleased with her reaction as she returned the picture. He seemed to have recovered from the drive and whatever tension he'd had since they met. He looked at her.

"I want you to talk now," he said.

Like David, she, too, had come prepared. "But I have to start with the past," she said, slowly, "and you said..."

"I'll listen," he answered, gently.

"And if I can't talk," she said, "will you understand if I cry?"

He didn't answer.

"I brought something for you," she said.

"But I,- I didn't bring you anything."

"It's not like that," she said, taking the souvenir box from her purse.

She saw his surprise when she opened the ring box that contained his ring. "You still have that?" he asked. The surprise was mixed with pleasure as he took it from the box. "I want you to keep it, Julie," he said, gently.

In a London Fog

"No, darling," she said, the word escaping of itself, "It was never really mine to keep. It was from your finger. It should be yours again."

He smiled as he put it on his finger. It almost fell off. "Well, now," he said, "I may need that chain now."

"You can get it resized," she said.

He examined the coins she had put in a plastic bag, seeming to check and appreciate their value. "You should keep these."

"I never learned to spend them, David."

She gave him his old book on the British police and the black and white studio photos he'd had taken for her.

"The pictures were done for you, Julie," he said, but he was looking at them, examining them, as if searching for the strong young man he had once been. He obviously wanted them.

"I made photocopies for myself," she said, as he replaced them in their envelope before putting it in his breast pocket, "You don't think I'd give back old hard face, do you, without keeping him for myself, too?"

She gave him the 9x12 watercolor she'd done from that photo. On the back she had written "The Real David." In the right hand corner she had signed it Love always, Julie Martine.

"I told you he loved me best."

She had packed it in a cardboard roll to keep it safe. "I couldn't pack the frame," she said. "Take care of him." *He needs tender loving care now.*

"I'll see to that, Julie. "He seemed to like the painting even more than the photo. "I have just the place to put it, too."

She had an empty pack of Embassy cigarettes, and in it was the stub of a cinema ticket.

He looked puzzled.

"You were smoking these then," she said.

"We never went to a cinema, did we?"

"No," she said, "That's where I ended up the day I was running away from you."

She gave him a small lamb of peace, an inexpensive jewelry piece for his lapel, and was so glad she'd brought it because he understood what she meant. He put it on as a tie tac.

When the souvenir box was empty she said, quietly, "I kept the record."

That's when she cried. "I'm sorry," she said. "I didn't mean to cry. I told myself I wouldn't cry. I don't know why I'm crying "

"Yes, you do," he said. "I wanted to come to you, Julie. You have no idea how close I came, and then it was too late."

"It wasn't too late. It was never too late. The door was always open." Her voice was choked with tears now.

He remembered the song and with it the words. *Half A World Away*. "The song is still ours, Julie. It will always belong to us."

"What hurt me most," she said, struggling to hold back tears that were suddenly mixed with pain, "was that you weren't there for me when I needed your support. You let them destroy even our friendship. I never asked you to leave Addie. You knew I'd understand."

Suddenly she heard herself and saw the dismay on his face and she stopped. "I'm sorry, David," she said. "I didn't mean to say any of that but I couldn't stop myself. And now my face is a mess and I've upset you."

"I'll be fine," he said. "You have a right to cry, Julie. And your face is not a mess."

When the waitress came to take their plates David excused himself to go to the men's room while Julie composed herself. Neither had finished their food but when David was back he said he had eaten too much. He beckoned the waitress for coffee.

Now he wanted to know about her life.

"I went back to school," she said.

"You said that's what you would do if..."

"My mother thought I should go to Florida and find a rich husband."

"She was probably right," David said.

"Maybe, but college seemed safer and it kept me busy. After my parents died I began taking jobs around a full time college schedule. My daughter had already married and my son had gone to work in Greenland for a while. I didn't like being alone so, in a way, college was company."

When she paused he said, "In all those years did you..? Was there..? Didn't you meet anyone?"

"I didn't forget you overnight, David. Believe me, I tried. But everything and everyone felt temporary. And if I met anyone British I ran the other way. I even left a job as associate editor of a dog show magazine when a British editor was hired. I didn't want to be around anyone with a British accent, male or female."

"College," he said. "Was that a university?"

In her purse she had pictures she'd hoped to share with him showing the schools she'd attended. She even had a picture of the oil painting she had done of the elementary school where she had been working. He moved closer to her to share the overhead light. He looked at them while she spoke.

"For the first two years I went to the community college where I became involved in the drama department and helped write and direct stage shows. Art work was part of it. I found some of myself there."

"Yes," he said, softly, remembering her spontaneity, "that would suit you."

"My earlier work had involved real estate so I took a broker's class through Rutgers University. After two more years at another university I had a bachelor's degree and I went on to teach. I've been teaching since then. The money is good, the work is rewarding. In spare time I read, write and paint."

"What are you writing?"

"Aside from ditties and some lovelorn poetry, I've done a couple of things, human interest mostly. About a year ago I unearthed our old letters and..."

"You should have burned them."

"I almost did," she said. "but it would have meant burning you with them. That reminded me of Guy Fawkes so I couldn't do it. I put them in a cardboard box and locked the box away. Then one day, after I retired, maybe because I had too much time on my hands or maybe it was time to deal with it, as in 'physician heal thyself,' I took the box out of storage and began reading. It was painful reading and I shed a bucket of tears but, by the time I finished, I knew I could write our story. I even started writing it. I call you Seth in the story. But David had come to life; I wanted to know how he was, and I wanted to see him again. Then Italy beckoned and, you know the rest."

He liked the idea that she was writing the story but he didn't want to be called Seth.

"Too Biblical," he said.

"What name would you like?"

"My own name," he answered. "David."

"With another surname David is fine."

It could never be another name.

"Do you?" he hesitated. "Do you have someone in your life now?"

"No. No one special," she answered.

After he'd made another trip to the men's room Julie asked if he was ready to leave.

"Not yet," he answered. "We spent so little time together, Julie. I was always rushing away from you. We can linger a little longer."

Talking became easier. At times, if she again mentioned the past as she spoke, he stopped her.

"It's too painful," he said.

Yet once in a while, as he relaxed, when he recalled their time together he laughed softly. "We had nothing at all, did we, Julie? But we were happy for a little while, weren't we?"

Another time he said, "You never asked me for anything. I always remembered that."

When she was quiet he encouraged her to talk. "I always loved your voice, Julie."

She didn't know what he thought of what she said, but he listened quietly. He said that he listened to every word. She was sure he did, too.

When he spoke of his cardiac problems she told him she'd had a bilateral mastectomy. She said it as a way to comfort him but he looked at her without saying anything.

"Do you know what that means, David?"

He nodded as if to say yes, but she wasn't sure he really understood.

At one point, interrupting something she was saying as he looked at her, he said, "You're more mature but you haven't changed. You still have the same vibrancy and the same warmth as my Gipsy. And you're still beautiful."

Gipsy. She wanted to cry.

"Italian genes," she said.

"In spite of my memory problems," he said, "I would have known you if we passed on the street." *I would have wondered if I knew you.* "And if we had never met I would still look at you twice." *It only took once for both of us the first time.*

"When you went out of the country in your traveling, "Julie asked, changing the subject to something safer, "did you take Addie with you?"

"No," he answered. "She wanted to stay home. I bought her a dog. A Yorkshire. He's waiting for me at home now. The last time I saw her alive I gave her yellow roses." He never wanted to see yellow roses again.

Julie wasn't sure what he was saying. "Would you like me to do a painting of her?"

"No. I did what I had to do and I saw that she was cared for, but I don't want to look at her picture for the rest of my life."

He was quiet for a moment. She almost heard tears in his voice when he spoke again. "I did love you, you know."

"And I loved you," she said, softly.

"When you called and I heard your voice on my answering machine and when we spoke on the phone the first time I felt the same as I did years ago. I was shaking when we hung up. That's what upset Hilda," he said.

"And you told her about us?"

"I probably said more than I should."

"That's why she's jealous," Julie said.

She had the sickening feeling that it was Hilda who had made those two mysterious calls.

By the time they were ready to leave they were speaking as friends. The fire was gone but the caring spark of love was still there.

He asked about her plans.

"I may add Spain to the trip," she said, with Richard in mind, "but I'm scheduled to visit relatives in Italy first so I don't know how that will work out. All I know at the moment is, because I landed here first, I will return to England before flying home."

On the drive to Emma's, he lost his way time and again, and he stopped to urinate in darkened areas again. He was worried about being out late.

"Hilda looks in on me," he said, "and the Yorky is waiting for me."

Sitting next to him and knowing how painful it was for him to drive she wished she could drive for him. *But it was Hilda who could drive on the wrong side of the road.*

Though their meeting ended well, it was clear he had been under an emotional strain, and the driving didn't help. He looked exhausted when they reached Emma's house.

"I hope you'll send me a card from your travel," he said, as he pulled to a stop. "Phone me when you get back and we'll go to lunch in London."

Less reserved by the end of the evening he gave her a light kiss on the cheek when they parted at the door. *Oh, my darling.*

"If you don't get back to England I'll write or call to stay in touch after you return to America." He looked so tired as he drove away she prayed he'd at least make it home safely.

She hated having to return to Emma's house but, in conscience, she had no choice. His health and driving problems aside, how would he explain taking her to a hotel in London when he got back to Hilda?

Robert invited her to the lounge after he opened the door. He and Emma were watching a Eurovision song contest on TV. Emma, wine bottle in hand, was calling out to the performers on the "telly," as if they could hear her.

"You won't get this in America," she said, when she saw Julie. "This is strictly a European show."

It was a song contest called "Best Songs of Europe," so Emma may have been right. Ireland won with *"Why Me?"* Another song, that was called *"One Step Out of Time,"* seemed to delight Emma.

"That fits your romance with David," she said, gleefully.

Sadly, she was right about that, too.

9 May Sat. Fortunately, Emma was "ill disposed" when Penny phoned about ten the next morning so there was no phone interference. Julie had been up since eight.

"How did it go with David?" she asked.

"We managed to talk, Penny. And we will talk again but, Penny, he's a very sick man. It was hard to see him like that."

""I'm sure it was," Penny replied, sympathetically. "If you're up to it I'll pick you up for early dinner at my house tomorrow and we can talk. And you can finally meet my family."

"Yes, that would be very nice." Julie said, weighing the idea of asking Penny for help to get away from this house when she came for her but, after 25 years, it would be an unfair imposition. It would be over soon anyway.

"I thought you'd want to join us, with Denise and her husband, for a drive and lunch near the coast," Emma said, with some annoyance later when Julie told her of her plans for the next day.

Denise, however, told Julie that her son wasn't feeling well and she had shelved that idea anyway. "But I'll get Mum to drop you off here today so we can visit while they run errands."

Denise had been a cute, blonde, nine year old when Julie saw her at the pool with her parents and little brother, Rich, Jr. Denise now looked so much like her mother that it was startling. What troubled Julie was that she seemed to have a drinking problem as well. She was friendly enough but it was early afternoon and she was already obviously tipsy.

She didn't know why that surprised her. "The Eastenders," show revolved around the Pub, and Pubs were a neighborhood staple for both men and women in England. She had been surprised to see liquor bottles, complete with glasses, out in the open, in homes wherever she visited even years ago. It seemed that nothing had changed. If anything, it seemed more prevalent. *I'm stewed, high, drunk, David wrote in some of his letters.* She had never seen him that way.

10 May Sun Penny arrived around noon. Robert spoke to her at the door but did not invite her in. Emma was conspicuously missing, in her bedroom/office.

Julie apologized for their behavior.

"No apology necessary," Penny said cheerfully. "It's not your fault."

Penny, now fifty-five years old, was still the lovely woman she had been at thirty. There was more maturity but she was still the same tall, thin and gangly woman with corn blonde hair, and a friendly, welcoming smile. The letters between them had formed a bond and the years melted away as they greeted each other.

When they were in her car Penny said bike races and road closings had held her up.

"I cannot get used to riding on the wrong side of the road," Julie said as Penny drove in and out of country roads and beautiful country lanes. She stopped at her fairly new, flower rimmed, hillside terrace house in Biggin Hill in Kent.

"Biggin Hill was once a famous airfield in WWII," Penny said. "Row houses of all descriptions are called terrace houses," she said, in answer to Julie's question. .

David and Addie had had a terrace house.

Penny's husband, James, was a tall, good looking man, who had been an Inspector at the Wallingford Police Station. Their two grown sons, also tall, were Mark and Kevin. They were friendly, nice looking adult teens. ..They knew of Julie as their Mum's invisible friend who sent letters from America.

"Like most children," Penny said, as she put plates on the table, "it was hard for them to think their mother had a life before they were born."

One of the best meals she'd had in England in 1966 had been the roast beef and Yorkshire pudding Penny made. Now, years later, early dinner (which probably meant tea) at Penny's was a slice of white bread with a slice of American cheese, a cold boiled potato, a beet and a lettuce leaf. And, of course, tea. Healthy enough and enough to eat but no wonder she was so thin.

A large bull mastiff was confined to the kitchen as they looked through photo albums and shared their family life. Once the boys had gone off to play football (soccer?) they talked about her meeting with David.

They were sympathetic about his medical problems. James, retiring from the police force, was interested in the work David had done after he'd retired and curious about what he was doing now. Penny understood why, with all his problems, David probably needed Hilda in his life.

"I do, too," Julie said.

"Still not easy, is it?" said Penny.

"No, it isn't, Penny."

With James driving they toured a bit of Kent before taking Julie back to Emma's house in Sussex.

David had driven her around Kent one day.

When they hit a speed bump Penny said the English who denigrated the British police referred to it as "a sleeping policeman."

"Considering how hard they work," Julie said. "they deserve more respect than that."

From David's book on the British police she'd learned that the entire Metropolitan police force, in every station, is part of Scotland Yard no matter what their position in the force. James reinforced what she'd read.

They walked her to the door when they reached Emma's house. Julie would have invited them in but, at 9PM, Robert was in his nightclothes when he opened the door. He said Emma was already in bed. It was the first time they'd gone to bed that early since her arrival.

Julie was embarrassed. James and Penny were gracious saying they wanted to get right home anyway. Julie had let Emma and Richard have parties at her townhouse without interference when they were in America.. If Emma wanted to make a point she'd made it. Once I leave this house, Julie thought, Emma will be history, ancient history.

11 May Mon. It would have been less expensive to fly to Spain first, but with Emma's appearance when Julie dialed the phone the following morning, the very mention of Spain would mean Richard and would put Emma in a frenzy. By the time Julie was finished with the travel agency she was scheduled to leave at 5AM for Heathrow to board Alitalia to Rome the next day. She would transfer to the Bari Airport.

Spain would have to wait.

She spoke Italian when she phoned Italy to arrange for a cousin to meet her in Bari. The young relative who took the call understood her dialectal Italian. Emma and Robert didn't understand a word. Just as well when she referred to Emma as an *umbriago* and said Robert was nice jerk in Italian.

Tomorrow couldn't come soon enough.

That evening, with her bag packed, she wrote out cards to Jason and Tina. She would mail them from Heathrow tomorrow. She also wrote one to David saying how nice it had been to see him again.

"I'll be in Italy when you receive this card," she wrote, "but I'll stay in touch so you can share my trip. I'm not sure where I'll be staying on my return but I'd like to be closer to London. I'll call after I make the arrangements. Best wishes. Love, Julie." She ended with a P.S. "Hello to Hilda."

12 May Tues Emma was still in bed, for which Julie was truly grateful, when Robert met her in the lounge at four in the morning. Always quiet, even quieter at that hour, Robert was silent.

Julie, alert to being on the wrong side of the road, was wide awake.

The Crawley she had seen under construction in 1966 was a lovely area now, with stores arranged for easy access and foot traffic.

She hadn't seen Brenda or Donny but. through Denise, she'd learned that Brenda had become headmistress and Donny had married a girl from Yugoslavia. After Donny's visit to America when he was twelve years old, she couldn't imagine him married to anybody. His hyper activity could only be borne by his mother. Poor girl, she thought as they reached Heathrow.

After an awkward thank you she waved goodbye to Robert when they reached Immigration.

She was glad he was already gone when she reached Security. Not only did she trigger an alarm for her necklace, which she removed, but she had to produce the earlier card from Security regarding the metal sutures in her body. Her suitcase caused another problem. It was taken from the counter and given to a uniformed customs agent nearby. She was asked to step out of line.

"What's wrong?" she asked.

"Your bag is neatly packed," he said, "though not in the usual pattern, so we have to check it." Continuing conversationally he went on. "What was the nature of your trip to England?"

What do you tell a customs agent about an old lover? She couldn't think of anything else.

"I came to see someone I loved," she said, truthfully. Her smile was suddenly mixed with tears as she said it. "but he's sick and...".

When he pulled out a brightly lit flashlight that she'd packed in the bag without turning it off she was too embarrassed to explain, but it stopped her tears. She realized she'd probably put it there in a hurry after feeling her way around the dark bathroom earlier. She smiled hoping she didn't look as idiotic as she felt.

"Will you be seeing your friend again?" he asked, kindly, as he returned her suitcase.

"I hope so," she answered.

Their Second Meeting

2 June 1992 London, England. She converted Italian lire to English pounds in Heathrow, and used almost all of that to arrange for a gypsy taxi from the airport. She later learned that 27 pounds was much too much for the taxi, and she shouldn't have been asked to pay for a reference. "Black taxis are more legitimate," she was told.

After three weeks in Italy, where she'd used Traveler's Aid to locate *pensiones* when she wandered without her relatives, the idea of bed and breakfast hotels appealed to her especially if she was being a tourist. Traveler's Aid in Heathrow gave her a list of hotels that included a number of B&B hotels in London.

The list included hotels she knew from home, the Marriott, the Hilton, and even an old name in London from years ago, The Dorchester. They had the luxury she'd want but since she expected to be out more than she was home she was reluctant to spend the money just for a place to sleep. She almost changed her mind when the taxi stopped at the Stanley Hotel on Belgrade Road in London, but it was close to Victoria Station and the cost was only 34 pounds a night, with breakfast.

The B&B hotels on the street were once stately old homes owned by a wealthy class of people. It was there that the television show, "*Upstairs, Downstairs*" had been filmed. Now, less elegant and in need of repair, many of those old homes were owned and run as B&Bs by men and women from India, some who adapted English names for their less pronounceable names.

The Stanley Hotel was strangely familiar. Had she been here before? Was this, or a place like this, where David had taken her just before she'd moved to Penny's flat? They'd made love there. They'd cried together there. It had been a roof over her head. *I never knew where I was when I was with you, David. I just knew you were there.*

Her second floor room shared a bath in the hall. There was no phone in the room. Had she known it when she was at Heathrow she would have bought a cell phone. Now it meant having to use the public pay phone in the downstairs hall for outgoing calls and receiving calls at the reception desk. The public pay phone took getting used to but it seemed much easier to use now.

Still, though it was clean and adequate, and it came with memories, the *pensiones* she'd found in Italy would put them to shame.

After dropping her suitcase Julie's first call on the downstairs pay phone was to her cousins in Italy. There was an audible sound of relief in their voices. They wanted to know if she was eating. She said yes but, like Dorothy in the Wizard of Oz, she knew she wasn't in Kansas anymore. Italy and wonderful Italian family midday meals were far, far away. From the sublime to God knows what.

She called home to speak to Jason. No answer. She left a message telling him where she was. She'd call back.

She called David at home to tell him she was in London and as usual she had to leave a message. Telling the machine that she was staying in London she left the reception desk phone number. She might not be on his doorstep but when he was in his office they were at least in the same city, and he wouldn't have to drive if he wanted to see her.

She had no intention of calling Emma but she knew Emma might be looking for her if she didn't make a contact so she called Denise.

"I tried to call your mother," she said, in a bold faced lie, "but her phone was busy so you can give her the message. Just tell her I wanted to thank her for her hospitality. I'm calling from a pay phone so I won't be calling back." *And she'd better not hold her breath waiting for an answer if she writes.*

She phoned Penny to say she was back. They'd catch up with each other later.

Finally she went up to her room. She was up for hours writing notes in her journal and nibbling on crackers left from the plane. The television in the room provided background noise. She wasn't sure what was on. English accents instead of Italian. At last, with thoughts of those she'd left behind in Italy, she fell asleep.

3 June 92-Wednesday- In the basement breakfast room she had a choice of orange juice, cereal, bacon and eggs, toast and coffee or tea. In Italy she'd had a choice of flaky croissants and delicious cappuccino as well. She ordered what she

recognized as Indian women cooked and served the food. One, called Ruby, who had taken her name from the scullery maid in the television show, was one of the servers. Orange juice made from a powdered substance was not very good. The coffee was barely palatable. She would try to remember not to order either of them again.

Two Americans from Las Vegas were at her table. There was also a man from Beirut who was eating everything available. He said he wrote a book and was trying to get a publisher in London. A British couple was in for 2 days to see the play, "*Miss Saigon*." Julie made a mental note to try to see the play as well. Family groups and various singles or couples were at other small tables around the room.

One of the Indian serving women pointed upstairs and put her hand to her ear to tell Julie she was wanted on the phone at the reception area. The receiver was handed to her by Sam, the young Indian man at the small counter.

David was returning her call. "I am so glad to hear from you," he said. "I received your cards from Italy. I was delighted that you were having such a good time."

"I had a wonderful time," she said. "And it gave me a chance to use my Italian."

David seemed to think she was in private quarters somewhere.

"I wish I were," she said, "but I'm in the lobby speaking on the phone at the reception desk and there are people all around me."

"Then we'll talk over lunch," he said. "I'll call around 10AM." He paused. "No," he said, "I think lunch would be better later.",

"Any special time?"

"I'll have to ring you again," he said. "I'll leave a message if you're not in."

She had tears in her eyes when she returned the phone to Sam.

"Sad news?" he asked.

"No. Just feeling sentimental."

She phoned Bianca, a travel agent she'd met in Italy, who was arranging her flight to Spain. Bianca told her to hold on. In a few minutes she had Julie booked on Dan Air on the 5th.

"Go to their representative's desk in the South Terminal at Gatwick Airport. Ticket will be waiting. Bon voyage, Juliana. Ciao."

Whatever the B&B lacked in appearance was at least compensated for by its proximity to Victoria Station, three blocks away. Julie walked there to change American Express checks into British pounds. She then stopped at the Post Office to mail a box of miscellaneous items to Jason. There was some undeveloped film, some things from Italy, and clothes she wouldn't need any longer. She had enough wash and wear in the carryon for Spain.

She had tried to post it from Italy, but was uncertain when the woman there said, for security reasons, they'd have to open her undeveloped film, and she would probably lose all the pictures. Julie managed Italian but the language dialectal difference made things unclear so she'd decided to send it from England.

David called just as she got back.

"Take a black taxi to Cort's Restaurant and Wine Bar on Chancery Road at 12:15," he said. "I'll meet you there and pay for the cab."

The driver of the black taxi greeted her with a smile when she got in his cab. "I saw you walking near Victoria Station earlier," he said, adding, almost apologetically, "and I wondered about your age. I thought you were nicely dressed and couldn't help thinking, Now there's a woman who cares about herself, no matter what her age."

"What a nice thing to say," Julie said. She was wearing black slacks, a black and white striped blouse and a bright red jacket.

A very slender more dignified David in a pale grey business suit was waiting on the sidewalk in front of the restaurant. In the sunlight she saw a handsome elderly man who seemed more relaxed than he had been at their first meeting. He paid the driver and actually leaned forward to kiss her cheek as she stepped out of the cab. It was almost a proprietary kiss, as he had kissed her long ago.

Hello, my darling, it said.

"It's good to see you again," he said, taking her arm, "but you have no right to look this lovely after so long."

Italy had done wonders for her morale. Three well to do Italian men had approached the family trying to meet her. If a 67 year old woman, who'd had her 68th birthday on a train in Italy, could appeal to a Count, a rich pasta manufacturer, or a wealthy landowner because she looked luscious to them she knew she looked good to David today.

She liked the way he was looking at her. She felt good, too. Her dark hair was wavy and shining in the sunlight, her dark eyes were sparkling, her bright smile was friendly and her figure, with the help of the prosthesis, was as shapely as ever. The warm sunshine was bringing her vitality out of the night shadows of their first meeting, and the cabbie's words had helped.

"It was as if I'd been kicked in the solar plexus when I saw you. get out of that cab," he said, his voice dulcet and tender. *Oh, David..*

"That's a good sign," Julie said, smiling at him. "It means you still remember."

David was clearly seeing her as he once did, almost for the first time, at their second meeting. He sat back and looked at her as lunch was put on the table. He poured wine in their glasses. "I never forgot the way we were, Julie."

"Neither did I, my darling." she said, making no effort to hide the endearing word. "And I didn't forget your birthday."

She'd sent him a birthday card with the statue of David pictured on it while she was in Florence. "In the event that I don't see you on June 6th," she'd written. Now she gave him a small but identical statue of David that she'd bought there.

"I was surprised that you remembered the date," he said, fingering the little statue as he looked at it. "I remember that your birthday is in May because I thought it made you only a month older than me, but I never remembered the day."

"Funny how we remember things", she said. "June 6th was the anniversary of D Day in Europe. It was also the date that Robert Kennedy was shot and killed. Somehow your birthday became an important part of that."

"Because of what happened to us?"

"Possibly. But I didn't want to hurt you. I just wanted to put my arms around you and wish you a happy birthday, that's all. I missed hearing from you. I was always easy to please, you know."

"I was pleased to get your cards from Italy," he said. "I looked forward to getting them. It was like.." He stopped. "I missed hearing from you, too, Julie. But I was glad to think you were having such a nice time."

They were quiet, seemingly engrossed in their food and wine for a few minutes.

"Now that you're not playing cops and robbers," Julie asked at last, "what does your work entail?"

"It's a paper chase now," he said. "I manage an office for a Direct Marketing Company with headquarters in Dallas, Texas."

She knew the company.

"I might be in Dallas for a convention in October," he said. "I change planes in New Jersey at Newark Airport. I've been through there a couple of times already."

She was stung at the thought that he'd been so close and hadn't tried to see her, that he'd practically been on her doorstep and had walked by.

"Do you know how close you were?"

"I knew," he said. "I thought of you, but I was afraid you'd slam the door in my face or slam the phone in my ear."

"You're not as brave as I am, Gunga Din," she said with a sigh. "I called you after 26 years. And I flew across an ocean to be with you. Twice. Wasn't it worth taking the chance?"

When he didn't answer she said, "I thought of flying back to England after your letter. I thought of surprising you by just showing up at the station to wait for you.

"Why didn't you?"

"Hardface persuaded me that you didn't have any options. If I thought it would have made a difference I would have done it."

"You didn't think I loved you enough?"

"If I had done that to you what would you think? Besides, I didn't want to be that homeless and alone in an affair like that again. I probably should have run away from you the first day. A better option for me was to rent my own flat without telling you I was there. Once I was settled, maybe even with a job, I would have found a way to run into you. Then, with my nose in the air, I might have walked right past you. Or maybe I *would* have slammed the door. We'll never know now, will we?"

"I might fly up to see you while I'm there in

In a London Fog

October unless," he stopped. "Are you seeing some one special?"

"If you mean special like someone I love, the answer is no, I'm not. Anyone that special would be with me right now."

"I'm here right now," he said, quietly.

"Yes," she said. "But I don't know what to do about you anymore."

They were quiet for a moment.

"What are your plans now?" he asked.

"I'm leaving for Spain on the 5th."

That seemed to upset him. "What are you doing, jet setting all over the world?"

He was jealous! Tell me to stay, David.

"I'm visiting Richard and his family."

She had to refresh his memory and remind him again that he'd met Richard in the States.

"What kind of work does he do?"

"He's an engineer for an oil rigging company, presently in Norway."

"I'm glad you're enjoying yourself," he said, at last. "I want you to be happy, but I think you're coping."

"Coping? Probably. But if I'm coping it has nothing to do with you. You're an invention," she said. "A character in a book that I created from a make believe memory."

"I'm real, Julie. We were real. There was nothing make believe about us."

So why are you letting me walk away?

He wanted to know if she had a word processor to help with her writing. When she said yes, that she even had a program in her computer to help, he said, smiling, looking every bit an aging John Boles. "Then you can change Seth to David in the book easily enough, right?"

"Of course."

"Will you send me a copy?"

"I'll deliver it myself," she said, "I'll dedicate it to 'The Real David.'"

That triggered a memory.

"I sent you that card with roses." He paused. "Did you know Cora died?"

"I'd have no way of knowing," she answered. "Our paths haven't crossed for years. When?"

"Only a few days ago," he replied. "She had a massive heart attack."

"She was dead a long time ago to me, David, so I can't say I'm sorry. But, considering the timing, it has gone full circle now, hasn't it? She must be spinning in her grave that we're sitting together at this moment."

He didn't say anything.

"Did you know she left her husband and daughter in England and that she followed Russ to America when he was transferred, even though he had a wife and four children waiting for him there?"

"No," he answered. "I didn't know a thing until after the court hearing. They thought I knew but, quite frankly, I was very surprised."

"At the time I met them," Julie said, "I was working to save my new house from foreclosure. Around that time I had a prom party there when Jason was graduating from high school. Neighbors with graduates attending the prom were invited to the party. Cora and Russ invited themselves.

A neighbor, one who had done some of the flowers for the party, also attended. She later told me that, in the guise of an interest in her flower arrangements, Russ had gone to see her and he didn't have flowers in mind. And these were the people pointing fingers at me?"

"I made a mistake by not coming to you, Julie." He spoke regretfully. "If only you knew how close I came."

"I did know," she answered. "That's why it was so painful. Had we been allowed to come to our senses on our own, without interference, we might have died on the vine in the natural course of events between us. And we would have remained friends. Beyond an immediate physical attraction at that time, one that was just getting started, we had little else between us from the start."

He flushed at that. "Three weeks. We had so little time alone," he said.

"That's true enough, my darling," she said. "But love had become part of it. In time we would have found our own way one way or another."

"Yes," he said. "I'm sure of it."

For a fraction of a second she knew, by the look in David's dark blue eyes, that if she said just the right thing he would have followed her back to her B&B that very day.

"I have longed for you, David. Yes, even now. And yes, I am coping, but, right now, as things are, I wouldn't know what to do with you. You'd have to slay a dragon for me now."

He smiled. "What kind of dragon?"

"You said I never asked for anything. Now I'd want everything. That includes a tomorrow. Yesterday is gone and you have a young Hilda in your life for tomorrow. Some scars don't show, David. Some do. The ones that don't show are the most painful."

"I would kiss those scars, my darling," he said, softly. "You're still my Gipsy."

"But it would still leave me alone. I don't ever want that again."

They were quiet. Considering the state of his health she was glad he had a Hilda. Each in their own way they were both coping with the hand their lives had dealt them.

"Hilda wanted to come with me today."

"You should have brought her."

"She couldn't have handled our conversation," he said.

"No, I suppose not," she said, suddenly remembering those two strange phone calls she'd had just after she'd spoken to him.

"Does she live with you, David?"

"Not really," he said. "She's learning to work in the office, and she helps me with grocery and driving and other things."

And other things. In a discussion group at one of her classes she'd heard forty plus single women advised not to ignore older men who were now widowers. "They're not ready right away, but don't wait too long. They're usually snapped up in the first three years. Remember they're not used to taking care of themselves and they're feeling old. That's where you come in."

One Step Out of Time. Emma was right.

"I'm glad you have someone to help you," she said. *I couldn't even light the water tanks..*

They had covered a lot of ground in their second meeting. David was relaxed, seeming to enjoy the comfort level they had reached. When she gave him a copy of the picture they'd taken at Emma's house he smiled and looked at it almost as though he was examining it. *Was he seeing a nice looking older woman with Julie's voice and a younger man in the elderly man's face?* He looked at her before he put it in his breast pocket.

"I'll never understand why you gave me your love, Julie. I wasn't good enough for you."

"You weren't ready for me, David. That's not the same thing. You were good enough. You were just too good for your own good, and you didn't know your own worth."

"Yet you loved me."

"Not always." Julie smiled. "But your sex appeal was a mitigating factor. I can breathe better now, but my heart still knows when you're around. Besides I knew things would change as you got older."

"Do you think I've changed?"

"In some ways," she said. "But underneath that dignified exterior I think you're still the man I knew and loved. *And still do.* You've always been a workaholic so that's not news, but that tells me that you're either running scared and showing authority or hiding from life."

"I never thought of it that way."

"How do you see yourself now?"

"I like women," he said, "but I consider myself a male chauvinist now."

Julie grimaced. "I saw the signs."

"I think I'm weak when I'm kind."

"I suppose that's true at times," Julie said, "but real kindness shows strength."

"I consider myself streetwise from all those years as a British police officer."

"You probably are," she said.

They talked about Spain again.

"You will like it there," he said. "Where will you be going in Spain?"

"El Escorial. It's an hour out of Madrid."

"I go to the islands."

"Where, exactly?" she asked.

"Tenerife. We were there a few months ago. I have a place there." He seemed somewhat embarrassed as he said it.

She thought about that. Was he embarrassed because they'd done so little when they were together? Or was he ashamed that he might be perceived as overstepping his class?

"I'm pleased you have more in your life now," she said, earnestly. "You earned it. You should have had it long ago."

He smiled. "We like it.

A young girl, who probably looks great in a bikini, has to be just what the doctor ordered.

. "I'd like to meet Hilda," she said. "I just don't think I could handle it right now."

"Nor could I," David said.

Lonely is lonely and at the moment his undivided attention was nice. Considering that she had traveled 3000 miles, twice, she told herself she deserved it anyway.

"I think Hilda has already called me a couple of times," Julie said. She explained the two calls. "Before it goes any further maybe you should check your telephone bills, at home or at work."

"I'll take care of that, Julie." He sighed, seeming to age in the next instant.

By the time he'd described her, somewhat apologetically, Julie saw Hilda as a young woman who would keep the home fires burning and give him clean white shirts just as Addie had done. And she liked to embroider doilies. If not always as compliant she would satisfy his needs in much the same way. He'd be a kind and good man and she would benefit from the fruits of his lifelong labor because he needed her and she was near.

"I understand," she said, talking through the lump in her throat. "Right now she's an important part of your life."

"I'm somewhat happy with my life now," he said, "but Hilda wants to get married. I will not succumb. I will not remarry. Ever."

Wanna bet? Julie thought.

"I have a home in Surrey now," he said, "I think Janet will move back with her baby."

But Hilda will want the house. That's the carrot on the stick, my darling.

They'd dealt with things well on their second meeting. The wine, her time away in Italy and the cards she'd sent from there, as well as the ease he felt with her now had made it easier for him to open up and talk about everything.

"I'll send you cards from Spain," Julie said. "I'll add a smile for Hilda."

"I'll write when you go back to the States. I write, probably better than I talk."

"I can't argue with that," Julie said. "They got me to cross an ocean for you."

He smiled at her reaction. "You must have thought I was potty."

Potty. A world of separation in that word.

"Never," she said. "I loved you, David. I loved your heart and soul as much as I longed for you physically. That's why it was so hard to say goodbye. I still can't say it."

"I never wanted to lose you, Julie.

"Maybe that's why I came back," she said."

Lunch was over. It was now 2:30. Somehow they'd finished a bottle of wine between them. Fortunately, Julie had eaten a full meal. He asked, considerately, if she needed to use the ladies room. She did. He went to the men's room. He beckoned a taxi to take her back to her hotel.

"I'll call before you leave for Spain," he said. "Call me when you get back." He put his arms around her and held her for one long minute as if he didn't want to let go before he kissed her cheek.

"Don't let anything happen to you, Julie," he said, quietly.

She turned her face to kiss him on his mustached lips before she turned away. At his surprise she said, "Take care of yourself, too, David. I don't want to lose you either."

He may have felt ten feet tall after that lunch. Julie hoped he did, but the thin, nice looking elderly man that walked away was soon lost among the pedestrians on the crowded walkway.

She wanted to cry, for David being ill, for his needing Hilda, for herself for looking so healthy and being so lonely, and for not taking him back to the hotel with her.

It had been a pleasant lunch, more than she'd expected, less than she'd wanted but, faced with the reality that she would be on her own that evening and the next day, she was lonelier than ever. The thought of how her time had been filled in Italy didn't help either.

She sat outside on the stone ledge near the steps of the B&B when she was back. Three young men, in their 20's, sat near her. They were on a world tour since finishing their college education. All very nice. One from Sweden, two from South Africa. Marketing majors. They were having car problems. They had twice had their tires blocked by the police so they could not drive anywhere. They were caught in a Catch 22 re: parking on the street, not knowing the rules, and when they paid the first fine (38 pounds) they were booted again and had to pay a second fine. At this point they were stuck with a rental car they had not been able to move all day. They wanted to get to Wimbleton. She wished she could go with them.

In the lounge of the B&B the man from Beirut stopped to say he was not confident of success in selling his manuscript, and he was running out of money. In her room she turned on TV. British game shows. News. Crime and local gossip mingled with yellow journalism. She was appalled at the gossipy trash that was, as in 1966, still headlined as news in newspapers . Tabloid papers at home, many owned by well known Britains now, were onsupermarket shelves. Most of it was about superstars in both countries, and about people and events in England. Right now it was about Princess Di and a book she had written "To Tell the Truth." There were some things on European happenings, and brief mention of American politics. Television shows were no better. Except for some curiosity about the programs themselves she saw little of interest.

She was called to the reception desk phone around 8PM. David.

"I just wanted to tell you I had a very nice time at lunch with you today, Julie."

"So did I, David."

He had the dates mixed up.

"I thought you were leaving for Spain tomorrow," he said. "I don't like to think of you being alone. *I never wanted to be alone either...*"

He paused. "I wish we could spend the day together but I have work on my desk and I can't get away. Have you made any plans?"

"I'd go to Wimbleton with some traveling college students but their car has been booted."

He was sympathetic. "...but I don't want you to sit in your room all day.. Take one of the bus tours. You'll enjoy it and you'll get to see the sights. We didn't see them all, you know. Some will refresh your memory."

It's not my memory that needs refreshing.

"I've already picked up the brochures in the lobby," she told him. "I may take the London Plus tour bus."

"Yes, that's very nice. You get on and off anywhere you wish all day." There was some hesitation. "I'll phone you again tomorrow," he said finally. "Maybe we can have a cup of tea when you return."

"Bring Hilda with you," she said.

"I'll think about it," he said.

"If you're going to be with her, we have to become friends or she'll never allow a friendship between us," she said.

"She'll have no say in the matter," he said, firmly. "Our friendship goes too far back."

Oh, David....

She found a seat in the lounge after the call. She was lonely but at least she wasn't alone. There was a couple from Mexico. She was a translator. Her husband, like Julie's cousin, Michele, in Italy was an orthopedic surgeon. They had given a talk at a seminar in Paris. The Beirut man joined the group. He spoke about losing most of his hearing because of the bombing and shelling of Beirut.

She paid her bill in full before going to bed. It amounted to 22 pounds.

Would that be 66 dollars, David?

4 June 1992 Thursday. She was up and ready for breakfast by 8:30AM. She took photos in the breakfast room and met more people there. Some were eager to talk, others, touring as couples or groups, were planning their day.

She walked to Victoria Station after 10 AM. It was a grey, rainy day. She used her red umbrella for the first time. She could have used one in Florence, where it rained for three days when she viewed the real statue of David, but she had left it in her cousin's villa when she was in *Corato*, the green, fig tree, mountainous area that was once home to her parents.

She bought a ticket to Gatwick Airport to have it ready for the following morning and stopped at British Air to check on her departure date for the USA. Her ticket was good for six months but her money, whether pounds, lire, pesos or dollars, wouldn't last that long.

David was being nice but he was also a sick man who was keeping her at arm's length because he was involved with someone, a younger someone now. The world had opened up to him as well. She was happy for his sake and she understood but understanding didn't help her loneliness. If anything it intensified it.

"Because she understood he came and found her; His soul was darkened and she gave him light; Because she understood and gave so fully; The darkness turned to light just overnight; And with the sunshine greener pastures beckoned; He turned away and gaily waved his hand. And for his leaving he felt no compunction; Because he knew that she would understand.

An understanding heart can hurt forever.

By the time she'd accomplished what she'd set out to do she suddenly didn't feel well. She paused at the top of the escalators to take a picture when she was at Victoria Station again, but as she aimed her camera she nearly lost her balance. She made it to the lavatory in the Station just in time.

At breakfast she'd forgotten about the foul water when she drank some of the orange mix that doubled as juice. Her normally sunny mood was affected by the discomfort. The grey rainy day didn't help. Sick or not she didn't relish the thought of being alone in her room either.

She bought a ticket for a London Plus Bus Tour just to stay outside, but she didn't feel up to getting on and off at the various stops. All seats on the upper level had been taken by hardy souls or young people ignoring the chill and the rain. She didn't enjoy being alone on the lower level of the red double deck bus, but she was outside and could at least view some of the world.

A Christian woman tour guide gave Julie a card with her ministry address. "You seem very sad," she said. "Call if you want to talk."

For the rest of the tour the woman guide kept an eye on her as she addressed the tourists on both levels as the bus moved along.

Julie would have told the woman it was her stomach, not her heart that was in trouble. But when she saw the street sign marked Chancery Lane her eyes filled with tears.

Alone is alone wherever you are, darling.

When she returned to the hotel she called Jason at work from the lobby pay phone.

"All is fine," he said. "Don't worry. It's great that you're having fun." He'd received her card from Rome yesterday. "Came by oxcart, I guess."

David called around 8PM. "I hope you have a nice time in Spain. If you think you can handle it," he said, "try to see the bullfights. Nice atmosphere. Do have a good time and send me a card from Spain. I'm sure you'll enjoy it. We'll have tea when you come back."

"I'll take pictures," she said.

"I'd like to take you to see my house when we see each other again, but that might not be a good idea. I'll bring pictures of the house and maybe some of my daughter, even of my Yorky if you'd like to see them."

"I'd love to see them," Julie answered. "You should bring Hilda with you as well."

"She's very jealous of you, Julie."

"I don't know what you're telling her, but I'm old enough to be her mother."

"You really don't look your age, Julie. Not at all, and with your spirit and your vivaciousness no one would believe it."

"It's still those Italian genes, David."

"Or the fountain of youth," he said.

Tell that to my stomach today, she thought. She wasn't sure she should eat anything with her stomach still queasy, but she was hungry, not for crackers and fruit, but for real food. The only decent meals she'd had in England, with the exception of Penny's long ago meal of roast beef and Yorkshire pudding, were those she'd shared with David. Oh, for real home cooked food.

With her red umbrella overhead she walked to a wine and bar restaurant she'd seen around the corner of the hotel. She ordered roast pork, vegetables and a glass of wine. It looked great on the plate, but the vegetables were soggy and tasteless and the pork was fatty and greasy. The wine was the best part of the meal.

She paid the grand sum of 11.50 pounds which, by her calculations, made it $23.00. David was probably paying more at the Chancery Road restaurants. Decent as it was, she hoped he was on an expense account because he would be paying for the location, and getting rooked with the meal.

No wonder Catherine DeMedici brought her chefs with her when she traveled, claiming later that the English had never learned to cook and the French covered their mistakes with sauces.

She stopped to buy a bottle of water on her way back to her B&B hotel. In Italy they'd had bottled water in decorated glass bottles in the refrigerator or on the table with each meal.

"We don't drink from the aqueduct," Michele had told her.

5 June 1992 Friday – She was up early. She had a light breakfast of toast and egg whites, without .juice or coffee, not even her own. She had no way to heat the water and didn't trust anyone to do it for her.

Finally, she took her purse and her carryon suitcase to Gatwick Terminal at Victoria Station for a Dan-Air flight to visit Richard and his family in Spain.

In a London Fog

Their Third Meeting

After three weeks in Spain it was as if she'd come home when the plane reached England for the third time. She knew where she was; she knew where she was going, and she was glad to be back.

She took the Gatwick Express for a ride back to Victoria Station. She picked up a USA Today and an Evening Standard at the terminal shaking off Maralisa's oppressive presence with a sigh of relief as she made her way.

England may not speak the Universal English of America, she thought, and many words were spelled differently, but it was understandable old English and she welcomed the sound of it around her. It was a liberating sound because she no longer had to concern herself with everything she said around Richard's wife, Maralisa, whether in her pidgeon Spanish or her American flavored English.

She again booked herself into the Stanley B&B Hotel, this time for 22 pounds a night.

Would that be $44.00, David?

It wasn't her first choice. She was ready for the luxury of the Hilton now. Once committed, however, she made the best of it. Room 38 was on a lower level and, as before, it had a "telly" without a bath or shower and no telephone. She had to go up the stairs to reach the telephone in the hall. The shared hall bath was right outside her room.

The rooms on that floor may have once been the servant's quarters when the house had servants below stairs. The walls were paper thin. She heard the couple in the next room having intercourse. At least she heard the movement and the man huffing and puffing. From the sound she guessed him to be a fairly fat fellow. Poor woman. In the lobby later she saw a number of rotund men with and without women, but she didn't bother to guess which one had been in the room adjoining hers. She didn't really want to know.

She called Jason from the hall pay phone to tell him where she was and had to leave her message on the answering machine.

"You can update Tina," she said.

When she phoned Penny to say she was back she said, "I'm almost a native now. As soon as I feel up to it I will take the train to Biggin Hill by myself." *I would have learned it all, David.*

After she called David, and left a message on his answering machine, she had touched base with those who at least cared something about her welfare and she didn't feel like a stray. Before going back to her room she went to the store.

She bought cold bottled water, and only those food items that were packaged or had skins on them, nothing she would have to wash first before eating. As in her Irene Dunne flat she ended up with a couple of oranges, some biscuits (crackers or cookies) a piece of cheese and a few bananas. They would keep her digestive system intact until she figured out how to eat a decent meal in England.

Maralisa's meals with Spanish or French flavors had been very good with wine on the table as in Italy. Julie had even prepared one meal herself, a

Julia Child's French-Italian meal of 40 cloves of garlic chicken cooked in white wine. The garlic, still tasty, but soft, was spread on crusty Italian bread that went with the meal. In local restaurants they'd had tapas or French bread stuffed with fried and breaded *calamari*. It was a gastronomic adventure, and was anything but English cooking.

In the hotel lobby she picked up some of the tourist brochures. Her hands were full as she carried papers and bags down to her room. She would go through them later.

If her B&B offered nothing else it was at least well located. She could walk to Victoria Station enjoying the people and buildings around her. Buses, subway and trains were a stone's throw away to get anywhere.

If Michele and Nina were well she would have gone back to Italy, to a *pensione* in *Corato*, to try her wings there, but she didn't want to be underfoot while they sought medical treatment.

She had done what she came to do. Unless David gave her a reason she wouldn't need the extra two months in England.

It was time to go home.

At Victoria Station she went to the Midland's Bank to get $200.00 from Visa. (100 pounds, not saving any money at this rate). She then went to British Air to change her departure date from Sept. 14th to Monday, July 6th. The cost to make the change in her flight was 67 pounds ($125.00).

At Tourist Info she booked Tours Plus for the next two days. This time she would get on and off the red, double deck buses at various spots during any phase of the tour. Willy-nilly she'd already managed a preview.

It was worth doing right, especially because her shoes had given out. She also wanted to book an evening cruise, and maybe check into seeing a play, maybe *Miss Saigon*. She didn't like the idea of being out alone at night but the theater district was within walking distance. I'll check into that tomorrow, she thought.

She bought an Air Bus ticket at five pounds ($10.00) to get to Heathrow Airport on Monday. The idea of being up early enough to get to the bus bothered her. The trains ran there also but she thought this would be more scenic and offered more views to take home with her.

Finally, before leaving Victoria Station, she shopped for British souvenirs. She looked at them and fingered them with sadness. They didn't look like toys. She didn't feel like a tourist. She was leaving part of herself behind for a second time.

Miniature red double deck buses, black taxis, the British red telephone booth, miniature London bobbies, and a couple of snowballs showing the Tower of London and the River Thames. London emblems for key rings and nail clippers. Maps of the underground and Victoria Station to frame.

Everything held a memory.

She got the picture she wanted from the top of the escalators looking down into the station. She wanted the photo but she also wanted to paint the scene when she was home.

In a London Fog

She noticed a woman in a security uniform watching her. With all that's going on in the world I can't blame her, she thought. A car bomb had gone off in Madrid while she was in Spain. On the plane back to London she'd sat with an Australian woman called Pat whose purse had been robbed at a Madrid department store two hours earlier. ",,,but they didn't get my ticket or passport." A prominent politician had been assassinated in Rome while she was in Italy. David had been unable to call her at Emma's because of a bomb scare at Victoria Station on his way home to Surrey.

We may all be looking for love, even for our lost love, she thought as she went on her way, but we'd better look over our shoulders as well. It's nice to know that someone is watching our backs even when they turn an eye on you.

Back at the hotel she called her son from the pay phone to bring him up to date.

"You might get back before some of your cards," he said. "They're arriving late but I've been keeping up with you by getting pictures developed as I get the film." He'd had most of them developed at a cost of $72.00! "All pictures were good but the pictures from Italy showing the family apartments and their villas were wonderful. One was like a palace. Grandpop would have loved it," he said."

$72.00. It would have been twice that much in pounds. The lire had been almost double the dollar, too, so she'd sent the other rolls home with some clothes. She'd had one roll developed while she was in Italy hoping she could have photos with her when she saw David again. It would give him a glimpse of her Italian roots. He'd said he'd bring photos, too, when they saw each other again. She looked forward to seeing them.

After she checked for messages she went to her room to wash her hair in the corner sink. The water was cold but she managed. With the help of Clairol she also managed to freshen the color of her hair. Sorry about that, Maralisa, she thought, remembering what dark haired bleached blonde Maralisa said. I will let the silver out when there's enough of it. Meantime I'm glad to keep my own dark color, thank you.

Hair washed, brushed out, bouncy and somewhat clean, all of which took more than two hours, she went up to the lounge. People were going out to eat. Julie still had fruit and biscuits in her room and she'd had fish and chips at Victoria, but she wanted something else, something tasty. But it was raining now and she didn't want to wander in it without a destination.

Sam, the very nice Indian man at the reception desk read her mind. He brought her a cup of tea and later, when he was eating pizza, he gave her a slice. It was hot and it hit the spot at once. Last night, before she'd gone to her room, he'd given her a slice of cake to welcome her back. Now she asked why he was being so kind.

"You are a nice lady," he said. "And you too much alone. I don't like to eat and not share." She made a mental note to remember to bring something back for him the next time she was out. She wanted to get out; she wanted to go out for the evening just once while she was in London, but it was dark and it was raining. Even at home she wouldn't wander alone at night.

"*You're still an alien, David said.*"

Richard had greeted her with a gift of *Obsession* perfume when she got to Spain because she had searched for and found David after so long. He was sure David had put the phone book in her hand. "He wanted you to find him," he said.

At dinner that evening they spoke of his frail health and she told them about Hilda.

Stefan, the French teen cousin visiting the family in Spain was touched by the story. "If I was older," he said. "I would marry you."

"*Merci, Stefan,*" she said. "*J'taime.*"

Alone or not you take yourself with you wherever you go so, yes, my darling David, I held myself together but I am still coping. I didn't want to grow old alone just as you don't, but it's easier for a man especially if he has enough to offer a younger woman who wants it all.

You had nothing but, oh, how I loved you.

Back in her room she went through the papers, watched the news on the BBC, saw a television talk show ala Johnny Carson on another channel, and watched a few other shows. With the first note of *God Save the Queen* on the telly the groaning in the next room began.

Noise from the street woke her at 7AM. After a quick dash to the pull chain bathroom in the hall, she used the sink in the room to wash up. She had a breakfast of bacon, eggs and toast in the morning room of the hotel, remembering not to drink the juice or the coffee. The day ahead was hers. On her list of things to be done was to find a shoe store. .She was still in the breakfast room when David phoned.

"I just got your message," he said. "We had been away, in Maidenhead, for two days."

Maidenhead. Sounds nice, she thought, with a stab of longing.

I'll be busy today but if it's convenient for you tomorrow," he said, "we can meet at Cort's Wine Bar on Chancery Lane again. Then we might walk around and I'll show you the sights. If you'd like we'll go to the Dicken's House."

"I'll be on the Tours Plus bus today," she said, sounding cheerful. "So that will be fine. And Dickens House sounds good for tomorrow if it's not too much walking."

"Too much walking?"

"I've worn out a pair of shows."

"Get off the bus on Oxford Street," he said. "It's changed a bit but you might remember the street."

Oxford Street?

Tours Plus, filled top and bottom, pulled away from their stop by 10AM. A very nice tour guide was on with them. They were given brochures listing all the buildings they were to see and learn about. Should they want to get off the bus they could tour the site then get on again as the bus came around. As far as Julie was concerned it was the best buy in London, and a good guide was worth every penny or pound he was paid.

As they passed the "Seaforth or Seaview House, Julie wasn't sure which name he'd used, he said, "This is where records of births, deaths and weddings are kept." Then, with a chuckle, he added, "This is where we hatch them, match them and dispatch them." He answered questions from those brave enough to ask.

"The water? Don't drink it. Just remember, when you see a tony waiter pouring water from an elegant crystal pitcher, it has gone through us first. Ask for bottled water in restaurants."

As they passed a gigantic display of an American group called the Chippendales, Julie volunteered her own story. She told of the American housewives who got their out of shape and overweight husbands to appear in a calendar, calling themselves the Chubbettes.

Everyone laughed. Her bubbly manner had dealt with Maralisa's heavy handedness at the dinner table that way. Stefan, the fourteen year old French cousin visiting Madrid, would have loved that story.

"He will love you forever," his mother said.

The tour had started off well enough. Julie got on and off the bus again and again when they reached places she wanted to visit, but rain was in the offing. The first drop appeared as she got off the bus on Oxford Street to look for a shoe store.

It wasn't until she passed a shop where coats were displayed in a window that she thought of what David said. *"You might remember it."*
Oxford Street?
Was this where they'd bought her London brown coat? She didn't remember. Strange that he did. But she had been looking at him. ..*I never knew where I was when I was with you, David.*

Translating size ten to the equivalent in British sizing was no better than it had been in Madrid. Sales clerks did not understand when she asked for help. And it didn't help to try shoes on either. So much for waiting to reach an English speaking world to buy the shoes. It might have been easier in Italy. Finally, needing shoes badly now, she bought a pair that seemed good enough. Not a good fit, but not falling apart either.

She paid 15 pounds for the shoes. That was $30.00 American. A similar pair of shoes at home would have cost no more than seven dollars.

It was pouring rain when she returned to the bus stop. Umbrellas were everywhere. Unfortunately, she had left her new red "brolly" at the hotel. She saw a Fish and Chips shop across the street from the bus stop. She made it across the street and back without stumbling into puddles in her new shoes.

Drenched and chilled, carrying a bag stuffed with fish and chips, as well as a bag of potato chips and crackers, she didn't wait for the Tours Plus bus. Instead she got on the first bus going in the direction of her hotel. The windows of the bus were fogged from passenger breathing and that, coupled with the rain on the windows, made it difficult to see outside. Once she was seated she turned to the woman beside her and asked if she would tell her when they reached her Belgrade stop.

"Of course," the woman said, cheerfully, adding, "Oh, you're an American, aren't you?" Without waiting for an answer, and aware of the food Julie was carrying, she said, "I'll bet you don't like our food, do you?" Julie just smiled. "Oh, that's all right, dearie," the woman said. "I have American friends who came here, and they didn't like it either."

Julie had had an interesting day. She had seen Westminster Abbey up close for the second time. *It wasn't the same alone.* She had seen St. Paul's Cathedral, Buckingham Palace, Fleet Street, the Towers of London and more. *None were the same as she remembered.* She–had shopped on Oxford Street by herself, not sure if she had ever been there before. She stopped at the reception desk to give Sam the bag of potato chips before going down to her room.

By 7PM she was sitting on her bed with a chair pulled up close to use as a table, eating her still warm fish and chips and watching the telly. Call them what they will, she thought, chips are still French fries but I don't know why.

While she ate she wrote on London cards to send relatives in Italy. "*Sperare tutti bene.*" (Hope all is well). "*Piange per non vista.*" (Miss you.)" It actually translated to "I'm crying because I can't see you," but the meaning was clear.. More sincere words were never written. She was flooded with thoughts of them and the way things were when she was with them, their warmth, their generosity, their sincerity, and those wonderful midday family meals.

She wondered about Michele and Nina, both around her age. Was Nina still undergoing treatment in Milan? Had Michele's problem been diagnosed? She wanted to phone, but the idea of trying to communicate in Italian on the public hall phone gave her pause. She would call when she was home.

She wrote on postcards showing London to the teens, Juan and Stefan, in Spain, with regards to Maralisa. She also wrote one to Richard, who had gone back to Norway as she was leaving Madrid.

They'd parted in the airport, and out of earshot of Maralisa he had given her a message for his two grown children in England.

There was no sound from the adjoining room as she wrote the cards. Female American voices speaking English in the hall attracted her attention. She opened her door. They were two young girls on a college break. They didn't know which door opened to the bathroom. She pointed it out to them and asked where they were from.

"You probably never heard of it," said one, with some snobbery in her voice.

"I must admit I'm somewhat bedraggled but try me." Julie said, smiling.

"Cherry Hill, New Jersey," they said as they dashed into the bathroom.

Bingo. My home town.

She spent the next few hours putting herself together again and getting ready for the next day.

2 July 1992 Thursday- He would have told her to take a taxi but, using the Tours Plus bus to get there, she met David at 1PM in front of Cort's Wine Bar. In spite of what seemed a fresh tan she was again struck at how frail he looked. He was still a very good looking man, and he held himself up with dignity but it didn't seem to come easily. He looked even more fragile than he did at their first meeting. Julie thought he looked troubled.

"Are you all right?" she asked.

"I'm fine," he said, kissing her cheek. "You look smashing."

Maybe they were getting used to each other as they were now. Maybe it is the way they would have been had they grown older together. The shock was gone but the caring remained. She saw it in his smile. She saw it in his eyes. He saw it in her.

He should have seen me yesterday, she thought. With few clothes to choose from in her carryon bag she was again wearing the black slacks, but with a silky white blouse, her red jacket, her new shoes, and dangling gold earrings she'd bought in Spain.. Her dark hair was brushed into soft fluffy waves and, even with just a spit bath, she felt ready to enjoy the world.

"Let's not go in the restaurant right away," he said, taking her arm. "Let's walk a bit first."

The sun was shining. Except for the pinch of her new shoes it was a lovely day to stroll and see the sights. The street was crowded with those on lunch breaks amid whatever tourists were around. Julie was sure his office was close by.

"We took off to go to Maidenhead for a two day holiday. It's a lovely place to relax and get a tan. Now that we're back we have a lot to do."

"You should have brought her with you," she said. *I'm glad you didn't.*

He smiled. "I enjoyed your cards," he said, as they walked. "I was pleased you were having such a nice time."

A nice time? In Spain? Of course he would think that from the cards she'd sent. Touristy. Picturesque. Some funny. Having a wonderful time. Trivia.

"Whatever made you think I would enjoy the bullfights? It was a gory spectacle."

He smiled, "We didn't like it either."

He seemed lost in thought before he spoke again. "Which country did you like best?"

"England feels like home because you're in it," she said, "It's my torment and my comfort zone, but Italy is right up there."

"Why?"

"Outside of the fact that three wealthy Italians, and one of them a Count, wanted to meet me," she said, smiling, "it was as if I had been born there."

He seemed intrigued but he didn't say very much. "Why didn't you like the Count?"

"Unless he looked like you," she said, with a smile, "with the power to fix things the way I want them he would have had to at least be a Duke."

He smiled, a somewhat half smile encouraging her to talk while they walked.

"I stayed with relatives in my parent's hometown of *Corato*. I could hear my father's voice when I saw the names of the streets. All the streets are named for well known writers, Dante among them. I understood the customs, the language, the people and the music. And I loved the food."

He led her to a small bench to rest while she talked. "We'll go to an Italian restaurant for lunch. What else did you do?"

He sighed as he sat down. "Do you mind if we take the Dickens House off the agenda?" he asked. "I'd rather hear you talk."

"No, I don't mind," she said, a little confused. She didn't care if she ever saw the Dickens House. *Talk to me,* she thought as she chattered. "In Italy, I left my cousins behind to go to Milan to see other relatives, and I wandered from there on my own taking trains to Venice, Florence and Rome. I stayed in Italian *pensiones* in each city. Then I took a six hour bus trip from Rome back to the south of Italy, near *Bari*, where my cousins were waiting and worrying about me being alone."

"I'm sorry you were alone," he said, gently. "I worried about that, too."

Did you, darling? "I never really felt alone when I was in Italy," she said. "Except, maybe, in Venice. That is no place for a woman with a romantic nature to be alone. I wanted to be serenaded while on a gondola with you."

"I wish I could have gone with you," he said, quietly.

"I wanted you with me," she said. "That's why I sent you a card from there. I knew, if you remembered, you'd like it."

"I never forgot the way we were," he said, smiling. "I didn't need a postcard showing a marble statue with a man and woman in a very seductive embrace to remind me."

"I was eating at a restaurant outside the Hotel Geremia which is right on the canal, hearing the gondoliers, watching people walk by, hearing the music and, when I thought of you, I couldn't resist that card."

"Hilda didn't like it."

"I wasn't thinking of Hilda. I was thinking of you with me in Italy.

"I don't know Italian."

"I know enough for both of us. Besides you don't need to know Italian. The atmosphere speaks and many people speak English. It's also rather funny when they don't."

They had started to walk again.

"I told my cousins about you," she said. "They would love to meet you."

"Why did you do that?"

"When they asked why I'd gone to England, I said one thing in Italian while I was thinking something else in English. The one relative who spoke English translated what I said in a way that confused things even more, and you became the romantic figure in my life. Of course, they were right but, rather than go into detail of why I was alone, I let it stay that way. From that moment on they asked about my David at every meal. As far as they were concerned I was a very unique woman to be traveling alone anyway."

They were turning into the doorway of an Italian restaurant now as he responded. He seemed pleased that he had been a topic of conversation.

"You are a unique woman," he said, as they went inside. "You're very special to me."

"Don't, David," she whispered. "I'll cry."

Even as he smiled she was sure she'd seen tears in his eyes. *Oh, David.. what's wrong?*

The music was Italian. The atmosphere was Italian, and the broiled fish and steamed vegetables were Italian enough. She was hungry; the food was good, the wine was poured in style and she was with David. That was more than good enough. She smiled appreciatively.

Except for his interest in what she was saying he hadn't said too much. When she was quiet he prompted her to continue talking. She showed him some of the photos taken in Italy, pointing out her cousins, Michele and Francesco, both tall, white haired, good looking, unlined, men in their late sixties or early seventies.

"Francesco is now retired," she said, "He had been an Immigration official at the Port of Brindisi. Michele is an orthopedic surgeon. He hasn't been well recently."

In one photo she was sitting among the wives and grown daughters.

'You're the family beauty," he said.

She laughed. "They said that, too."

"Why didn't you like Spain?" he asked.

"I didn't get to see very much. I was confined to Richard's house in El Escorial. There were a number of local events, a religious parade, even a fiesta, and I went through the 1000 year old monastery that brought tourists. I might have enjoyed it more on my own. And it was awkward to be with Richard's second wife, Maralisa. "

"She was probably jealous of you."

"You're right, and it was uncomfortable. It was like being back with Emma. I couldn't even bridge the gap with language. Richard was no help at all. In fact, he's developed a nervous tic in his Spanish speech pattern that showed the strain he's under. She had no reason to be jealous of me. They were aware of my search for you so it was no secret that I loved someone in England even before I got there. Richard is convinced you put that phone book in my hand when I found you."

"I probably did," David said, quietly.

"I was never interested in Richard nor he with me. She's the same age as Hilda, for heaven's sakes. Why would she be jealous of me?"

"Hilda's jealous of you," he said, smiling.

"Didn't you show her my picture?"

"She thinks you're a stunning woman," he said. "Sophisticated and elegant."

"That does make me sound old."

"She's right, you know. You always were. But I still see gipsy in your eyes. And, today, with those small golden earrings.."

"Spanish gold," she said, "the only thing I bought in Spain. It went with this." She took a small tissue wrapped ceramic doll from her purse. The doll was dressed as a flamenco dancer in a dancing pose with arms overhead. Her dark hair was long, topped with a mantilla, and she wore dangling gold hoop earring.

"I thought of you," she said, standing it in front of him. "She belongs with the David statue."

"Hilda won't like it," he said.

"It's for your birthday, not hers."

He was staring into space.

"Did you bring your home photos with you?'

"I'm sorry. I didn't even remember them. I was somewhat distracted this morning."

"I've noticed," she said.

Conversation wandered but it was clear that something was on his mind, even though he'd managed to keep her talking, not that that was such a hard thing to do. Outgoing and gregarious, and stifled by her circumstances, she was bubbling with things to say about the trip she had made alone, especially to David who wanted to listen. But she wanted him to talk, too.

"David, talk to me."

"I like your voice." he said, quietly..

"There's nothing special about my voice."

"Oh, yes, there is," he said. "Your voice *is* you. It's a kind voice. gentle and soft and.."

"American?"

"Not just that," he said. "I've heard many American voices. Yours is a happy voice. I remembered that. I missed your voice."

"I missed yours, too," she said. "I'd like to hear more of it, especially when you're being down to earth David, and not British proper."

They talked about languages and British-English as opposed to American English. Julie told him of a book she'd picked up at Victoria Station which said much the same thing. He was sure an American had written it.

"No," she said. "It was written by an Englishman." She made a mental note to send him the book before she left.

"I would like to meet Hilda before I leave."

"Maybe another time," he said.

"Time was never our friend, David. I'll be leaving in a few days."

"Leave? Why? Why are you leaving?"

"I've been invited to visit everyone's home but yours, David. I can't stay in a bread and breakfast like this one indefinitely."

"I've been boorish," he said, regretfully.

"In that regard, yes," she said, sadly. "I would like to have seen your house, to have had a cup of tea with you there, even with Hilda."

"You don't understand," he said.

"No, David, I don't. You're single now. You don't have to hide me anymore. If I'm nothing else I'm at least an old friend who should be welcome."

"Hilda sees you as a threat," he said.

"That's why I want to meet her," Julie said, "If she's going to be in your life I'd like us to at least try to be friends."

"You were the love of my life, Julie, and she knows it. She saw the photo we took in London. She knows what you've meant to me."

"But you're speaking about something that happened years ago, and you spend all your time with her now and she knows that, too."

"I lost you once. No matter how I feel there's nothing I can do about it now."

You said it was all best forgotten.

He seemed distracted again.

She finally blurted. "David, I know something is wrong. Are *you* all right?"

He answered slowly. "Yes. Yes and no. The good news is that I'm glad to see you again. I'm glad just to be sitting here with you. There are so many things I want to say but..." He paused. "The bad news is that I have to go to hospital Wednesday to have more cancer growth removed from my shoulder."

"More? Cancer? *More* cancer growth?"

"I have lymphoma, Julie," he said, quietly. "Hilda found the new lump on my chest this weekend. I expect I'll have radiation this time. My cardiac problems complicate things but I've had other growths removed in the past and it went well."

"Oh, David, I'm so sorry," she said. Her eyes flooded. "Weren't you ever going to tell me? Why did you let me talk so much? What can I do?"

There was a quaver in his voice. "I'll be fine, Julie. I have people to look after me."

"I don't have to go," she said, wondering if he meant Hilda or his daughter or other relatives. "I still have time. I can stay, David.""

"Hilda will take care of me, Julie. She knows what to do."

"I can't leave you, not like this. Oh, David, I wanted to leave you happy this time." Tears were spilling down her cheeks now.

"Please don't cry, Julie." He tried to brush her tears away. "I don't deserve even one of your tears. Just seeing you again has made me happy, darling. I'll try to see you before you leave. And I'll stay in touch."

"Oh, my darling, I'll be so far away again." She was struggling for control. "How will I know how you are after the surgery?"

"I'll have Hilda call you," he said.

Just as she would have been underfoot in the face of Michele and Nina's medical problems, she would be in the way and no help to David with Hilda running things. How sad to be leaving on such a note. He lit a cigarette as she watched.

"That isn't helping," she said, unable to stop herself.

"I know. But it's a little late to stop now." He was lost in thought for a few minutes.

Their plates, with whatever was left on them, were taken away. Julie toyed with the stem of her wine glass as she waited for him to say something as he stared into space.

"My brother, Derek, died of cancer not long ago. He died three months from diagnosis. But I can't let myself think like that."

There was a look of desperation on his face before he spoke again.

"I have a pension from my work with the police, and I also have an old age pension, but I worked hard for this position. I'm trying to hold on to this job for the next two to three years. The pension from this job will be better than both of the others put together."

"I'm sure," she said. "I know how the American Social Security system works. I'm on it now myself. Americans still complain but it has to seem like a windfall for you now. You worked too hard for too little for too long, darling."

"Yes," he said, "I know how hard you tried to get me to do what I'm doing now, but regrets are futile, aren't they? ."

We would have grown old together…"

"I'll be in Dallas on the 24th of October," he said. "My flight will take me to Newark Airport for transfer to Dallas. I'll write or call to let you know. Maybe we can meet."

"The 24th of October?" Her breath caught in her throat. "David, that was the date that I flew to you from America years ago!"

He seemed surprised. "I've forgotten so many things but how could I forget that date?"

"Maybe because by the time I saw you your calendar said the 25th. Oh, David," she said, as her eyes flooded, "I'll meet *you* at the airport this time, on my side of the ocean, and I'll take you home to see where I live. You might remember it. I haven't moved very far."

"Why?"

"It's a nice area and a pleasant place to live. They've even put in a new pool. You once wrote that the area reminded you of Kent or Surrey And you wanted my new address if I moved so, when I finally had more rooms than I needed, I went from the townhouse at 146B to a one floor apartment at 146A next door. Everyone knew where to find me, even the mailman."

"I didn't have the cheek to show up, Julie, but you were never out of my heart."

"You could have tried," she said, softly. "I don't know why you belong to a gaming club," she added. "I don't even know what a gaming club is unless it's like a casino, but you're not much of a gambler, are you?"

"No, I suppose I'm not."

They were talking about his house as they were leaving the restaurant. She told him Richard had given her a message for his two grown children in England.

"At the time of their divorce," she said, "Emma was to sell the house and give them their father's share of the proceeds. There would still be enough to take care of her."

That message struck a chord with David. He was in somewhat the same quandary. Julie actually saw the dilemma in his face. If he was to depend on

Hilda his house in Surrey had to be part of it.. But his grown daughter was coming home to live.

Poor David.. He needs help right now. I hope those around him will give it to him without any strings. *And, God, please give him a long life to let him enjoy his pension.* He has earned every pound, every dollar and every penny of it.

He wanted to put her in a taxi to send her to the London Museum, which she'd planned to see, but she put on a happy face and opted for the Tours Plus bus. Her ticket was still good.

After a lingering hug, one that would have ended sooner if either of them had let go, they went their separate ways. When she reached the corner and looked back his frail frame had already been swallowed up in the crowded street.

Finally, alone, walking until her tears stopped her when she was standing somewhere near the black metal fencing of 10 Downing Street, the home of the Prime Minister of England, with no one anywhere around, she let her tears flow.

David was a good and decent man. He always was. It was sad to wonder if she was leaving a dying man. Unless he came to her there was nothing she could do for him except walk away and hope they'd always be friends. She begrudged him nothing. .In her heart of hearts she wished him years of life and happiness. *But to be leaving like this..*

Their third meeting had been pleasant but tinged with sadness, and their tender parting had been somewhat subdued. Julie had hoped to have someone take a last picture of them together, or at least get one of him before they said *adieu*, but she was so taken back by his health news that she forgot all about taking pictures.

She'd left him knowing that she would always love him. The future would be forever part of a life that included him. If she had to accept him as an old friend she would. It would, at least, allow her to wish him well from time to time, to let him know she cared about him.

She spent the rest of the afternoon on the Tours Plus bus to see more of the places she had marked off on her brochure. Seaview or Seaforth House (*she never got the name right*) was checked off but she put it off until another trip. Browsing there would take too much time. She still had the Tate Museum to see and, maybe, Kew Gardens.

From time to time tears came unbidden and she cried without being able to stop the tears.

Why am I crying, God?

It was late when she returned to her hotel. She picked up a vegetarian pizza from a–nearby pizza shop. She had two slices and gave the rest to Sam at the reception desk.

Later she phoned Penny from the pay phone in the hall. She left the hotel number with her son, Kevin, for a return call. She walked across the street for a newspaper and a couple of canned sodas. Sam had a message waiting. Penny had returned her call. Julie gave Sam one of the sodas and called her back.

Penny had just returned after a hassle with

authorities trying to get her car from a locked parking lot at the library. "And the police were no help," she said. That was sort of a joke since her husband, James, was with the police in another district.

"Take the train from Victoria to Bromley, South," Penny said, "I will pick you up there. It's approx 8 miles from my house. I have some errands to run anyway, one of them in Surrey, where David lives. I can show you more of the real England," she said. "I will call tomorrow to confirm if all is okay for a Sunday visit."

In her room, emotionally exhausted, Julie read the *Evening Standard*, until she cried herself to sleep. .

3 July 1992 Friday- She was called to the phone in the reception area around 10:30AM.

"I worried about you last night," David said. "Did you sleep well?"

"I wish I knew how to lie to you," she said. "But after reading the newspaper, I cried myself to sleep and then it was morning so I suppose I slept well enough."

"I do feel boorish for not spending more time with you, Julie," he said. "But I'll be out of the office next week, so I have a lot to get ready."

"I don't want to understand but I do," Julie answered, swallowing hard. "Just take care of yourself."

"I don't like to think of you wandering around London alone, darling."

"I've been managing," she said.

"I want you to know I'm here for you should you need me. If I'm not in just leave your name and I'll return your call."

Just to know you're there for me.

She told him what she'd done after their lunch, but she didn't tell him she'd seen it all through her tears.

"I'm pleased you enjoyed the tour."

"With Sam watching over me," she said, explaining the man at the desk, "I'm doing fine. "I'm more concerned that you take care of yourself."

"I'll write," he said. "I find it easier to express myself on paper."

"Yes, I know. I wish you could write one that would get here before Monday."

"I'll do what I can, darling," he said.

They were about the same age, David and Julie, and Richard as well. She'd had her share of problems, both medical and personal, and she'd had to deal with them alone, yet she felt as sorry for David as she did for Richard as she hung up. Both had younger women in their lives.

Richard's strain had been obvious. She prayed for David. *Let him be content, God.*

She kept busy. Her ill fitting British shoes were not a walking tour lifesaver so she bought another ticket for a final ride on the London Plus Tour bus. Rain began shortly after she boarded.

The bus was half empty. This time she looked out at places she'd seen on her own, not just those she'd seen years ago, with David. She could

In a London Fog

have given her own talk on the tour. She didn't leave the bus.

Rain or not it was a ride touched with memories. The bus passed places she had seen years before, at another time of year. Westminster Abbey, St Paul's Cathedral. She had been there for Guy Fawkes Day, the Remembrance Day parade. She had seen Queen Elizabeth place flowers at the Senatof while David held her hand. As they played *"God Save the Queen,"* she heard *"My country tis of thee.."*

The tour bus passed, but did not go onto Chancery Road where she'd met David for lunch yesterday. *Which building held his office? Would she see him with Hilda under an umbrella?* She blew a kiss toward the court yard as the bus went by.

She stopped at Victoria Station when the tour ended to check on the train to Bromley South. There was a problem. The line was down. She bought a Big Mac with French fries at an American McDonald's there. The price was six pounds. *Is that really 12 American dollars, David? For a hamburger?* Horrendous. It wasn't all that good either. She bought oatmeal cookies and soda to go. Before going back to the hotel to eat she picked up a copy of the *Evening Standard.*

When the rain stopped she went to the corner store to buy a couple of boxes of biscuits. One for Sam and one to take with her to Penny's. She had bullfighter key rings for Penny, James, and their teenage boys.

She called Penny from the hall phone about 9PM to let her know about the train problem. "I was told the Bromley South line was closed, and that I'd have to transfer from Blackfriar."

"I'll find out about a different train from Victoria," Penny said. "And I'll let you know."

4 July 1992 –Saturday. She was suddenly homesick. It was the same feeling she'd had when she was in England in 1966 as Thanksgiving approached at home. There was no where else she wanted to be but home for Thanksgiving. She got home in time then, heartsick and lovesick, but right now, as America was having a coast to coast fireworks party in celebration of Independence Day, she was in England, lonely and alone, still heartsick and lovesick, amid dead silence.

There was no mention of Independence Day on TV and only a tiny item in the newspaper even referred to it. Buried in the middle of the paper was a story about an English Lord who was dressing as a cowboy and inviting his friends in for an American style barbecue for the 4th of July. And they say we don't have news about them in our press! Guess they're still bearing a grudge. Like Thanksgiving, there is no other more American day than Independence Day. Maybe Guy Fawkes Day does it for them.

She played mental memory games trying not to think or worry about David. Remembrance Day had been Armistice Day at one time. It later became Veteran's Day. Memorial Day, which was once called Decoration Day, now signaled the unofficial start of summer. And in September school started after the Labor Day holiday.

She had just come up from the breakfast room when she was called to the phone in the reception area. *David?*

It was Emma's daughter, Denise. "We've been away for a couple of days, Aunt Julie," she said. "I want to thank you for the card you sent from Spain. How did you find my Dad?"

Julie told her, briefly, of Richard's concern regarding their share of the house but, standing there, with others needing attention around her, it was difficult to go into detail. "I'll write a letter to explain further," she said.

"Does your mother know I'm in London?" she asked.

"No, she thinks you're still in Italy."

"Leave it that way." Julie said.

Penny called around 11AM. "I will pick you up at the Croydon Station now," she said. "The other line has ongoing work. It will take about half an hour, with two stops along the way so it shouldn't be too bad."

"I think I'll be fine," Julie said.

"We'll be in David's area," Penny said. "Would you like to see his house?"

"I'd love it," Julie said, "But I don't want to cause him any more problems than he has now."

"We'll just drive by," Penny said.

She had the day and evening to be on her own. At first she walked around. She went to the theater district near Victoria Station then to Tourist

Info re: ticket to *Miss Saigon*. If she took the "tube" to another area she might be able to get a half price ticket "assuming there are any available."

She opted not to gamble on a maybe. I'll see it in New York, she thought. Whatever it costs here will be half that at home.

Continuing to walk around she found a pier with a sign offering a boat cruise on the Thames to the Thames Barrier. That's where the water was held back to prevent flooding. She liked being on the large, ferry like boat. It reminded her of the more romantic water taxi in Venice. And, in a smaller way, it was somewhat like the boat that sailed from Liberty Island to the Statue of Liberty in New Jersey.

The people around her were singles, couples and families with children, most of them tourists. A man, sitting with a woman across from her, asked where she was from. When she said Cherry Hill, New Jersey, he laughed, introducing himself and his wife. "We're from Mt. Laurel," he said. Very close. Both worked at the Post Office in Bellmawr. He knew her brother, Ray, there. Said he often picked him up when he had car problems. The man, called Ben, was now retired; His wife, Mary, was sleepy and quiet in a somewhat bored way. Julie tuned her off her radar to enjoy the water ride.

When they returned to the dock Julie found that she had lost her little wrist purse. In it was about five dollars worth of thick English coins. She remembered hearing a thud. She was annoyed with herself for not checking. But she still had her waist pack and enough money for the inexpensive bus fare at 5:30 on the No. 11 bus from Westminster. I'm getting around almost like a native, she thought.

David would have been proud of me.

Except for the hotel breakfast that morning she had grazed from carts selling fruit or ice cream along the way. She stopped at the corner store across from her B&B for a box of crackers and a bottle of water. She still had fruit in her room.

Eating on the run like this, and moving about, has done wonders for my figure, she thought. Eating as I did in Italy with all that walking had done the same thing. I'd better remember that when I get back to home cooking. It's the walking that helps keep the pounds off.

5 July 1992 Sunday- Julie was up for breakfast by 8AM. After walking the three blocks to Victoria Station, and following Penny's instructions, she found the correct train and sat back to enjoy the ride. People left the train at various stops. Everything was fine until they reached the Croydon station. She panicked when she couldn't find the latch on the door to exit the train. A man who had already exited told her to reach to the outside of the door to find the latch.

"Turn it to release the door," he said.

Gee. Why was there no sign? she thought. She felt like an idiot. As she walked to the exit of the station a conductor looked over at her.

"Were you the lady who didn't know how to get off the train?"

"Yes," she answered, "I'm sorry to say."

"Are you all right now?"

"I'm fine," she said, smiling, amazed that her shaky legs didn't betray her.

Penny was waiting with her son, Kevin, at the station.

"We're going on a little tour ," Penny said, when they were in her car. "I'd like to show you around so you can see the real England before you head home." Driving on the wrong side of lovely tree lined roads and curving flower bordered lanes, she added, "but I have a stop to make for Kevin first.

When she stopped at a 'Toys R Us' store, where Kevin was buying something, were it not for the British accents, she could have been in the same store at home. They passed a very pretty tall building with layered floors as she drove away.

"It's known as the Wedding Cake building," Penny said.

That's exactly how it looked. Julie was sure there was a romantic story behind it.

David had mentioned that he took the train to and from Croydon so she knew she was in the general vicinity of where he lived. It was nice to imagine him living there, and if he was recovering from surgery it was nice to picture him resting in such green and flowering surroundings.

"Do you know where he lives in the area?" Penny asked.

"He lives in a town called Shirley," Julie said, looking in her purse for her address book. They were passing a pharmacy as she read the address aloud.

In a London Fog

"This is his street," Penny said, suddenly.

"Oh, Pen," Julie said, "

"And there's his house!"

Julie's heart pounded. In part it was the thought that she was near his house and in part the thought that she shouldn't be there. Not like this. Not like his old camp follower.

It was a small, but lovely, deep red brick ranch like, bungalow with a wooden top painted a muted ruby red. In a parking area in front of the house was a small, red, Citrion car. A white fence bordered a green lawn on the side of the house. Since David's Saab was no where around Julie assumed he was out somewhere with Hilda. In view of his medical problems she hoped it was a restful weekend somewhere, but they could have gone shopping and might return to think she was snooping. She would have died of shame if that happened. As it was, by the time she caught her breath, she was flustered and unnerved, and suddenly in tears.

Kevin took a photo with her camera as his mother turned the car around.

"Penny," she said, when they were finally away, "Thank you. I would never have done that on my own. But," she repeated, feeling like a 68 year old teenager, now that they were on another road and the deed was done, "Thank you very much."

Dotting the i's and crossing the t's can take many forms, even unexpected ones. It placed him somewhere. He was not just a sick aging man on a crowded street in London now.

It was just a house, but it was *his* house. She had moved to an apartment from a house that had been twice as nice and twice the size. But his was a nest that he'd fashioned himself. It was his home. He wouldn't be calling it Gipsy Cottage now, but she could imagine herself living there with him, central heating or not.

"*Some place that's known, to God alone, Just a spot to call our own...*"

She spent the afternoon with Penny. She went with her to Keston, a drive that took them near Shirley, to see a conservation country show. It was an outdoor show to raise money to save the environment. It had a different name but the same things were going on at home.

By the time they returned to the house and sat down to eat dinner Julie thought she had figured out why the English didn't know how to cook. They'd rather plant flowers than learn to cook. They eat for sustenance and convenience, not taste. Lunch was a slice of melted cheese on a piece of toast with tea. Dinner was cold cuts, tuna, beets, lettuce and a cold boiled potato. English cooking. Adequate and healthy, the kind of summer day fare she might have had at home.

As they ate she shared the highlights of her trip to Italy and Spain and she gave them the key chains. Mark had a football game (soccer) waiting so he couldn't stay around. Before he left she took photos of the four of them, James and Penny, Mark and Kevin, and they took pictures of her with them.

Later they spoke about David.

"I don't know much about Lymphoma," Julie said, "I just know it's a blood cancer that develops in stages. I didn't think to ask him so I don't know what stage he's in."

"It must be terrible for him," Penny said.

"I'll look it up on the Internet when I get home," Julie said. "Not that I know what good it will do but I'd like to be informed. He said he'd stay in touch and we'd like to remain friends, but Hilda sees me as a threat so that might be a problem."

They were sympathetic to his health problems and said they would let her know if they learned anything and then, too soon, it was time to leave. Saying goodbye is never easy especially when your worlds are so far apart. She could never thank Penny enough for her kindness and for her genuine friendship through the years.

They drove her to the Croydon station at 7PM. She was at her hotel before eight. Am I getting around England well now or what? she thought. She stopped at the desk to check out in the morning.

"We hope to see you again," said Sam, pleasantly.

Sam knew she'd spent her evenings alone in her room. The days kept her busy enough. From time to time he had suggested things she could do, but alone at night on a London street is still alone in a big city. She had avoided trouble by being careful. In his own way Sam's kindness showed respect.

She spent the next hour packing. I've become quite good at it, she told herself. Clothes ready for tomorrow. All else in carryon. Shoulder bag for items that might be useful on the plane. Money, passport and camera in waist pack. She was packed to go home.

After she changed into her light summer nightgown she sat on the bed and cried.

A Late Visit

One of the teachers at school had advised her to schedule David as her first, not last, stop when she got to Europe. "You don't know how that will end," she was told. "You can be sure of bringing home happy memories from Italy." She was right. But she had seen David three times, first, middle and last letting David become part of her entire trip. It had been a mixed blessing.

She was still crying when she heard a knock at her door. She gasped as she opened it.

He had a single red rose in his hand. He handed it to her. "I wanted to come to you at least once before you left," he said. "I thought the rose would help."

"Oh, David," she said, softly.

Looking around he said, "We were in a place like this once, weren't we?"

"Twice," she said.

Her bra with the prosthesis was on the bureau. He didn't say anything as he looked at it.

He took her hand as he sat on the bed. "Sit with me, darling," he said, gently.

She burst into tears. "David, we can't."

"I just want to hold you," he said.

His arms went around her when she sat next to him. He moved the straps of her nightgown from her shoulders.

"David, no," she whispered. "Don't..."

He moved until his lips were on the scars on her chest, then he replaced the shoulder straps and he kissed her. It was a sweet, tender, kiss. He held her gently as he spoke.

"We're both scarred, Julie," he said. "Inside and out. You thought I didn't understand what you told me but I did. We were more than that. I loved you then and I love you now just the way you are."

"I never stopped loving you, David," Julie whispered, trying to control her tears. "Even when I thought I hated you I loved you."

"You should have hated me but you don't know the meaning of hate, Julie. I gave you so little, darling. Then and now. Nothing I say can make up for it but I'm sorry I ever left you so alone."

"You didn't know what you were doing anymore than I did." Her eyes flooded as she spoke. "You wanted me and I know you loved me but my world, for all its temptations, wasn't your world. You've learned to fit it all in but I'm as lost as ever."

"I never wanted to lose you, Julie, not ever."

"But you needed Addie then; you need Hilda now." *You need your nest, David. A British nest.*

As her sobbing subsided but with tears in her eyes, she said, "I'm sorry that I never learned to drive on the wrong side of the street. I'm sorry that

I never learned to use British money. Oh, David, I couldn't even light the stove and..."

He stood up, pulling her toward him to kiss the tears on her face. "No matter what our problems were, my darling, we had more that would have kept us together than anything that separated us." He wiped her tear streaked face with a handkerchief before splashing his own face with cold water from the corner sink.

He squeezed her gently. "We could have dealt with those things long ago, darling. We just never had enough time, and we still don't. My health and that pension must to be considered now."

"Does Hilda know you're here?" she asked.

"Yes," he answered. "She's not happy about it but she knows you're leaving."

"Oh, my love, to leave you like this.."

He stroked her hair as he spoke. "I never thought I'd see you again, Julie. The miracle is that you came back."

She saw tears glistening in his eyes.

"We must go on, darling. I want us to stay in touch but no matter what happens I want you to be happy."

As he prepared to leave her tears fell again.

"Please take care of yourself, David. Reach across the sea if you need me or if you just want to talk. I'll want to know what happens after your surgery on Wednesday. Oh, my darling, may all your birthdays be happy ones and may there be many more of them."

"For both of us," he said, holding her again.

"Have a safe flight home. And don't worry."

She could not stop her tears.

"There's nothing we can do now, Julie. That's the problem. I'll write and stay in touch. We may even see each other in October so please don't cry. Just remember me."

"I'm not the one with memory problems, David. How do I forget?"

He held her close before he turned away.

She watched from the foot of the stairs as a tall, thin man in a grey suit carried his frail, dignified body up to the lobby. When he was out of sight all she had left of him were the petals of the rose that had been crushed between them. She held the fragile petals to her lips drawing in the aroma to hold on to him as she went back to her room.

He had come by train from Croydon. He would return the same way. Hilda would meet him at the Croydon station to drive him home. She had forgotten to tell him she had seen his house, but she could picture it all now.

6 July 1992- Monday She had not slept well but she was up and dressed and in the lobby, bag and all, by 7 AM. She didn't bother with breakfast. That could start stomach problems.

Her thoughts were of David's visit and of his coming surgery. He'd be in the hospital in a couple of days and she'd be back in America. In sudden panic she wanted to call him.

Don't worry, he said. Famous last words.

Sam dialed the number for her and let her use the phone at the desk. Even at that early hour she reached his answering machine. She burst into tears as she wished him well."I love you, David," she said at the end. *"Ciao."*. That covered it all. She was still crying when she hung up.

In a London Fog

Chapter Six Leaving England

Suddenly, with the 5 pound ticket she'd purchased in advance in hand, she was rushing to get to the stop to meet the Air Bus to Heathrow. In spite of all her preparations that last minute call caused her to miss the bus. She reached the bus stop just moments after the Air Bus pulled away. She actually watched it go.

Now she had to rush to get to the underground train from Victoria Station. She only had a carryon with wheels and a shoulder bag, even so, it still slowed her down. Once she located the proper train going in the right direction and, obviously looking unsure, a pleasant looking young man helped her board. He was going to Heathrow as well. He said his name was Badi, that he was a student in London and was going home during school break.

"Where are you from?" she asked.

"Kuwait."

He could not have been nicer but with warnings all over the airports, and being asked constantly if anyone had helped with your bags she felt a shiver of fear. She was sure it didn't show and they reached Heathrow with no problem. Still, she was glad when they parted company. Unless he pasted something invisible on the handle of her carryon, all was fine. She was where she was supposed to be and she was on time.

All was fine until she reached baggage control. She didn't know what the problem was but she was calm. She had no reason not to be calm. As far as she was concerned, she liked knowing security was doing their job. The first time it had been the metal of her sutures. She wasn't okay then and she wasn't seen as okay now, not even with the note from the first security check about her sutures. She had even been asked to step out of line when she was leaving England to go to Spain. That time it was a problem with her suitcase.

She practically had to strip this time. Finally, with young security women still looking askance, she was free to go to her plane. She was already in the boarding area when she realized she had left her waist pack on the counter after her baggage came through. That waist pack held her passport, her camera, which was filled with recent photos, and what was left of her Traveler's checks.

She panicked.

A pilot standing nearby said, "This queue will take some time. You'll have plenty of time to run back."

Run was the word. She had to reach almost the end of the building to get to the baggage check out again. When she got there she had to go to the British Air customer lost claim area, which was some distance away, and prove her identity before she could get it. She was frazzled by the time she got back to the boarding area. They were announcing last call to board Flight 219 going to Philadelphia. A man behind her, who became her aisle seatmate, said the plane would be delayed. He was right. The plane was held up for 45 minutes.

"We're still in a queue," the pilot said.

She was still not out of the woods on this flight. Because she'd changed her original flight she seemed to have lost her requested aisle seating. She would have to take what was available. With the way her stomach had been recently she panicked again, but she tried to be polite.

"If you won't help me," Julie said, smiling, as she spoke to the airline attendant, "I'll probably get sick and someone on the plane will have to do something to assist me right at the seat."

Reluctantly, and with some annoyance, the young woman gave Julie a seat number in another area of the plane. When she reached it, however, it was another window seat. At Julie's consternation the man in the aisle seat very pleasantly gave up his seat and moved to the window seat.

Julie was grateful, but felt every bit a spoiled American. She apologized.

"It's no problem," the man said. "I take the flight quite often and just settle into whatever is available."

He was a British man called Levi. He was so easy to talk to that Julie's preflight jitters vanished.

"I live in Cotswald with my wife and children," he said. "Nice place to visit," he told her when she spoke of her trip, mentioning a stay at a London B&B. . "Nice B&B there."

A steward came by with champagne almost as soon as they were aloft. In short order Julie had a total of five glasses of champagne, all without breakfast. It was free; it came with little tidbits of food, and everyone around her was imbibing, eating and talking now. She almost didn't notice that they were now airborne and that she was on her way home. But she did have to use the lavatory.

"I wasn't given champagne or food like this on the flight in," she said, on her return.

"That's because," said Levi, who seemed to be looking at her approach as men look at attractive women, "you were transferred to business class. Companies pay over $2000.00 for these seats."

No wonder David liked it. From nothing to everything. For Julie it was an accidental piece of luck. She sat back enjoying the moment and looked around. They were mostly businessmen, a few women, no children and no bedraggled hippie types. Most were in business suits, a few in shirt sleeves and ties. Julie fit in quite well wearing the black slacks, a white blouse and the tailored red jacket that had almost become her uniform in the last few days. Her short dark hair was just right.

"Were you in England alone?" Levi asked.

"Most of the time," she answered, "But a dear friend lives there. I saw him a few times."

"And he let you go?"

She would have burst into tears again if she tried to explain so she just smiled and looked away.

The man in the aisle seat across from her, a university professor, said he was returning from Greece and Italy where he had spent a month studying the Mediterranean diet.

Although her visit to Italy had been closer to

the Adriatic she had been near enough and she knew the food and the variations.

"You mean people still don't know it's the best diet in the world?" Julie said, shocked. "And you're being paid to study it? "

Home – USA

She went through customs in Philadelphia without a single alarm bell going off. *Boy, are they going to hear from me.* She found the Rapid-Rover station and got a seat in the next van going in her direction. American flags and posters from the Independence Day celebration were still around as they left the Philadelphia terminal.

In Europe she had become aware of terrorists and armed men around but street crime did not seem a problem. Once the van left the airport in Philadelphia, however, she found herself thinking of street crime. It was not a pleasant homecoming thought. Maybe that's how the natives of each country saw it, she thought. *Pickpockets in England, robbers in Spain, gypsy thieves in Italy. Guns in the hands of hooligans in America.*

She was home by 3PM (USA time). 9 or 10PM GMT. Her neighbors, especially the little old ladies who sat under shady trees every day, glanced curiously in her direction. Until they saw her emerge with her suitcase from the Rapid Rover van they hadn't known she'd gone anywhere. Julie waved a greeting as she went to her door. In spite of a certain amount of busy-body curiosity they didn't think it unusual not to see her because Julie kept to herself writing or painting when she wasn't working anyway.

Julie was home. She was inside her own apartment and, as David once wrote, she felt totally cut off from a world that included him.

Except for some unopened mail on the dining room table, and the box she'd mailed back from England, which was open but sitting on her bed, all was as she'd left it. Were it not for that box it was if she had not been away.

It was only after she made a beeline for her own bathroom that she finally knew she was home. Hot water ran from modern chrome faucets. The modern toilet flushed with a turn of a chrome lever, or a push of a button. She knew it again when the phone rang and she was able to pick up her own phone and answer it herself.

It's the little things, and the important people who make it home. *Oh, David, we could have shared our lives anywhere.*

Jason phoned to see if she had arrived yet.

"Well, I'll be darned!" he said when she picked up the phone. "You're home!"

She took a picture of him coming through the door around 6PM. He was smiling from ear to ear. Now that is a welcome I can live with, she thought. Just as in Italy, it was real.

When *Bonanza* appeared in living color on television, with Hoss, Ben and Little Joe speaking American cowboy English, not dubbed in Italian or Spanish, she again knew she was home.

"The Post Office called me when the box you sent got here," Jason said. "They wouldn't deliver it. I had to go there to open it myself before they'd let me have it."

"Why?"

"They heard something ticking inside so no one else would open it."

"Ticking?"

"You sent your alarm clock home and it was still going strong when it got here," Jason said, by now laughing as he told the story.

Julie laughed, too, as she remembered how carefully she'd packed everything, including how she'd wrapped that clock in something to muffle the sound since she couldn't turn it off. It was only an inexpensive bedside alarm clock, and it was still ticking away! Amazing.

"Some terrorist I'd make," she said. "Considering all the mistakes I made, it is a miracle I didn't trip over myself and blow everything up!"

Jason, who worked with computers now, enjoyed cooking and he already had the gravy ready for a simple spaghetti and meatball dinner. He added a salad for her first meal at home. It was good, old fashioned, Italian style home cooking. They even had a glass of wine together before he left to go home.

American voices came from television but after Jason left she was as alone as she had been in London. It's my own fault, she thought, even as she took a hot shower before she went to bed later. I should have been more socially active instead of burying myself in school books all those years.

She took another hot shower when she got up. She'd had three months of spit baths at sinks or oddly fashioned showers. She had to wash away the residue in order to finally feel clean. Even the elegant bathroom in Michele's apartment, although it had a bidet, had complicated, hand held shower things to use. It was almost luxurious to be washing her hair, almost drowning in her own shower.

It took time to readjust from Greenwich Mean Time to East Coast Daylight Saving time.

She tried to put things where they belonged even as thoughts of David intruded. When she drove her own car, another welcome sign that she was home and driving on the right side of the street, she went to the Cherry Hill Mall to buy cards.

She bought USA cards to send to everyone in Europe. Some were of the Statue of Liberty, some showed the American flag flying over the White House, and some were of her own Cherry Hill home town. She dropped off film to be developed and had prints made from those Jason had developed earlier.

How wonderful to see them again, especially those taken in Italy seemingly so long ago. She wrote that message on cards she sent to the relatives in Italy. Each card got individual messages.

In her cards to David she told him of her visit to Shirley, and of Penny driving past his house. She wished she had told him when he came to the hotel, but she could barely think let alone talk. She told

In a London Fog

him of the picture that had been taken there. It was easy to be honest with David. He would understand. He might also have understood if he'd found her there that day, but she wouldn't have liked seeing herself with her nose pressed up against a glass looking in from the outside. "It's a beautiful house, David," she wrote. "I can picture you living there." It was on her last roll of film so it was still being developed. "I'll send you a copy," she wrote.

By the time he got anything she sent his surgery would be over. Why hadn't she thought to ask the name of the hospital so she could call herself? Now she could only hope for a call or a letter. In Get Well cards to him she enclosed copies of pictures she would have shared with him when they met. One showed her with relatives near the beautiful villa in Italy. Another was with Richard in front of his small Spanish casa. She hoped he enjoyed her cards.

After going through the pictures Jason had had developed she spent hours sorting them out to save in albums and to send copies to everyone, everywhere. She sent a card to Maralisa and the boys in Spain and another card to Richard in Norway. Best wishes and regards to all. Were it not for Richard she would not have sent one with Maralisa's name on it. She sent a note to Denise with her father's message adding a PS to tell her mother Aunt Julie had returned to America.

On Saturday, on the 11th of July, she received a phone call from England. Her heart almost stopped.

"Hello, Is this Julie?"

"Yes." Julie answered.

"This is Hilda, David's girlfriend. He has asked me to ring you to tell you the surgery went well." *Thank you, God.*

"Oh, I am so glad," Julie answered.

"I've seen him every night in hospital," she said. "I will be collecting him and taking him home tomorrow. *Sunday.* He said not to worry. He will write when he has a chance."

"I'm pleased it went well," Julie said. "I'll look forward to hearing from him, but assure him a letter can wait if he needs rest."

"I will be staying with him next week to look after him, and he will go back to work the next week so all will be well." Hilda said.

"I'm sorry we didn't meet while I was there," Julie said. "I'll write to David. Maybe I should write a letter to you, too."

"You got that right," she said, firmly.

Zing. Foolish girl. Poor David.

"Thank you for calling, Hilda. Give David my love, and best wishes to both of you."

What else could she say except goodbye?

Hilda got her message across like a British Maralisa, firm, insecure and uncertain. It had to be awkward for her. She wished David had brought her to lunch at least once. Given a chance we might have become a little friendly, Julie thought. I'll do my best but I doubt it now.

When the relatives in *Corato* received their cards and photographs they wrote back saying,

"The sky rained memories in the photos from Juliana in America now."

By the time she finished organizing all the photos, some she was keeping in albums for herself, some she would distribute to family members, and others she was sharing with friends, she ended up with two albums for Italy, half an album for England, and a quarter of an album for Spain.

David's pictures went into a special album that still contained their airport photo, even some of the early pictures that had been taken at the pool.

Their honeymoon pictures showing them standing together on the River Thames were there. They had been taken the same day in the same place. The missing one was the one she had sent him before her trip and she didn't have a copy or a negative. She was sorry she hadn't taken the time to make a copy for herself. She'd made prints of the airport picture but the colors of the others had faded with time. She enhanced the colors with her computer as best she could.

The neighbor ladies who sat outside and saw her coming and going marveled aloud at her energy. "Where do you get it?' they asked.

"Hormones," Julie answered. Why not? That's what her doctor said.

Whatever else is wrong, she thought, I don't want to cope. She just couldn't settle down. Besides a body at rest tends to stay at rest and she didn't want that either. She was reading; she was writing to everyone; she was fixing the photos, and she was climbing the walls.

David phoned, stiff upper lip and all, about three weeks after Hilda's call. "I want to thank you for your cards and pictures," he said. "I was like a boy waiting for your mail."

Julie's cheerful greeting did not mask the tears in her voice. "You are a boy, my darling," she said. "I can't tell you how happy I am to hear from you. How are you feeling?"

"I feel fine," Julie," he answered. "All has gone well. I should be back to work soon."

"Is Hilda home with you?"

"Not today," he said. "She's been taking care of me but there's work waiting at the office so its best she got back."

"Thank you for having her call me after the surgery, David. She delivered your message with no problem but I got the feeling that she thinks I should be writing to her."

"I told you she was jealous of you, Julie."

"Even though I'm not underfoot now?"

"I talked to her about the two phone calls you received before your trip, and I checked the phone bills. You were right. She made the calls herself from here. She was quite upset that she'd been found out. She won't be doing that again."

"I hope I didn't cause a problem for you, David. I just thought you should know."

"She caused the problem, not you, Julie. As for writing to her? That's up to you, but it's not her place to dictate the matter."

"I'll keep things as they are for now," Julie said. "I'll write to you. You can share my letters with her as you wish."

"Now that you're home again," David said, "Have you put your feet up?"

"Not really," she said. "It's hard to settle down. The walls keep closing in on me. I don't seem to have any direction right now."

"You haven't started on the book?"

'It's in my head. It's in my heart. But no, right now I'm too close to it." She sighed. "And, if you don't mind, I'd like to know what the doctors had to say about your health."

"This is a slow moving lymphoma," he said. "I may end up dying of something else. But it can flare up as it just did. With care and medication it can be controlled. They think I have a few good years left."

"Enjoy them, David. Don't work yourself to death. Take Hilda to Venice and think of me."

He chuckled at that. "That would defeat the whole purpose, wouldn't it?"

"Not for me," Julie said.

"Among the pictures you sent was the picture taken of my house. That's one of the best photos I've ever seen of the house. I like it so much I may enlarge it and have it framed."

"It was a quick and accidental shot," Julie said, "but I'm glad it turned out well."

"I wish you could see inside the house. I did a lot of work there.

"Maybe, someday," Julie said.

Before they hung up he said. "I'll write to you as soon as I feel up to it, Julie. I miss talking to you. I miss hearing your voice."

"I miss you, too, darling," she said.

Staying busy wasn't easy.

From pictures taken when she visited Penny she did an oil portrait of Penny with James in his police uniform and sent it to them with love. She didn't even attempt to do one of David again. It would have been an emotional disaster for her.

We must go on, he said.

She forced herself to go anywhere and she worked hard at looking happy wherever she went. She drove to Atlantic City and walked the boardwalk just to see and smell the ocean. With the help of friendly people along the way she had pictures taken. She enclosed one of them with best wishes in a card to David. She had a box of salt water taffies shipped to his home with a card enclosed that said To David and Hilda.

Julie had seen many places in Europe, places she liked and places she didn't, but now she wanted to touch base again with places uniquely American. Tina had been born in New York; but she took a day trip there just to see the sights. She took the Liberty cruise to see and touch the Statue of Liberty. She toured Ellis Island and had her parent's names inscribed on the Immigrant Wall of Honor. She took an overnight trip to Washington, D.C., where she had worked during WWII. She visited Tina in Chicago and they saw the sights there together. They went to a stage show in a little theatre. They took a cruise on Lake Michigan and did a tour on one of the red London double deck buses being used there. *It hurt to see them out of place..*

She sent cards to everyone, including David. "Wish you were here." "Wish I was there." "Miss you." "Be happy." "Stay well."

She was surrounded by people but she couldn't have felt more alone. *A Step Out of Time* was right. She had been at the wrong place at the wrong time for too long. She was running in circles and she knew it.

She couldn't even think of writing the book.

"I'm pleased to think of you having such a good time." David wrote when he acknowledged receiving her cards. He had gone back to work. "It's best to stay busy." It was stiff upper lip shorthand. *I know how you feel.*

She went to singles club meetings a few times. Most of the men, her age or older, were surrounded by much younger women. . The few women her age chatted in lonely groups. Some danced together. A few joined the younger ones in line dancing. She went to book seminars and poetry readings, even reading her own work from time to time. She went to outdoor concerts. She exhibited her own art work at art shows.

It was when she joined a charity group that she found something of a niche with people of various ages as she participated in raising funds for noteworthy causes.

At the end of August the charity focus was on a Polo Match for one of the hospitals in the area.

The publicity revolved around the participation of British Major Ronald Ferguson, the father of Fergie who had married, and later divorced, Prince Andrew of the royal family of England. His team was competing with an American polo team. On the day of the Polo Match Julie sat at a table in the main tent among those who had paid to attend. Food and drink, which included champagne, was plentiful; denim clad musicians played guitars, and cameras flashed particularly when Major Ferguson entered the tent while those doing divot stomping slammed their feet on the polo ground outside.

One woman, intending to take a picture when Julie was near Major Ferguson, got a shot of Julie standing near someone else instead.

Julie was able to pose the woman with Major Ferguson to take the picture with her own camera. They exchanged addresses. The photo Julie received showed her with a fairly tall, nice looking man in his late forties or fifties, who appeared to be with her. They held stemmed wine glasses filled with an amber colored liquid. The background showed the activity in the tent.

Julie was wearing the same dark slacks and matching dark shirt with the same bright blue jacket she had been wearing when she visited Penny. The lapel still had the little lamb of peace pin she'd bought for herself when she'd bought one for David.

On his late night visit he'd said, "No matter what happens I want you to be happy." The picture showed her smiling and apparently having a nice time so she wanted to keep it and, maybe, send it to

David along with a cheerful card to explain the event. Her only problem with that was wondering if, with his memory problems, he would misunderstand and think she was saying something else so she delayed sending it.

An Indian summer September welcomed children back to school, and Julie's phone rang almost at once. "If you still want to work, we have some classes that need coverage."

When she wrote David to tell him she would be working at the school again David answered saying that he might surprise her and show up at the school himself one day. "If you do," Julie replied, "classes will be cancelled for the day, and there will be an assembly program in your honor just to welcome you."

Julie's search for him and the cards she'd sent back from England had captured the imagination of everyone in the building. Her cards on her trip had been posted on the main office bulletin board at school. She brought in her photo albums to share with them when they had free time. They enjoyed the few pictures she had taken in Spain, bullfights and all, and they were impressed at the pictures of Italy and the lifestyle of her relatives, but the main curiosity was about David.

On her first card she had told them of his cardiac problems and of his four strokes. Now she told them he was also being treated for Lymphoma. A catch in her tear choked voice told them how she felt without her having to say much more.

"Work will help," they said.

It did, but as October came, with the date of the 24th shown in red, she wondered why she hadn't heard from him. He answered his phone at home on her first try when she phoned.

"I can't imagine getting on an airplane right now," he said when she asked if he was still planning to go to the convention in Dallas.

"You sound exhausted," Julie said.

"I am, Julie. I've had some radiation, and I'm in the middle of a chemotherapy cycle at the moment. Fatigue seems part of it. And," he added, "I haven't heard from you for a few weeks. That doesn't help, you know."

"But David, I've sent a number of cards. I don't write every day, not even once a week, but I have been writing to you."

"Then someone is nicking the mail," he said, "and I don't think it's the postman."

"You think Hilda..?"

"She's punishing me through you."

"I can't be any threat to her from here, David, and I'm not planning to kidnap you."

"She wants to get married but I don't."

"I won't tell you what to do but maybe if she thinks I'm involved with someone she'll keep me out of it and you can decide for yourself."

She told him about the Polo Match photo mixup. "I'll send you the photo along with one of Major Ferguson surrounded by fans. If Hilda sees them she might .."

In a London Fog

She heard him coughing as he tried to answer. "Don't count on it, darling," he said, when he caught his breath.

"I don't know what else I can do, David," she said, her heart aching for him, "But I want to be able to reach you, and I want you to write to me even if you just want to say hello again."

"Code word? Gipsy with an i?"

"y or i." she said. "I'll know it's you."

She sent the mixup photo with one of the Major Ferguson photos and enclosed a happy note for both of them.

There was no reply.

A few weeks later, in an envelope with David's return address, she received a photograph. It showed David in a brown suit, sitting on the arm of a modern. white, lounge chair, with a smiling Hilda, seated in the chair beside him. She was wearing a lovely white pants suit. The background showed a window on clear white walls. She was pretty. She looked happy. He looked very nice, but unnaturally puffy, as if he had put on weight.

There was no message, no note, no code.

But the picture was telling her something. She was sure it had been taken in his house. It said the photograph had been taken by someone with them. It suggested an event to be celebrated. She didn't know why it took so long for her to realize what she was seeing before it dawned on her but, in that moment, she knew the picture had not come from David. The picture was undated so she couldn't say when it happened but David had given

Hilda what she wanted. This had to be their wedding party.

She was pleased for David's sake. He was a sick man. He would get what he needed. As his wife she would benefit from his income and from his American social security when he died. She would also get dower rights in his property.

She put the picture on the back page of her David album. She didn't cry. She was angry. She was angry with herself for wanting to cry. She was angry with the Hilda who wanted to hurt her. And, for a moment, she was angry with David for being sick and not telling her himself.

He phoned from his office weeks later.

"We had been away," he said, without saying where they'd gone. She didn't ask.

"I didn't know she'd sent the picture, Julie. Not until we got your card. I'm sorry if it hurt you."

"I didn't let it hurt me, David. I understand. I want you to be happy."

"I never wanted anything less than that for you, Julie," he said.

"I know that, David."

"Does this mean you're feeling better?"

"Yes," he said, "Much better. The drugs seemed to work. I'm on new medication now. The side effect of the drugs I was on was water weight."

"   "Are you able to fly again?"

"Not on any long trips," he said.

"Will that affect your job?"

"No. It's all paperwork now."

"Does Hilda still work in the office?"

"She prefers to keep the home fires burning now." He laughed as he said it.

"Will it be difficult for you if I send a card once in a while?" she asked.

"Not at all," he answered. "She knows we're friends. Old friends." There was a catch in his voice as he continued. "I'll always want to hear from you, Julie. And I'll call or write when I can, with or without code."

"I will, too, David. And I'll remember to send you a birthday card."

"I never remember your birthday."

"Any day in May will do. Or choose one you prefer."

"October 24th," he said, quietly.

She burst into tears when she hung up.

We had been so frightened, David. We had no idea what was ahead of us.

It was weeks before she received another envelope with David's home address in the return corner. It contained another unsigned photograph that had obviously been taken at that same wedding party on that day.

This picture had an attitude. It showed David, in the same brown suit, leaning from the arm of the white lounge chair, his arms outstretched, as if his hands were reaching for Hilda's white clad rear end while she was bent over in the chair. That was the entire picture. All that could be seen of Hilda was her white clad rump with David's hands reaching in that direction.

The message was clear.

He wants me, not you, it said.

She might give him what he needed. She might even give him what he wanted. But it was the kind of thing Cora would have done. It could have come from Maralisa or even from Emma. She might talk to David about it someday but it was not something he would have done. It was obviously from Hilda. Maybe she was clearing out a bad shot of that party and wanted to trash it in Julie's direction if only to hurt her. It didn't. It saddened her for his sake. It would have shamed him. He deserved more respect than that. So did I, Julie thought. There were tears in her eyes as she shredded the picture.

Fate may tear you from my arms, But never from my heart..." She heard their song as she threw the shreds in the trash. It didn't belong in her album, not even on the last page.

Ciao

Epilogue

One problem with getting intimately involved with relatives and faraway friends is the hold they have on your affection as you part, especially when you are leaving them knowing they are ill, and knowing you may never see them again. There is a very real tug on your heart as you walk away.

Michele and Nina died within two years of each other after Julie left Italy. Nina died of ovarian cancer, Michele died of an inoperable brain tumor. Richard died years later in Spain of respiratory failure.

David and Julie exchanged cards if only to say hello or happy birthday. David's cards arrived around October 24th. When his cards didn't come Julie sent a thinking of you card. He responded with little note cards sometimes with only the word gipsy with an i. If nothing else it told her he was alive if not well enough to write more. *They never sent each other a Christmas card.* When his cards stopped she knew, without knowing anything else, that he would have written if he could.

In 2008, as David's birthday approached, Julie sent a Thinking of You note card addressed to him at his house, care of any family member. In it, along with a request for information, she enclosed a small picture of herself. It showed an attractive, silver haired woman with an unlined smiling face. On the back she wrote 83 years old. If the postal service got it right it would arrive on his birthday.

She put her home address on the envelope with her email address on the note card.

"I hate waiting for our mail to catch up."

Maybe they should have left it at the magic of their love letters. Only desire and a surprising love that had grown with it had held them together. A powerful physical attraction, no matter what it promised, had not been enough. The love that came with it was painful.

As the plane left England on November 14th, in 1966, mainly because David had put his life on the line, she'd felt as much an emotional obligation as an emotional connection. What happened to him later told her he'd felt the same way. In the face of love magic moments had not been enough. It had been a bittersweet remedy.

A week later she received an email.

"Received your card with a picture of yourself on what would have been David's 78th birthday. David died on November 16, 2004." It was signed Hilda Gregory.

Julie cried at knowing what her heart had already told her but she wanted to know why he died, how he died. She wanted to know what only those who love want to know. David would have wanted someone to tell her.

There was no one to ask and nothing but memory to comfort her. It was a sad comfort.

Those we have held in our arms for a little while, if we truly loved them, we hold in our hearts forever. Rest in peace, dear David.

God be with you.